The Sparrow's Secret

Journeys Through Grief and Nature

Elara Tannin

Table of Contents

Chapter 1
New Beginnings

Alex Martin, having lost his wife to cancer, sought solace in the budding hues of spring at Greenhaven's expansive parks, where nature began its annual awakening. With binoculars in hand, he isolated himself among the early blooms, his eyes scanning the treetops not just for the rare feathered creatures that returned with the season, but also for a glimpse of the joy he once shared with Lydia. Each chirp and flutter above stirred a bittersweet symphony of memories, making the presence of his late wife palpable in the crisp morning air.

As the sun climbed higher, casting longer shadows over the dew-speckled grass, the park slowly filled with the enthusiastic murmurs of other birdwatchers. Families with eager children, couples sharing binoculars, and solitary figures like Alex, each lost in their observance of nature's spectacle. He watched them from a distance, their laughter and camaraderie a stark contrast to his silent mourning. The easy bond among the group members, highlighted by shared jokes and snacks, seemed a barrier too vast for Alex to cross.

Yet, amidst the crowd, a figure detached herself from a lively group and approached him. Elaine Roberts, with a warm smile and an open face, carried a palpable aura of empathy shaped by her own recent loss. Her brother, like Lydia, had been taken too soon, and birdwatching had become her refuge from the loneliness that followed such grief. As she introduced herself, her voice held a soothing undertone that seemed to acknowledge the unspoken sadness behind Alex's polite smile.

Their conversation began with the casual exchange of favorite bird sightings, but quickly deepened to shared experiences of loss and the unexpected comfort they found in the avian world. Elaine's presence, marked by genuine understanding and a lack of pretense, made it easy for Alex to lower the walls he had built around his grief. In the shared silence of watching a cardinal flit among the spring buds, a tentative connection was forged.

As the group prepared to move to a viewing spot known for its recent sightings of a rare migratory bird, Elaine turned to Alex with a spontaneous invitation. Her suggestion to join her not only promised a better vantage point but also hinted at a new beginning, a step away from the solitude of grief. Torn between the comfort of isolation and the emerging desire for companionship, Alex hesitated. The fragrance of spring blossoms filled the air, a subtle reminder of the renewing cycle of life that surrounded them. With a deep, fortifying breath, he accepted her invitation, taking his first step out of the shadows of mourning and into the uncertain yet hopeful light of new beginnings.

As Alex and Elaine made their way to the renowned viewing spot, a gentle breeze rustled through the budding trees, carrying with it the distant calls of returning birds. The park, vibrant with the hues of spring, seemed to pulse with life, each breath of wind and beam of sunlight reinvigorating the world around them.

Elaine, ever observant, paused by a cluster of budding lilacs, her binoculars hanging loosely around her neck. "This spot always reminds me of early mornings with my brother," she shared, her eyes not meeting Alex's as she lost herself in memories. "He loved the lilacs. Said they were the perfect backdrop for the indigo bunting."

Alex, encouraged by her openness, responded with a nod, feeling the weight of his own binoculars against his chest. "Lydia was partial to cardinals," he said, his voice soft with remembrance. "She loved their vibrance—said it was like a spark of life among the greens and browns."

Their shared memories hung between them, a tender bridge built on mutual loss and the solace they found in nature. Elaine turned to him, a smile touching her eyes. "It's beautiful, isn't it? How these small creatures can carry so much meaning for us."

"Yes, it's... therapeutic, in a way," Alex admitted, allowing himself a small smile in return. "Coming here, it's one of the few times the silence in my house feels a bit less overwhelming."

Elaine nodded, understandingly. "I feel the same. After my brother passed, the house was too quiet. Coming out here, listening to the birds...

it's like the world isn't so empty." She glanced around at the scattered groups of birdwatchers, their faces alight with excitement and anticipation. "It helps, being around others who share the passion."

"Does it ever get easier?" Alex asked, the question slipping out before he could weigh it down with the heaviness of his thoughts.

Elaine considered it, her gaze drifting to a pair of robins darting through the underbrush. "I don't know if it gets easier, or we just get better at carrying the weight," she replied thoughtfully. "But I think sharing it, like this, helps lighten the load, even if just for a little while."

As they resumed walking, their conversation shifted to lighter topics— their favorite birdwatching spots, the quirkiest bird behaviors they had observed, and the elusive species they hoped to spot someday. The path wound through a copse of trees, opening up to a clearing that offered a panoramic view of a small lake, its surface shimmering under the late morning sun.

"This is it," Elaine announced, spreading her arms toward the view. "We might catch a glimpse of the migrating teal if we're lucky."

They set up their equipment in companionable silence, each lost in the preparation of their binoculars and cameras. Soon, they were joined by a few other members of the birdwatching club, their arrival marked by muted greetings and the clinking of equipment.

"Hey, Elaine, brought a new friend?" one of the members, a jovial middle-aged man named Michael, called out as he approached.

Elaine laughed, waving Alex over. "This is Alex. It's his first time out with us this season," she introduced.

"Nice to meet you, Alex. Always good to see new faces," Michael said, offering a hand. "Elaine here is one of our star spotters. Stick with her, and you're bound to see something special."

Alex shook his hand, feeling a bit more at ease amid the friendly banter. "I'm looking forward to it," he replied, his interest genuine.

The group's chatter filled the air, mixing with the calls of distant birds. As they discussed recent sightings and swapped stories of rare finds, Alex found himself drawn into the camaraderie, his earlier hesitations fading into the background.

"So, Alex, Elaine tells me you're quite the bird lover," Michael continued, his tone inviting. "Got a favorite?"

"Ah, the cardinal, I suppose," Alex said, glancing at Elaine with a small smile. "For sentimental reasons."

"Excellent choice," Michael nodded approvingly. "Bold and beautiful. We get a few cardinals around here. With any luck, we'll spot one today for you."

As the morning wore on, the group's excitement only grew, their shared enthusiasm acting as a balm to Alex's grieving heart. Laughter and light-hearted disputes over the best bird calls wove through the air, pulling him further from his solitude.

It was in this newfound sense of belonging, amidst the laughter and shared anticipation of the next great sighting, that Alex found a flicker of the peace he had been searching for—a reminder that, like the seasons, life too might find a way to renew itself.

Amidst the fluttering leaves and the symphony of chirps, the group's attention turned skyward as a sudden rustle from the tree line signaled the arrival of something significant. Elaine, with her keen eyes, was the first to spot the flash of vibrant color against the green. "There!" she exclaimed softly, pointing towards a small clearing where the sunlight pierced the canopy in golden beams. The group followed her gaze, spotting the elusive teal as it settled by the water's edge, its feathers shimmering like a gemstone set against the muddy bank.

The bird was rare, a migratory visitor that graced Greenhaven with its presence but once a year. Its arrival was a coveted moment, anticipated by all who held their breaths in the hope of witnessing its tranquil beauty. Alex, new to this collective ritual, felt a thrill of excitement—a pulse of life that, for a moment, seemed to fill the void left by Lydia's absence.

With measured steps, the group advanced, their movements deliberate and respectful of the natural theater unfolding before them. Cameras clicked softly, binoculars were adjusted, and whispers passed between the members like a sacred chant, each word a tribute to the spectacle they were privileged to observe.

Elaine remained close to Alex, sharing insights in hushed tones. "Teals are known for their shyness. It's rare to see one so close," she murmured, her words laced with a reverence that echoed the awe reflected in Alex's wide eyes. As the bird dipped its head into the cool water, ripples danced across the surface, distorting its reflection into an impressionist's painting—nature's artistry at its finest.

The scene was more than a mere birdwatching triumph; it was a moment of collective communion with nature, where human hearts beat in sync with the wild rhythm of the world outside their grief and solitude. Alex felt the tension of the past months dissolve, washed away by the simple purity of the moment. He glanced at Elaine, seeing not just a guide in this new world of avian wonders but a kindred spirit, someone who understood the silent language of loss spoken in the quiet corners of their lives.

The teal, perhaps sensing its audience, soon spread its wings, a preparatory gesture that stilled the air around. With a sudden burst of grace, it took flight, its body slicing through the crisp morning air with effortless precision. The watchers stood in silent homage as it ascended, tracing a path toward the distant hills, its presence a fleeting gift to those it left behind.

As the bird disappeared from view, the spell it had woven broke gently, leaving a trail of soft exclamations and smiles in its wake. The group slowly gathered their gear, the atmosphere light with the afterglow of their shared experience. Elaine turned to Alex, her eyes sparkling with unspoken stories and whispered histories of feathers and flights.

"Moments like these," she said, "they remind us that there's always something beautiful on the horizon, even when the skies seem most empty."

Alex nodded, feeling a resonance within him that went beyond the words spoken. The morning had transformed from a simple venture into the woods into a pilgrimage of sorts, a journey back from the edges of his grief to a place where beauty and remembrance coexisted in peaceful coalescence.

As they made their way back to the park's entrance, the chatter of the group resumed, now filled with plans for the next outing and recollections of past excursions. Alex found himself more engaged, asking questions and sharing observations, his voice no longer just a whisper in the wind but a note in the lively melody of the group.

The sun climbed higher, warming the earth and casting long shadows that danced lightly across their path. With each step, Alex felt a gradual lifting of the shadows that had clouded his heart, a lightening of the spirit facilitated by the natural world's simple, enduring rhythms.

As they reached the park's edge, where the city began to reclaim its territory from the wild, Alex paused to look back at the trees, their branches swaying gently as if waving goodbye. He knew he would return, not just for the birds but for the peace he had found among the feathers and flights—a peace that whispered of new beginnings in the language of lifted wings and shared skies.

The late morning sun had climbed its apex as Alex and Elaine returned to the heart of Greenhaven Park, where the birdwatchers began to disperse with the satisfied ease of a successful outing. Alex felt a certain reluctance to see the morning end, the serenity of the park offering a stark contrast to the solitude that awaited him at home. He lingered near the park's entrance, watching as Elaine spoke briefly with other club members, her laughter a light note floating on the breeze.

Elaine then turned to Alex, her smile still lingering. "I hope today was worth the early start," she said, her voice carrying a hint of hope that he had found some measure of joy in their shared morning.

"It was more than worth it," Alex replied, sincerity marking his tone. "Thank you, Elaine, for... everything today."

She nodded, her eyes reflecting a depth of understanding. "It's good to have you with us, Alex. Birdwatching is better when you can share it."

As the others left, Elaine invited Alex for a cup of coffee at a nearby café, a suggestion he readily accepted. The short walk to the café was filled with a comfortable silence that spoke of an ease forged through shared moments of wonder and reflection.

The café, a cozy place with walls adorned with photographs of birds and local landscapes, welcomed them with the rich aroma of coffee and the soft murmur of its patrons. They chose a table near the window overlooking a small garden where a couple of feeders attracted the less shy city birds.

Sitting across from Elaine, Alex allowed himself to relax, the warmth of the café seeping into his bones. They ordered their drinks, and as they waited, Elaine shared stories of her past birdwatching adventures, each tale woven with threads of joy and sometimes poignant strands of loss.

"It's more than just watching birds, isn't it?" Alex found himself saying, his thoughts vocalizing a new understanding. "It's about connecting— with nature, with each other, with parts of ourselves maybe we've forgotten or lost along the way."

Elaine nodded, her expression thoughtful. "Exactly. It's about finding a way to move forward, to not let the grief become all-consuming. We find little pieces of what we've lost in the world around us, in the flight of a bird, the turning of the seasons."

Their drinks arrived, and as they sipped their coffee, the conversation turned to the rhythms of nature, the cycles of life that promised renewal and rebirth. Alex felt a resonance with the world beyond his grief, a world that Elaine painted with her words, inviting him to explore and embrace.

As the afternoon waned, their conversation dwindled to a contented silence, each lost in their thoughts. Alex looked out the window at the small birds flitting about the garden, their movements quick and full of life. It struck him then, the simplicity and complexity of healing, mirrored in the fluttering wings of the birds outside.

They parted ways with a promise to meet again for the next club outing, and as Alex walked home, he felt less burdened, more hopeful. The day had opened a door he had thought was shut tight by Lydia's passing—

the door to a world vibrant with life and the possibility of new connections.

He walked the familiar streets back to his home, the sounds of the city a gentle background to his thoughts. Inside him, something had shifted, a lightness like the flight of the teal they had watched that morning. Maybe, just maybe, this was the beginning of his path through grief, with each step guided not just by the memory of Lydia but by the new experiences and friendships that awaited him in the wings of the birds he was learning to know and love.

Chapter 2
A Chance Meeting

The second chapter of Alex's journey through grief and towards healing opened on a luminous morning at the Birders' Café, a quaint establishment nestled at the heart of Greenhaven. The café, with its rustic charm and walls adorned with bird-themed decor, had become a sanctuary for those whose passion for birdwatching extended beyond the mere observation of wildlife. Here, the community of birdwatchers gathered not just to share sightings but also to weave their personal stories into the fabric of collective memory and camaraderie.

As Alex stepped inside, the aroma of freshly brewed coffee blended with the soothing undertones of a classical melody playing softly in the background. The café buzzed with the energy of a morning crowd— retirees discussing the nuances of migratory patterns, young enthusiasts comparing notes on their latest equipment, and locals who just appreciated the good coffee and warm atmosphere.

Elaine was already there, seated at their usual spot by the window overlooking the small garden that hosted an array of bird feeders. She waved Alex over, her smile brightening the already light-filled room.

"Morning, Alex! I saved us the best seat in the house," she greeted, her voice carrying the warmth of genuine affection.

"Thanks, Elaine. It looks perfect," Alex replied, taking the seat across from her, his eyes briefly catching the movement of a pair of finches darting through the garden.

Their conversation started lightly, with Alex sharing his attempts at setting up a bird feeder in his own backyard. "It's more complicated than I expected. I had to consult a few 'how-to' articles just to get started," he confessed, eliciting a soft chuckle from Elaine.

"Oh, I remember my first time setting up a feeder. It was quite the spectacle. The birds were wary for days," Elaine shared, her laughter mingling with the clink of their coffee cups on the saucer.

"But I guess it's all about patience, isn't it? Whether it's waiting for birds to come or... dealing with life in general," Alex mused, the conversation edging towards the deeper currents of their shared experiences.

"That's very true," Elaine agreed, nodding thoughtfully. "Patience teaches us to appreciate the moment when it arrives, no matter how long it takes."

Their order arrived, and as they sipped their coffee, the topic shifted to the upcoming activities of the birdwatching club. Elaine was particularly excited about a planned field trip to a nearby reserve known for its diverse avian population.

"We're hoping to spot the Great Blue Heron this time. It's been spotted there recently, which is quite rare for this region," Elaine explained, her eyes lighting up with the thrill of the chase.

Alex listened intently, his interest piqued. "I've read about them but seeing one in person would be incredible," he said, the prospect adding a spark to his voice.

As they continued to talk, a group from the birdwatching club entered the café, their lively banter filling the room with an infectious enthusiasm. They joined Alex and Elaine, expanding their table into a lively roundtable of discussions about the best birdwatching spots and the most memorable bird encounters each had experienced.

"So, Alex, Elaine tells us you're getting quite the hang of this birdwatching business," Michael, a club veteran, said with a friendly nudge.

"I'm trying," Alex replied modestly. "It's a whole new world for me, but it's been... refreshing, to say the least."

"It's more than just a hobby, isn't it? It's about the connections we make—with nature and with each other," Maggie, another club member, added, her voice rich with the wisdom of years spent in the pursuit of feathered wonders.

The conversation deepened, weaving through topics of nature's healing powers and the solace many found in the silent watchfulness required to glimpse the most elusive of birds. For Alex, each story shared and each connection made at that table wove him tighter into the fabric of the community, grounding his recent losses in a tapestry rich with new beginnings and renewed hope.

As the morning waned into afternoon, the group made plans to meet for the upcoming field trip, their voices a blend of excitement and anticipation. Alex found himself looking forward to it with a sense of purpose he hadn't felt in a long time. The café, with its chirping patrons and fluttering stories, had become a bridge from his past to his future, each visit strengthening the bonds he formed with his new companions and with the world that continued to unfold before him.

Under the golden wash of the late afternoon sun, the Birders' Café gradually emptied, leaving Alex and Elaine to the quiet contemplation of their next steps. They lingered over the remnants of their coffee, the earlier vibrancy of shared conversations giving way to a gentle, reflective silence.

Outside, the cafe's garden played host to an array of birds, the feeders swaying gently in the breeze, bustling with the activity of sparrows and finches. Alex watched them with a newfound appreciation, their small lives unfolding with a simplicity and urgency that mirrored his own shifting emotions.

"I'll be heading to the reserve tomorrow to scout the area before our trip," Elaine mentioned, breaking the silence with a practical tone, her eyes scanning a small notebook filled with lists and observations. "It's always good to have a fresh update on the terrain and bird activity."

Alex nodded, his mind already on the lush landscapes of the reserve that he had seen in brochures and heard described vividly during today's gathering. "That sounds like a good plan. I wish I could join, but I've got a prior commitment at the library."

Understanding flickered in Elaine's eyes as she closed her notebook. "Well, there'll be plenty of opportunities, Alex. And who knows? Maybe you'll spot something unique at the library too, some rare bird in a book," she joked lightly, eliciting a small, appreciative smile from Alex.

As they parted ways, the quiet of the café enveloped Alex, leaving him to his thoughts. He decided to take a slow walk through the park, the route home meandering past streams and over bridges where nature was often at its most persuasive. The late afternoon light cast long shadows, stretching the shapes of trees across his path, their branches whispering secrets of resilience and renewal.

His walk became a meditation, the rhythmic crunch of gravel underfoot a grounding beat to his introspective melody. The park, with its vibrant canopy and hidden alcoves, seemed to hold him in a gentle embrace, reminding him of the beauty of continuity and the cycles of nature that promised rebirth from the barest of branches.

At a small pond, Alex paused, watching as a heron stood sentinel in the shallow water. Its stillness was a stark contrast to the flurry of the smaller birds he had come to know in his backyard. Here was a creature that embraced patience, its entire being honed to the art of waiting, and in that waiting, a kind of peace that Alex felt echoing in his heart.

The heron dipped its head, breaking the surface of the pond in a smooth, purposeful motion, emerging with a small fish. The act, so full of grace and lethal precision, was a reminder of the balance of life—of taking and giving, of loss and sustenance.

Turning from the pond, Alex's path eventually drew him out of the park and onto the quieter streets that led home. The houses he passed, with their front gardens coming to life with the first hints of spring, spoke of the ordinary and extraordinary transformations that each season brought.

By the time he reached his front door, the sky had deepened to a dusky blue, stars beginning to prick the evening light, each one a distant world of fire and fury. Alex felt a quietude within, a settling of his spirits that had been tumultuous and raw for so long. Tonight, there seemed a promise in the air, a whisper that in the vast tapestry of the universe, his own thread of grief and recovery was woven with a strength and pattern he was only beginning to understand.

He entered his home, not with a sense of returning to a place of solitude, but to a space that was slowly filling again with the echoes of a life still vibrant, still worth exploring. The evening awaited him, not as an expanse of emptiness to be endured, but as a canvas to be filled with the new colors of his emerging passions and rediscovered joys.

The next morning brought a brilliant burst of sunlight that filtered through the library's tall windows, casting patterns of light and shadow across the rows of books where Alex found his solace and purpose. As he arranged the volumes returned from the weekend's lending, his thoughts meandered back to the birds and the natural calm they represented—a calm he was learning to cultivate in his own life.

His reverie was interrupted by the chime of the library doors and the cheerful greeting of Sarah, a regular visitor known for her keen interest in local history. "Morning, Alex! I was hoping to catch you today. Got anything new on Greenhaven's past?" she asked, her eyes bright with the anticipation of discovery.

"Good morning, Sarah," Alex replied, smiling at her enthusiasm. "Actually, yes, we just received a donation of books from the estate of one of Greenhaven's earliest settlers. They include some journals that might interest you."

"Oh, that sounds wonderful!" Sarah exclaimed as she followed him to the new acquisitions section. "I love the personal touch in journals. The history feels alive, like listening to voices from the past."

As Alex handed her one of the leather-bound volumes, he shared his own newfound appreciation for the narratives held within the natural world. "I've been spending quite a bit of time in nature myself lately. It's like a different kind of history, written in the land and the skies."

Sarah looked up from the journal, intrigued. "That's a beautiful way to put it. Do you think you'll incorporate some of that into your work here?"

"I'm considering it," Alex admitted. "Maybe a series of talks or workshops about the natural history of Greenhaven. There seems to be a growing interest in the community."

"That would be brilliant," Sarah said, her tone encouraging. "And it ties together with the historical aspect beautifully. History isn't just about people and buildings, right? It's about how those people interacted with their environment, how they shaped it and were shaped by it."

"You're absolutely right," Alex agreed, feeling a spark of excitement at the idea. "It's all connected. The more we understand, the better we can appreciate our place in the story."

Their conversation drifted to potential collaboration ideas, weaving together their mutual interests in history and nature. Sarah suggested incorporating local schools in the project, "To get kids excited about their town's history and environment. It's a great way to teach them the importance of preservation and appreciation."

Alex nodded, inspired by her vision. "I like that. It makes the past relevant, and it gives them a sense of belonging to something larger than themselves."

As they continued to discuss the possibilities, more patrons drifted into the library, some nodding greetings to Alex, others pausing to see what had Sarah so animated. It wasn't long before a small crowd had gathered, drawn in by the enthusiasm of their conversation.

One of the patrons, an elderly gentleman named Mr. Jennings, chimed in with his memories of Greenhaven's landscapes. "I've watched this town change, but the hills and the streams, those have been constants. It's good to see new generations taking an interest."

"Absolutely," Alex responded, feeling a deep sense of community binding them together. "Every story adds a layer, doesn't it? Whether it's in a book, a personal tale, or a bird's flight across our skies."

The impromptu gathering slowly dispersed, leaving Alex and Sarah to finalize their plans. They agreed to meet again the following week, each tasked with fleshing out parts of their proposed project.

As Sarah left the library, her departure marked by a hopeful promise of future endeavors, Alex felt a sense of fulfillment that went beyond his usual duties. The library, a vessel of knowledge and community, seemed the perfect place to merge his old life with the new paths he was forging, underpinned by the rhythms of the natural world he was learning to read.

He resumed his work, cataloging and shelving, but with a renewed vigor, each book placed on the shelf a component of the larger narrative he was helping to build—not just for himself, but for everyone who found refuge among the stacks.

Later that afternoon, Alex found himself walking through the familiar rows of bookshelves, his thoughts circling back to the upcoming field trip with the birdwatching club. His interaction with Sarah and the patrons earlier had sparked a deeper interest in intertwining his newfound passion for birdwatching with his professional life at the library.

As he pondered these ideas, his solitude was interrupted by the arrival of Michael from the birdwatching club, his presence a welcome sight amid the quiet hum of the library. Michael approached with a grin, his hands tucked into the pockets of his light jacket. "Alex, I was in the neighborhood and thought I'd drop by. How's our newest bird enthusiast doing today?" he asked, his voice echoing lightly in the spacious aisle.

Alex smiled, setting aside a stack of books he was cataloging. "Hey, Michael. I'm good, thanks. Actually, I've been thinking about how to bring some of the club's activities into the library. Maybe set up a display or a small exhibit about local bird species."

"That sounds fantastic," Michael replied enthusiastically. "It could really raise awareness about our feathered friends and maybe draw more people into birdwatching. What do you need to get started?"

"I was thinking about gathering some materials—photos, maybe some info panels that describe their habitats, feeding habits, typical behaviors. Anything that gives a clearer picture of their roles in our ecosystem," Alex explained, his mind sorting through the logistics as he spoke.

"I can help with that," Michael offered. "I've got a collection of photographs and even some video clips. And I bet Elaine would love to contribute as well."

"That would be great. It's amazing how much birdwatching has opened up a new perspective for me. It's not just a pastime; it's about connecting with the environment and the community," Alex said, his enthusiasm growing as he spoke about his new passion.

"It really is," Michael agreed, nodding. "And speaking of the community, how would you feel about giving a talk during one of our club meetings? Share what you're learning, maybe get more folks interested in the historical and environmental aspects of birdwatching?"

Alex paused, considering the idea. "I think I'd like that. It would be a new challenge, but a good way to integrate my work here with the club activities. Let's plan on that."

"Excellent!" Michael clapped him on the shoulder. "I'll talk to Elaine and set things up. We can make it an event—'Birdwatching and Beyond' or something catchy like that."

As they discussed further details, Alex's confidence in his evolving role within the community solidified. This blending of his professional skills and personal interests felt like a significant step forward, not just in healing from his loss but in forging a new path that honored both his past and his future.

Michael's visit concluded with promises to send over the materials he mentioned and to touch base with Elaine about expanding their collaboration. After he left, Alex returned to his work, his actions more deliberate, each book he shelved, each record he updated, now part of a larger project that connected him more deeply to the community around him.

The day wound down with the golden light of sunset streaming through the library's front windows, casting long shadows over the desks and chairs. Alex looked around at the quiet nooks, each filled with knowledge waiting to be discovered, and felt a profound connection to this place which had served as a sanctuary during his darkest times.

Now, it was not just a refuge but a launching pad for new initiatives that would, hopefully, bring the same solace and joy to others as they had brought to him. As he locked up for the evening, the echo of his footsteps a familiar sound in the emptying hall, he felt a quiet anticipation for the days ahead, each one an opportunity to add another layer to his story, and to the ever-unfolding story of Greenhaven.

Chapter 3
Shared Skies

As the day of the field trip approached, Alex's anticipation grew, not just for the birdwatching but for the deeper connections he was forming within the community. The morning of the outing was crisp and clear, the early sun casting a pale golden hue across the dew-sprinkled fields of Thornwick's hills, where the birdwatching club had decided to meet.

Elaine arrived with her usual cheerful demeanor, her binoculars already dangling from her neck. "Alex! Over here," she called, waving him over to where she and a few other members were unloading their equipment from the back of a large, muddy SUV.

"Morning, Elaine. Looks like we've got the perfect day for it," Alex greeted her, his own binoculars in hand.

"It couldn't be better," Elaine agreed, handing him a clipboard with a list of bird species they hoped to spot. "I've marked the ones we're most likely to see, but keep an eye out for anything unusual. You never know what might show up."

As they set off into the meadow, the group spread out, their eyes scanning the treetops and underbrush. The air was filled with the sounds of the awakening countryside: the distant lowing of cattle, the rustle of small mammals in the undergrowth, and above all, the varied calls of the birds.

"So, Alex, have you thought more about that library exhibit?" Elaine asked as they walked, her voice low so as not to disturb the wildlife.

"I have," Alex replied. "Michael's already sent over some of his photos, and I've been working on the information panels. I'm thinking of including a section on how local bird populations have changed over time, tie it into the broader environmental changes in Greenhaven."

"That sounds fascinating," Elaine said, genuinely interested. "It's a great way to make people realize how everything is connected. The birds aren't just part of the environment; they're indicators of its health."

"Exactly," Alex nodded. "And it's something that can appeal to all ages. I hope it might inspire more people to get involved, or at least more aware."

Their conversation paused as a flash of color darted through the bushes nearby. Elaine raised her binoculars swiftly. "There! A male Eastern Bluebird. See, on that branch?"

Alex lifted his binoculars, focusing as directed. The bluebird was vibrant against the green, its movements quick and fluid. "Got him. That's a beautiful sight."

"They're amazing creatures," Elaine said, watching as the bird flitted away. "Persistent, resilient. They have to be, with the way their habitats are shrinking."

"It's sad, though, how much harder it's becoming for them," Alex reflected, lowering his binoculars. "It makes places like this, and days like today, even more important."

"Indeed, it does," Elaine agreed. "And your work at the library—helping people connect the dots between what they see in their backyards and the bigger environmental picture—that's just as crucial."

As they continued along the path, their group reassembled around a small pond, a known watering spot for many bird species. The chatter was subdued but excited as they set up their viewing stations, everyone eager to see what the morning would bring.

"Mornings like this remind me why I started birdwatching in the first place," Alex shared with the group, feeling a bond with these enthusiasts who took so much joy in the natural world.

"It's the same for all of us, I think," Maggie, one of the elder members, commented. "It's not just a hobby, it's a passion. A commitment to these little guys," she gestured towards a pair of ducks paddling across the pond.

The group shared a laugh, their camaraderie evident in the easy way they interacted. As they settled in to watch, Alex felt a profound sense of belonging. This was more than just an escape from the grief that had once consumed him; it was a step towards something new, a chapter in his life that was just beginning to unfold. With each bird that crossed their path, with each rustle of the leaves, Alex found himself more entrenched in this world, his heart lighter than it had been in months.

As the morning wore on, the sun climbed higher, casting shimmering reflections across the surface of the pond. The birdwatchers remained at their posts, each member entranced by the ballet of avian life before them. Alex, more comfortable with each passing hour, began to recognize the calls and plumage of the birds they observed, his previous apprehensions replaced by a growing confidence.

"This is turning out to be quite the morning," Alex remarked to Elaine, who was jotting down notes in a small waterproof notebook.

"It really is," she agreed, smiling at his enthusiasm. "You're getting quite good at this, Alex. I think you've got the makings of a serious birder."

"Thanks to a good teacher," Alex replied, giving her a grateful nod. "I'm learning from the best."

Their light-hearted exchange was interrupted by a sudden commotion among the reeds at the far end of the pond. A flurry of wings and a splash announced the arrival of a new visitor.

"Look over there," Michael called out, pointing towards the disturbance. "That might be our elusive heron."

The group's attention shifted as they watched a Great Blue Heron gracefully navigate its way through the reeds. Its slow, deliberate steps and intense focus were a lesson in patience and precision.

"There's something truly majestic about herons," Elaine whispered, her binoculars trained on the bird. "They have this calm dignity about them, don't they?"

"They do," Alex agreed, mesmerized by the sight. "It's like they're completely in tune with their environment."

As the heron settled at the water's edge, the group took turns observing through a spotting scope Michael had set up. The bird's every movement was watched with bated breath, its success in hunting a small fish met with quiet cheers.

"It's moments like these that really highlight why we need to protect these habitats," Elaine said as she stepped back from the scope, her expression turning thoughtful. "It's not just for our enjoyment but for their survival."

"You're right," Alex replied. "It makes you think about the bigger picture, the impact we have on their world."

Their conversation deepened into a discussion about conservation efforts in the area. Elaine shared insights from her involvement with local environmental initiatives, explaining the challenges and successes they had encountered.

"It's a constant effort," she explained. "We've managed to secure some funding for wetland restoration not far from here. It's projects like that which really make a difference."

"That sounds incredible," Alex said, genuinely impressed. "It must be rewarding to see tangible results from your work."

"It is," Elaine nodded. "And it's always a bit of a battle, but every small victory counts."

The morning gradually transitioned into afternoon, and the group began to pack up their equipment, their conversation light but filled with plans for future outings and projects. Alex found himself more engaged than ever, his initial interest in birdwatching blossoming into a passionate commitment to the environmental causes it supported.

As they made their way back to the cars, Alex turned to Elaine. "I'd like to get more involved, actually. Maybe bring some of this back to the library, like we talked about. It could really engage the community."

"I think that's a fantastic idea," Elaine said, her eyes bright with enthusiasm. "Let's sit down sometime next week and sketch out some plans. We can coordinate with the club and see if we can set up a series of talks or workshops."

"That sounds great," Alex agreed, feeling a surge of anticipation for the collaborative work ahead.

Their walk back was filled with ideas and laughter, the bonds of friendship and shared purpose drawing tighter with each step. The field trip had not only brought Alex closer to nature but had also woven him deeper into the fabric of a community that valued and fought for the preservation of the natural beauty around them. As they reached the parking lot and said their goodbyes, Alex felt a profound connection to his new friends and their cause, eager for the opportunities that lay ahead.

Back at the library, the calm after the morning's field trip provided Alex with a tranquil setting to reflect and plan. As he sat behind the reference desk, sorting through new material for his upcoming exhibit on local bird species, the library's door chimed and in walked Maggie, one of the elder members of the birdwatching club, her steps slow but determined.

"Alex, dear, I heard about your project," Maggie began, her voice a soft blend of curiosity and support as she approached the desk. "Elaine told me you're planning something exciting here."

"Yes, Maggie," Alex replied, his face lighting up with enthusiasm. "I'm working on integrating our birdwatching with some educational materials for the community. I want to show how our local environment is such a crucial part of Greenhaven's heritage."

"That sounds wonderful," Maggie said, leaning closer, her eyes twinkling with interest. "You know, I have some old photographs and documents from my own collection. They might be just what you need to give your project that extra bit of depth."

"That would be incredible, Maggie. Thank you," Alex said, genuinely grateful for her contribution. "Your experience and knowledge could really enrich this exhibit."

"I'll bring them by tomorrow. And I was thinking," Maggie continued, her voice dropping to a conspiratorial whisper, "maybe you could use this project to host a small event here. A kind of meet and greet for the community to learn about birdwatching and the importance of our natural surroundings."

Alex considered the idea, his mind racing with the possibilities. "That's a fantastic idea, Maggie. It could really help raise awareness and get more people involved."

"I thought you might like it," Maggie chuckled, pleased with his reaction. "I'll help you set it up. We can arrange a few displays, use some of those photographs, and I can even talk a bit about the history of birdwatching in Greenhaven."

"I'd appreciate that immensely," Alex said. "I think it would be great to have you share your stories. It would give the event a personal touch."

As they discussed the details, Alex felt a growing sense of purpose. The library had always been a place of learning and community, but now he was beginning to see it as a beacon of environmental awareness as well.

"Let's aim for next month," Alex suggested, pulling up the library's calendar on his computer. "We could tie it into the local school's curriculum on local ecosystems. Maybe get some students involved."

"Perfect," Maggie agreed, nodding approvingly. "Engaging the younger generation is key. They need to understand the value of their natural heritage."

As Maggie left, promising to return with her materials the next day, Alex felt more connected to his role not just as a librarian but as a custodian of both knowledge and nature. The project was becoming a confluence of his past interests in history and his new passion for birdwatching, each enhancing the other in unexpected and fulfilling ways.

He spent the rest of the afternoon planning the layout of the exhibit and the event, his thoughts occasionally drifting to the birds at the pond, their serene presence a constant reminder of what he was working to preserve. The library slowly emptied as the evening approached, leaving Alex in the quiet company of books and his budding plans.

With each decision he made, from selecting photos to plotting the event schedule, Alex wove a tighter weave into the community fabric, finding his place among those who shared his reverence for Greenhaven's natural beauty. As he locked up the library, the fading light casting long shadows through the tall windows, he felt a quiet satisfaction in the day's achievements and the promising ventures that lay ahead.

As the event day approached, the library transformed under Alex's careful direction. Each morning was filled with the shuffling of chairs, the meticulous arrangement of photographs, and the placement of informative panels that painted a vivid tableau of Greenhaven's avian life. With Maggie's help, old documents and photographs were interwoven with modern images and data, creating a timeline that traced the evolution of local bird populations and their habitats.

The heart of the library held a large map of Greenhaven, dotted with notable birdwatching spots, each marked by a small, detailed description of the birds likely to be seen there. This map became a focal point, drawing in visitors who would pause, point, and share their own experiences of sightings and the spots they held dear.

Outside, Alex had set up a few telescopes, aimed at the small garden where feeders attracted a variety of local birds. These viewing stations became especially popular with children, their excited exclamations punctuating the air as they spotted a cardinal or a cheeky squirrel.

On the day of the event, Alex felt a mixture of excitement and nervousness. As people began to fill the library, he found himself at the center of a gathering that buzzed with anticipation. Community members of all ages, from inquisitive school children to seasoned birdwatchers like Maggie, mingled and shared their stories.

Maggie, true to her word, was a wellspring of knowledge, captivating small crowds with tales from her decades of birdwatching in Greenhaven. Her stories, rich with personal anecdotes and historical context, helped bridge the gap between past and present, illustrating how much the landscape had changed and yet remained a vital part of the community's heritage.

As the afternoon waned, Alex took a moment to step back and observe the fruits of his labor. Families clustered around the exhibits, discussing the displays that detailed the migratory patterns and environmental impacts on local species. Teachers from the local school guided their students through a worksheet that Alex had prepared, encouraging them to learn through observation and engagement.

The event not only highlighted the ecological diversity of Greenhaven but also underscored the library's role as a community hub, a place where education and enthusiasm for nature could thrive hand in hand. Alex's efforts to integrate his newfound passion for birdwatching with his professional life had not only brought a new dynamic to the library but had also rekindled his own connection to the community.

As the last of the visitors left, leaving behind a trail of grateful nods and promises to return, Alex and Maggie shared a quiet moment of satisfaction. "You've done something wonderful here, Alex," Maggie said, her voice tinged with pride. "This is just the beginning, I think."

"I hope so," Alex replied, looking around at the now-quiet library. "It feels like we've opened up a new chapter for the library and for myself."

With the successful event behind him, Alex felt a renewed sense of purpose. The library was more than just a repository of books; it was a living, breathing space where the community could come together to learn and appreciate the natural world around them. As he locked up for the evening, the fading light through the library windows seemed to promise more such events, more opportunities to bring people together, and more ways to serve and celebrate the community he had grown to cherish.

Chapter 4
Mysterious Messages

In the days following the successful event, the library seemed to hum with a renewed vibrancy, its walls echoing with the traces of community engagement and environmental awareness sparked by Alex's initiative. With each morning's arrival, he could still sense the remnants of enthusiasm that had filled the air, as regular patrons and new visitors alike commented on the new displays or paused to examine the detailed maps that now adorned the library's main hall.

On one such morning, under the soft glow of the early sun that streamed through the high windows, Alex found himself organizing a new donation of books on local flora and fauna. This latest influx was a direct result of the event's success, inspired community members contributing to the library's growing collection on natural history.

While he sorted through the books, Michael entered the library, his presence as reassuring as ever. "Alex, that was quite the shindig you put on here," he began, his voice echoing slightly in the quiet morning. "I've had folks telling me they never knew we had such interesting birds right in our backyard."

Alex smiled, placing a book on the shelf before turning to Michael. "Thanks, Michael. It's been great to see so much interest. It makes all the effort worth it."

"Absolutely," Michael agreed, his eyes scanning the new titles on the shelf. "And it's got me thinking—maybe we should organize a series of guided walks? You know, really get people out there, seeing these birds up close."

"That's a fantastic idea," Alex replied, enthusiasm building within him. "It could really help build on the momentum we've started here."

As they discussed potential routes and schedules, the library began to fill with the usual morning crowd. Parents with young children headed to the children's section, while elderly patrons settled into their favorite chairs with the day's newspapers.

Alex's conversation with Michael was a spark, igniting a plan that soon took on a life of its own. Over the next few weeks, Alex mapped out a series of nature walks, each tied to a specific theme related to the birds they might encounter. He used the library's bulletin boards and online social media pages to announce these walks, inviting community members to join and learn more about the habitats that supported local wildlife.

The first walk was scheduled for a mild Saturday morning, the weather cooperating with gentle breezes and a cloudless sky. Alex, along with Michael and a few other volunteers from the birdwatching club, gathered at the designated meeting spot near a well-known local nature trail. As people began to arrive, Alex felt a surge of excitement mixed with a hint of nervousness about leading his first outdoor educational activity.

He carried with him several pairs of binoculars, generously loaned by the club, and a stack of informational brochures he had prepared, detailing the types of birds they might see along the trail. The group that assembled was a mix of ages and experiences, from seasoned birdwatchers to families with curious children, all eager to explore the natural beauty of Greenhaven.

As they set off along the trail, Alex led the way, pointing out nests and listening spots, while Michael shared anecdotes about the peculiar habits of some of the more common species. The children were particularly fascinated, their delight palpable as they spotted a red-tailed hawk circling overhead.

The walk proved to be more than just an educational outing; it was a communal experience that brought the participants closer to nature and to each other. Alex found himself not just imparting knowledge but also learning from the observations and questions of the group members, their insights enriching the experience for everyone involved.

By the time the walk concluded, the participants were sharing their own stories and observations, their faces alight with the joy of discovery. As they said their goodbyes, many expressed their eagerness for the next walk, their enthusiasm ensuring that this new venture would be a lasting addition to the library's community offerings.

Returning to the library, Alex felt a deep satisfaction. He had extended the reach of his passion for birdwatching into the community, fostering a connection not just with nature, but among the residents themselves. It was a confirmation that his efforts were sprouting new growth, weaving a richer tapestry of community life in Greenhaven.

The momentum from the successful nature walks infused the library with a palpable sense of excitement. To build on this newfound enthusiasm, Alex arranged a planning meeting at the library with key members from the birdwatching club, including Elaine and Michael. They gathered around a large table in the library's main reading area, surrounded by stacks of bird guides and regional maps, their faces bright with ideas and anticipation.

"So, what do we think about making these walks a regular monthly event?" Alex started, looking around the table at his fellow enthusiasts.

"I think it's a brilliant idea," Michael responded immediately. "There's clearly a demand, and it's a great way to keep the community engaged with our local environment."

Elaine nodded in agreement, her eyes scanning a list she had made. "Absolutely, and I think we can expand on the themes. Maybe focus on different aspects each month? One walk could be about bird migration patterns, another about nesting habits, or even a night walk for owling."

"That sounds fascinating," Alex replied, his enthusiasm growing. "We could really cover a broad spectrum of topics. It would keep it fresh and interesting for repeat attendees."

Michael leaned forward, his hands clasped together. "And we should think about involving local schools too. Maybe organize a few special walks designed just for students. It could be part of their science curriculum."

Elaine picked up on the idea. "Yes, and perhaps we could coordinate with the teachers to develop accompanying materials that they can use in the classroom. It would reinforce what the kids learn on the walks."

Alex jotted down notes as they spoke, his mind racing with possibilities. "These are all great ideas. How about outreach? We should promote these events more aggressively to reach a broader audience."

"Social media could be a big help," suggested Michael. "We could create event pages, share photos and highlights from each walk, maybe even livestream parts of the walks for those who can't attend in person."

"And let's not forget the local paper," added Elaine. "A regular feature could really help boost visibility and attendance. Maybe one of us could write a monthly column related to what we're doing?"

"Excellent point," Alex acknowledged. "I could take on that task, or we could rotate among volunteers."

The conversation shifted to logistics, with each member contributing their expertise. They discussed the best times and locations for future walks, considering factors like bird activity and the accessibility of trails.

"Timing is crucial," Michael pointed out. "We need to ensure that the walks are held during peak activity times for the birds. Early morning or just before dusk are usually best."

Elaine pulled up a digital calendar on her tablet. "Let's map out some tentative dates. We need to avoid major holidays and check the local events calendar to ensure we don't clash with other community activities."

As they penciled in potential dates, Alex felt a deep sense of gratitude for the group's shared commitment and passion. "This is turning out to be much more than just birdwatching," he reflected aloud. "It's about building a community that's aware and educated about their natural surroundings."

"Exactly," Elaine smiled. "And it's about stewardship, too. We're fostering a sense of responsibility towards our environment. Each walk is an opportunity to inspire that in our participants."

The meeting wound down with tasks assigned and a follow-up meeting scheduled. Everyone stood, gathering their things but lingering in the warm atmosphere of collaboration and shared purpose.

As they left, Michael clapped Alex on the back. "You've really brought something special to the table, Alex. This is just the beginning, I think."

Elaine echoed the sentiment. "Thank you, Alex, for taking the initiative on this. It's going to make a real difference."

Alex watched them leave, feeling both inspired and motivated. The library, once just a repository of books and a haven for quiet study, was becoming a dynamic center for community education and environmental activism, reflecting the evolving interests and values of Greenhaven's residents. As he turned off the lights and locked the door, he was already looking forward to the adventures and opportunities the next walk would bring.

With the series of nature walks now officially on the library's calendar, Alex found himself increasingly in the role of an environmental advocate as well as a librarian. Each upcoming event brought new responsibilities, weaving his passion for nature into the very fabric of his daily work. The library transformed subtly under his care, becoming a hub not only for literary pursuits but also for community engagement with the natural world.

In the weeks that followed, Alex dedicated himself to preparing for the first of these monthly walks, themed around the migratory patterns of local bird species. He meticulously gathered research materials, organized guest speakers, and coordinated with local schools to involve students. The library's main hall was rearranged to accommodate a new exhibit featuring maps, migration charts, and interactive displays designed to educate participants about the intricacies of avian migration.

The morning of the walk was crisp and clear, a gentle breeze stirring the newly blossomed leaves of the trees surrounding the library. Participants gathered early, their faces bright with anticipation, equipped with binoculars and notepads. Alex greeted each attendee with a warm smile, handing out brochures he had designed, which outlined the day's activities and learning objectives.

"Good morning, welcome! I hope you find today's walk both enjoyable and informative," Alex said to a group of arriving families, guiding them towards the starting point where Elaine was already giving an overview of what to expect.

The walk began with a short presentation by a local ornithologist, a friend of Elaine's, who explained the significance of the region in the broader migratory routes used by several bird species. His talk was punctuated by questions from an intrigued audience, their interest palpable in the hushed tones of their inquiries.

As the group ventured onto the nature trail behind the library, Alex led the way, pointing out signs of recent bird activity, from nests tucked into branches to the distinctive marks left by foraging birds on the ground. The trail wound through a variety of landscapes, each offering different habitats and, consequently, opportunities to observe a diverse range of bird species.

Children in the group were particularly captivated, their excitement bubbling over each time they spotted a bird or identified a call from their brochures. Alex watched them with a sense of accomplishment, knowing that these experiences were planting seeds of environmental awareness and stewardship.

The walk concluded at a large clearing, where Michael had set up telescopes aimed at a known nesting site. Here, the group was able to observe a pair of ospreys tending to their young, a sight that drew gasps and awed whispers. Alex took this moment to talk about the importance of protecting natural habitats, linking the survival of these spectacular birds directly to the health of their environment.

"This is why we do this," Alex said, gesturing towards the ospreys. "Seeing these creatures thrive is a reminder of what we stand to lose if we don't act to protect our natural spaces."

The group lingered at the clearing, not eager to end the experience, sharing observations and discussing what they had learned. As they eventually made their way back to the library, the conversations continued, a buzz of inspired plans and promises to return for the next walk.

Back at the library, Alex felt a deep satisfaction as he watched the participants disperse, their expressions reflective and content. He stayed behind to tidy up the materials and displays, his mind already running through ideas for enhancing the next event. The success of today's walk was a testament to the community's growing interest and his own evolving role as an environmental leader.

As he locked up the library, the quiet of the evening settling around him, Alex felt connected to his work in a way that transcended his initial expectations. He was no longer just a guardian of books but a facilitator of greater understanding and appreciation for the natural world. This role, he realized, was his true calling, merging his past and present into a meaningful path forward. As he walked home, the calls of the returning birds accompanied him, a reminder of the day's successes and the promise of more to come.

The ripples of Alex's efforts continued to expand beyond the boundaries of the library and its natural walks, reaching deeper into the fabric of the Greenhaven community. As the weeks unfolded, Alex and his team of volunteers, including Elaine and Michael, began to see the fruits of their labor in the increased engagement of the local schools and community organizations.

One late afternoon, as Alex was organizing materials for the next walk, focused on local conservation efforts, Elaine stopped by the library with a proposal. "Alex, I've been talking with the local environmental club at the high school," she began, her eyes sparkling with excitement. "They want to get involved with our walks, maybe even help us with some citizen science projects."

"That sounds fantastic," Alex responded, his interest immediately piqued. "What kind of projects are they interested in?"

"Well," Elaine continued, setting down a stack of field guides on the desk, "they're really eager to start a bird monitoring program. They want to learn about data collection and analysis, really get hands-on with conservation work."

"I love that idea," Alex said, his mind already racing with possibilities. "It could be a great way to not only engage them with nature but also teach them valuable research skills. We could integrate it with our walks, make each one a data collection opportunity."

"Exactly," Elaine agreed. "And it would give our walks an additional purpose, contributing to ongoing conservation efforts."

As they discussed the logistics, Michael joined them, his enthusiasm matching theirs. "This is turning into quite the community effort," he noted with a grin. "It's amazing to see how much impact your idea is having, Alex."

"I couldn't have done it without all the support," Alex replied, feeling a wave of gratitude for his friends and collaborators. "This is really a team effort."

The planning session extended into the evening, with Alex, Elaine, and Michael sketching out a schedule for the upcoming months and brainstorming additional activities that could be incorporated into the walks. They discussed potential partnerships with local scientists and wildlife experts who could provide guest lectures or guidance for the student projects.

As the details were ironed out, Alex felt a profound sense of accomplishment and anticipation. The library, once a quiet sanctuary for solitary learning, was now a vibrant center of community and environmental activism. He appreciated the irony that his journey into birdwatching, initially a solitary pursuit of healing, had led him to foster such widespread connections.

The next walk was scheduled to coincide with the start of the school's environmental club project. As the day arrived, Alex watched with pride as students equipped with notebooks and cameras joined the regular attendees at the nature reserve. The air was filled with the chatter of eager young voices mixed with the seasoned tones of experienced birdwatchers.

Throughout the walk, Alex led the group, pointing out bird habitats and explaining the importance of each species to the local ecosystem. Elaine and a guest ecologist provided insights into how each participant could contribute to the bird monitoring efforts.

As they reached a particularly scenic overlook, Alex paused, allowing the group to take in the view. "Each of you, with your notes and observations today, are contributing to something bigger," he addressed the group.

"You're helping to ensure that the beauty we see today can be preserved for future generations."

The walk concluded with a group discussion, where students shared their observations and asked questions about their findings. The enthusiasm was palpable, and many expressed their excitement for the next opportunity to contribute.

Walking back to the library, Elaine leaned over to Alex. "You started something special here, Alex. It's more than just about birds now. It's about empowering these kids, giving them a role in protecting their environment."

Alex nodded, his heart full. "It's been an incredible journey," he admitted. "And I think we're just getting started."

As the group dispersed, leaving behind echoes of their day's adventure, Alex stayed behind, locking up the equipment and gazing out at the quiet reserve. The setting sun cast a golden glow over the landscape, and the peaceful chirps of evening birdsong filled the air. This project, born from his grief and nurtured by his community, was a testament to the enduring power of nature and the human spirit to enact change. With a contented sigh, he turned towards home, ready for whatever the next day might bring.

Chapter 5
Suspicions Arise

As the seasons shifted, bringing with them the vibrant colors of autumn, Alex watched as Greenhaven transformed under the brush strokes of nature's palette. The community's burgeoning interest in the local environment, sparked by the educational walks and the library's exhibits, had begun to take on a life of its own. The library, once a quiet haven for book lovers, was now bustling with patrons of all ages, eager to participate in the next scheduled event or to simply learn more about their natural surroundings.

On a crisp October morning, with leaves crunching underfoot and a chill hinting at the coming winter, Alex prepared for a special session focused on the impact of seasonal changes on bird behavior. The library's main room was rearranged to accommodate a large screen for a presentation, and rows of chairs were set out facing the makeshift stage.

Elaine arrived early, her arms laden with additional materials and resources for the day's talk. "Alex, I've brought some new visuals that should help illustrate the migration routes we discussed," she said, unpacking her things.

"Thanks, Elaine," Alex replied, helping her set up. "Your visuals always bring the information to life. I think it really helps people connect with the data on a different level."

As they worked, Michael strolled in, a warm grin on his face. "This place is looking more like a nature center every day," he observed, surveying the setup.

"We're just trying to keep up with the community's enthusiasm," Alex said with a laugh. "It's amazing to see how much interest there is in these topics."

"Absolutely," Michael agreed, taking a seat and watching as more people filtered in. "It's a testament to the hard work you've put in here, Alex. Greenhaven's never been so tuned into its wildlife."

As the room filled, Alex took a moment to step back and appreciate the scene. Families found seats together, children pointing excitedly at the bird posters that lined the walls, while older patrons chatted amiably about their recent sightings and experiences in local parks.

The session began with Alex introducing the topic, his voice steady and clear as he welcomed everyone and expressed his gratitude for their continued support. "Today, we're going to explore how the changing seasons affect our feathered friends, particularly those who make the long journey south for the winter," he explained.

Elaine took over to delve deeper into the specifics, using the visuals she had brought to show migration patterns and how they shifted with climatic changes. "As the days get shorter and the temperature drops, birds receive signals to begin their migration," she detailed, pointing to a map that traced the routes from Greenhaven to various southern destinations.

Throughout the presentation, questions bubbled up from the audience. "How do birds find their way?" one young boy asked, his curiosity echoed in the faces of many around him.

"That's a great question," Elaine responded, pleased with the engagement. "Birds use a combination of strategies, including the sun during the day, stars at night, and even the Earth's magnetic field to navigate."

The discussion moved from the mechanics of migration to the challenges birds face along the way, such as habitat loss and climate change. Alex addressed these issues with a hopeful tone, emphasizing the community's role in conservation. "Every garden, every local park that we maintain and protect can serve as a pit stop for these travelers," he stated, encouraging personal action.

As the event drew to a close, the attendees lingered, reluctant to leave the warm, collaborative atmosphere of the library. Many approached Alex and Elaine to thank them or to ask further questions, their faces alight with newfound knowledge and understanding.

After the last guest had departed, Alex and Elaine stayed behind to tidy up. The success of the event was a reflection of the community's growing commitment to environmental stewardship—a commitment that Alex had nurtured from his own need to connect with nature after his profound loss.

Walking through the quiet, empty library, Alex felt a surge of fulfillment. His efforts to bring the community closer to nature had not only transformed the library but had also deepened his own connection to Greenhaven and its residents. As he locked up for the evening, stepping out into the cool air, the rustle of the autumn leaves seemed to whisper of the ongoing cycle of life, of change, and of renewal.

Autumn deepened in Greenhaven, painting the town with the fiery hues of orange, red, and gold. The chill in the air brought with it a crisp clarity, and the community's growing awareness and enthusiasm for the local ecosystem seemed to mirror the season's vibrant transformation. Alex's library programs had ignited a collective interest that now extended beyond the confines of scheduled events and into casual conversations and spontaneous gatherings around town.

One brisk morning, Alex arrived early at the library to prepare for a workshop focused on winter bird feeding—a timely topic as the colder months approached and food sources for birds became scarcer. He set up stations with various types of bird feeders and seeds, each display accompanied by detailed information about the birds that might be attracted to each type.

As he arranged the last of the feeders, Michael wandered in, his breath visible in the cool library air. "Morning, Alex! I see we're all set for another full house today?" he greeted, his eyes sweeping over the setup.

"Morning, Michael," Alex replied, giving him a nod. "Yes, it looks like we'll have a good turnout. People seem really eager to help out our feathered friends during the winter."

"That's good to hear," Michael said, helping Alex with the final touches. "It's these little things, isn't it? Putting up a feeder, keeping water sources ice-free. They make a big difference."

As the participants began to arrive, wrapping scarves a little tighter against the chill, Alex welcomed them with a warm smile, happy to see many familiar faces. The workshop began with a brief introduction about the importance of supporting local bird populations during the harsh winter months. Alex emphasized how residential areas could serve as crucial sanctuaries for wildlife when natural food sources were covered in snow.

Throughout the workshop, attendees moved between stations, their conversations a low murmur in the otherwise quiet library. Alex circulated among the groups, answering questions and sharing tips on feeder placement and maintenance.

"Remember, consistency is key," Alex advised a young couple setting up their first feeder. "Once you start feeding, try to keep it up throughout the winter. Birds come to rely on the food sources they find."

As the event wound down, the participants seemed reluctant to leave, lingering to chat with Alex and each other, their shared interest fostering a sense of community and collective responsibility. They discussed forming a neighborhood watch program for local wildlife, exchanging ideas on how to make their gardens more bird-friendly.

The library, once again, had transformed into a hub of activity and learning, the seeds of Alex's efforts now flourishing into a community-wide movement. As the last of the attendees left, Alex felt a deep satisfaction in the role he was playing in both educating and uniting the community.

After everyone had gone, Alex took a moment to reflect on the journey he had embarked upon. From grieving the loss of his wife to finding solace in birdwatching, and now leading a community in conservation efforts, his life had taken a path he could never have anticipated.

He gathered the materials from the workshop, storing them carefully for future use. The library was quiet now, the bustle of the day settling into the peaceful silence of an autumn evening. Alex looked around at the space that had become so much more than just a place for books. It was a place of connection, of growth, and of healing.

Stepping outside, Alex locked the library doors and paused to breathe in the crisp air. The town around him was changing, just as he had changed. The trees, ablaze with autumn color, stood as reminders of nature's constant cycle of renewal and resilience. With a contented sigh, Alex turned towards home, his heart light with the knowledge that he was part of something larger—a community committed to caring for the world around them.

With the first snowflakes of the season beginning to drift lazily from a steel-gray sky, the cozy warmth of the library offered a haven for the latest gathering. Today's session was designed to recap the year's activities and to plan for the upcoming spring. Alex, Elaine, and Michael sat around a cluttered table, steaming cups of coffee in hand, surrounded by files and notes, the air alive with the scent of fresh pine from a small tree set up in the corner.

"So, looking back, what do you think worked best this year?" Alex began, his voice filled with both curiosity and a hint of pride.

"I think the hands-on workshops really hit the mark," Elaine responded promptly. "People love getting directly involved. It makes the learning stick and the experience personal."

Michael nodded in agreement. "The birdhouse building workshop was a huge hit. I think doing more things like that—activities where people can create something to take home—is a great way to keep the engagement high."

"Absolutely," Alex mused, making a note. "And getting the schools involved has been a major success. Maybe we can expand that next year, offer some programs specifically tailored for students."

Elaine, flipping through her tablet, chimed in, "I was thinking about a possible 'Bioblitz' event where we could have families and school groups come together to identify as many species as possible over a weekend. It could be a fun competition but also a great data collection opportunity."

"That sounds fantastic," Alex replied, his eyes lighting up. "We could partner with local environmental scientists. Turn it into a real community project."

"And speaking of partnerships," Michael added, leaning forward, "I've been in talks with the city park's department. They're interested in our birdwatching trails and suggested we could help design new ones around the city."

"That's great news!" Alex exclaimed. "It would be a wonderful extension of our work here, and it'd provide more accessible locations for people to engage with nature."

"Exactly," Michael said, his voice enthusiastic. "And it ties back to our mission of conservation and education. The more accessible we make these experiences, the better we can foster a sense of stewardship in the community."

Elaine looked from Alex to Michael, her expression thoughtful. "Speaking of stewardship, how about we organize some regular clean-up days? Not only at the park but also along the river. It would help wildlife and give us a chance to talk about water conservation."

"I like that," Alex nodded. "It's hands-on, it's local, and it's incredibly important. Plus, it shows that we're committed not just to watching birds but to maintaining their habitats."

"As we plan for spring," Michael said, shifting gears, "we should also consider a series of beginner birdwatching sessions. Start right at the basics. We might attract a new crowd who might be intimidated by more advanced talks."

"That's a good point," Alex agreed. "Keeping things inclusive should definitely be a priority. Maybe we can do a few 'Introduction to Birdwatching' sessions in early March. Catch people as they start to look forward to spring."

"And let's not forget about our online presence," Elaine added. "Updating the blog more frequently with tips, stories, and updates could keep people engaged, especially through the colder months."

"I could set up a schedule for posts," Alex offered. "Maybe even feature some guest posts from local experts or other members of the club."

As they continued to brainstorm, the library's main room filled with the soft, ambient sounds of other patrons browsing and reading. The trio's discussion wove through the myriad ways they could expand and enhance their initiatives, each idea building on the success of the past year.

As the meeting drew to a close, they agreed on a rough plan for the coming months, their tasks and responsibilities laid out. They stood, gathering their things, but none seemed in a rush to leave, buoyed by the productive session and the shared anticipation of the projects ahead.

"I'll get started on the promotional materials for the spring sessions," Elaine said as she packed up her tablet.

"And I'll reach out to the parks department first thing tomorrow," Michael added, slipping on his coat. "Let's get those new trails mapped out."

Alex watched his colleagues with a sense of deep camaraderie and purpose. "Thanks, both of you, for everything. It's going to be an exciting year."

As they left the library, the falling snow seemed less like a curtain drawing closed on the day and more like a blank canvas, ready for the vibrant brushstrokes of the coming year's projects. Alex turned off the lights and locked the door behind him, stepping out into the quiet of the snow-covered evening, ready for the future.

As winter deepened, the frosty mornings became the canvas for Greenhaven's newest spectacle: the early bird sessions for beginners, hosted by Alex and his enthusiastic team at the library. The program was designed to attract those new to birdwatching, providing them with the fundamentals in a friendly and engaging environment.

One chilly morning, as Alex set up telescopes and laid out several field guides on a folding table outside the library, Elaine arrived, her breath visible in the frosty air. "Morning, Alex! How are we looking for today's session?"

"Good morning, Elaine! It's shaping up well," Alex replied, checking the alignment of a telescope. "I think we'll have a good turnout, despite the cold. The sign-up sheet was almost full yesterday."

"That's fantastic," Elaine said, her cheeks rosy from the cold as she helped arrange the guides. "These beginner sessions are such a great idea. It's the perfect way to introduce new people to birdwatching."

"I hope so," Alex agreed. "I wanted to create a welcoming space for everyone, make sure they feel comfortable and curious."

As participants began to arrive, bundled in scarves and hats, Michael joined the group, a thermos of hot chocolate in hand. "Brought some warmth for us," he announced, placing the thermos on the table with a grin. "Morning all, ready to spot some birds?"

The attendees greeted him warmly, grateful for the hot drink as they gathered around. Alex started the session with a brief introduction. "Thank you all for braving the cold this morning! We're here to learn the basics of birdwatching, which is not only about identifying birds but also about understanding their behaviors and environments."

Elaine took over to discuss the field guides and how to use them effectively. "These books are your best friends in the field," she explained, flipping through a well-worn guide. "They'll help you identify the birds you see by their color, size, and even their songs."

As the group listened intently, Michael set up a demonstration on using binoculars. "The key to good birdwatching is a steady hand and a sharp eye. Here, let me show you how to adjust the focus," he said, handing a pair to a young woman who looked eager to try.

"Like this?" she asked, peering through the lenses.

"Exactly, well done!" Michael encouraged. "Now, try pointing them at that tree over there. You might catch a glimpse of the early robin we spotted yesterday."

The session unfolded with a mix of theory and practice, the group moving from one station to another, their enthusiasm undampened by the cold. Alex, watching the interactions, felt a surge of pride. The community's response had been beyond what he'd initially hoped for.

As the morning progressed, the sun broke through the clouds, casting a gentle warmth over the group. Alex gathered everyone for a final talk. "As we wrap up today, remember that birdwatching is also about patience and respect for nature. It's about the quiet moments, the watching and waiting, and eventually, the seeing."

Elaine added, "And don't forget, it's supposed to be fun. Enjoy the outdoors, enjoy the learning, and share your experiences with others."

The attendees started to disperse, chatting among themselves about the birds they hoped to see and making plans to attend the next session. Alex and his team began to pack up, satisfied with the morning's success.

"Looks like we've got a few new birdwatchers in our community," Michael remarked, securing the lid on the now-empty thermos.

Elaine nodded, smiling. "It's a good day's work. And who knows? Some of them might be leading these sessions one day."

As they finished packing, Alex looked around at the clearing, now empty of telescopes and field guides but filled with the promise of future gatherings. The successful session reaffirmed his belief in the power of community education and his role in fostering a connection between the residents of Greenhaven and the natural world around them.

Walking back to the library to store the equipment, Alex felt content. The laughter and lively chatter of the morning echoed in his mind, a testament to the community's growing passion for birdwatching and conservation. The winter might have brought the cold, but in Greenhaven, it had also brought a new warmth, kindled by shared interests and newfound friendships.

Chapter 6
Undercover Observations

Spring brought a palpable renewal to Greenhaven, not just in the blooming of daffodils and the fresh green of the trees, but also in the vibrant energy circulating through the community. Alex, feeling the shift in the air, planned an ambitious event to kick off the season: a "Dawn Chorus" walk, intended to introduce participants to the magical morning songs of the local bird population as they announced the new day.

The event was set to begin at the break of dawn, and as Alex set up the last of the signs at the meeting point—a quiet clearing near the edge of town—Elaine arrived, her enthusiasm as bright as the morning sun peeking over the horizon.

"Alex, this is going to be wonderful. Have you heard the robins yet? They're in full song today," she said, unloading a box of field guides from her car.

"I have, it's like they knew we were coming," Alex replied with a laugh. "I think this is going to be a great introduction to bird songs for many of our newcomers."

As they were speaking, Michael pulled up with a trunk full of binoculars and listening devices. "Morning, you two! Looks like we've got perfect weather for bird listening," he commented, handing over the equipment.

"Couldn't have asked for a better day," Elaine agreed, helping to distribute the binoculars among the early arrivals. "Remember, folks, the key to enjoying the dawn chorus is to listen as much as you look."

The attendees, a mix of familiar faces and excited newcomers, gathered around Alex as the sky lightened, a pale wash of colors that hinted at the coming sunrise. "Good morning, everyone! Thank you for joining us at this early hour. You're about to experience one of nature's most beautiful performances," Alex began, his voice clear and welcoming.

"Today, you'll learn not just to identify some of the common bird songs, but also to appreciate the symphony they create together at dawn," Elaine added, taking over the introduction. "Each bird has its own unique call, and they use these songs to communicate—a bit like how we use words."

Michael chimed in, "And just to make it interesting, we'll have a little contest. Anyone who can identify three different bird songs during our walk will get a special prize at the end!"

The group chuckled and murmured in anticipation, their excitement palpable as they adjusted their binoculars and tested the listening devices.

"Let's start with some basics," Alex said as they began to walk along a trail lined with blooming dogwoods. "Listen for the robin—it's one of the most beautiful songs you'll hear today. It's a cheerful tune, often described as a series of melodious phrases repeated several times."

Elaine pointed to a nearby tree where a small bird perched, barely visible in the dim light. "There, that's a robin. Everyone, just listen for a moment." The group fell silent, the clear, lilting song of the robin cutting through the morning air.

"That's beautiful," one of the participants whispered, her eyes wide with wonder.

"It really is," Alex agreed. "And right over there," he gestured to another part of the wood, "you might hear the thrush. Their song is a bit different—more like a series of flute-like whistles."

As they moved deeper into the woods, the full chorus of morning birdsong enveloped the group. Every few steps, another layer of sound seemed to add itself to the morning's melody.

"How about that sound?" Michael asked, pausing to let a particularly melodious warble reach the ears of the group.

"That's a blackbird," Elaine answered, smiling at the rapt faces around her. "They have a very melodious and fluty song, quite distinctive once you learn to recognize it."

The walk continued with more stops, more listening, and lots of questions from the group about each new song they heard. The woods came alive with the sounds of nature, and the participants, guided by Alex, Elaine, and Michael, learned to discern the subtle differences in each call.

As they concluded the walk, the sun had fully risen, casting a warm glow that seemed to ignite the fresh leaves of the trees. "I hope you all enjoyed this as much as we did," Alex said, gathering the group one last time. "Remember, each morning these songs are sung right in our backyards. You don't need to come to the woods to enjoy them."

"Absolutely," Elaine added. "And keep practicing. Soon, you'll start recognizing these songs wherever you go."

As the participants dispersed, chatting excitedly about the birds they had heard and the songs they had learned to identify, Alex, Elaine, and Michael packed up their gear, satisfied with the success of the morning. The dawn chorus had not only showcased the beauty of Greenhaven's avian life but had also brought the community together, sharing in the wonder of the natural world as the day began anew.

As the success of the Dawn Chorus walk rippled through the community, Alex saw an opportunity to further enhance the birdwatching initiatives. He proposed a collaboration between the library and the local nature reserve to establish a permanent birdwatching station that would serve as both an educational resource and a recreational spot for the community.

Meeting with the reserve's manager, Janet, and Elaine, Alex discussed the plan in the library's small conference room, surrounded by maps and birding guides that were marked with potential locations for the station.

"Janet, thanks for coming down. We think this could really benefit both the reserve and the community," Alex started, spreading out a topographic map on the table.

"I'm intrigued," Janet replied, peering over the map. "You've got a good track record with these programs, Alex. What are you thinking?"

"We'd like to build a birdwatching station right here," Elaine pointed to a shaded area on the map, "near the eastern trail. It's an ideal spot because it's easily accessible and already popular with our morning walkers."

Janet nodded thoughtfully. "That does look like a good location. It's near enough to the paths to be accessible but still secluded enough to not disturb the wildlife. What kind of facilities are we talking about?"

"We're thinking a small pavilion with informative signage about the local bird species, and perhaps some permanent binocular stations," Alex explained. "Plus, educational materials that visitors can use to learn about bird behaviors and conservation."

"That sounds wonderful," Janet agreed. "Education is key to conservation, after all. How do you plan to staff it, or will it be self-guided?"

"We were thinking of a hybrid model," Elaine chimed in. "We could have staff during peak times, perhaps volunteers from our birdwatching club. Other times, we could make it self-guided with clear, informative panels and interactive elements."

Janet seemed to warm to the idea. "I like that. It keeps our staffing costs down while maximizing the station's educational potential. What about maintenance and funding?"

"We hope to fundraise through the library and local sponsorships," Alex answered. "As for maintenance, we'd set up a schedule with volunteers, and perhaps occasional support from the reserve's staff."

"Sounds like you've thought this through," Janet smiled. "Let's draft a proposal. I can take it to the board next week. I think they'll be as excited as I am."

Elaine and Alex exchanged a pleased glance. "We'll get on it right away, Janet. Thank you for considering this partnership," Alex said, gathering the maps.

As Janet left, Elaine turned to Alex, her expression thoughtful. "This could really be something special, Alex. A permanent station would be a lasting contribution to our community's environmental awareness."

"I think so too," Alex replied, feeling a surge of anticipation. "It's about leaving a legacy, isn't it? Something that will keep the community engaged with nature long after we're gone."

"Exactly," Elaine nodded. "And it's about deepening our connection with the natural world. Showing people the beauty and importance of these creatures that share our space."

The work that followed was intense. Alex and Elaine spent hours drafting the proposal, refining their plans, and reaching out to potential sponsors. They met frequently, discussing adjustments and preparing for the presentation to the nature reserve's board.

When the day of the presentation arrived, Alex felt a mixture of nerves and excitement. He and Elaine laid out their vision, explaining how the birdwatching station would serve as a bridge between the community and the natural world.

The board members listened attentively, asking insightful questions and expressing their appreciation for the thought and effort that had gone into the proposal.

As they awaited the board's decision, Alex and Elaine discussed the future possibilities. "No matter what happens, I'm proud of what we've started here," Alex said, his voice reflective.

"And I'm grateful to be part of it," Elaine added. "It feels like we're really making a difference."

When the call finally came, it was with good news. The board had approved the proposal, excited by the prospect of enhancing the reserve's educational offerings and its accessibility to the community.

As Alex and Elaine shared the news with Michael and the rest of the birdwatching club, the excitement was palpable. Plans were made, schedules drawn up, and the community buzzed with the anticipation of the new birdwatching station.

Through it all, Alex felt a deep sense of fulfillment. The project had grown from a simple idea to a community-focused initiative that promised to educate and inspire for years to come. As he locked up the library that evening, the setting sun cast long shadows across the quiet town, a silent affirmation of the day's success and the promise of tomorrow.

As spring unfurled its vibrant hues across Greenhaven, the new birdwatching station slowly took shape near the eastern trail of the local nature reserve. Alex oversaw the construction with a meticulous eye, ensuring that every detail—from the placement of the viewing scopes to the accessibility of the pathways—was perfectly aligned with their vision of making nature observation accessible and educational for all.

The structure itself was designed to be unobtrusive, crafted from natural materials that blended seamlessly with the surrounding landscape. Large informational panels, illustrated with vivid photographs and engaging facts about local bird species, were mounted along the interior walls. Each panel not only educated the visitors about the birds they might see but also offered tips on how to observe wildlife responsibly.

Outside, the viewing area was equipped with several high-powered binocular stations, strategically placed to provide optimal views of the nearby habitats known to attract a variety of birds. A small amphitheater, built from local stone, provided a space for school groups and visitors to gather for guided talks and presentations.

Throughout the construction process, Alex found himself at the site almost daily. He worked closely with the builders, sometimes helping to hammer in a nail or adjust a display. His dedication was driven by a deep passion for the project and its potential to enhance community engagement with the natural world.

One cool morning, with the station nearly complete, Alex stood back and surveyed the progress. The sun had just risen, washing the landscape in soft golds and pinks, and a gentle breeze rustled through the trees. A sense of accomplishment swelled within him as he watched a family of hikers pause at the station, the children's faces alight with curiosity as they peered through the binoculars.

"It's really coming together, isn't it?" Elaine remarked, joining Alex with a steaming cup of coffee in her hand. She handed him a cup, and they both took a moment to enjoy the peaceful scene.

"It is," Alex replied, his voice tinged with pride. "It's more than I hoped for. Seeing people already using it, even before it's officially open—it feels like we're really making a difference."

Elaine nodded, her eyes scanning the area. "This place is going to be a cornerstone of environmental education in Greenhaven. You've done something wonderful here, Alex."

Their conversation was brief, their attention soon drawn back to overseeing the final touches. They discussed the upcoming grand opening, planned for the following week, which was shaping up to be a significant community event. Local dignitaries, school groups, and birdwatching enthusiasts from across the region were expected to attend.

As the day progressed, Alex and Elaine coordinated with the reserve staff to finalize the event schedule, which included guided bird walks, live demonstrations, and a series of short talks designed to introduce visitors to various aspects of avian life.

The final days leading up to the opening were a flurry of activity. Alex found himself immersed in preparations, from checking every detail at the station to reviewing the speeches and materials for the event. Despite the busy schedule, he felt energized by the work, each task underscored by the anticipation of sharing this new resource with the community.

On the eve of the grand opening, the birdwatching station stood quiet and ready under the twilight sky. Alex took a solitary walk around the site, reflecting on the journey that had brought him to this point—from mourning his wife to finding solace in birdwatching and ultimately sharing that passion with Greenhaven. The station was a testament to the healing power of nature and the community spirit that had embraced his vision.

As he locked up for the night, the station bathed in the soft glow of the setting sun, Alex felt a profound connection to the place and the people it would serve. Tomorrow would be a celebration, but tonight, the quiet satisfaction of a dream realized filled the cool evening air, settling around him like a promise of new beginnings and continued adventures in conservation.

The day of the grand opening dawned clear and bright, the early sunlight casting long, dappled shadows across the newly completed birdwatching station. Alex arrived early, his heart a mix of nerves and excitement, as he made final checks on the setup. Elaine and Michael joined him soon after, their faces alight with anticipation.

"Alex, everything looks fantastic!" Elaine exclaimed as she walked up, her gaze sweeping over the area. "You've outdone yourself."

"Thanks, Elaine. Couldn't have done it without you and Michael," Alex replied, checking his watch. "Looks like we're all set. How are the refreshments coming along?"

"All ready," Michael chimed in, coming over with a clipboard in hand. "We've got the local bakery to thank for the pastries and the coffee smells great. Should keep everyone happy and warm."

"Perfect," Alex nodded. He looked around as the first guests began to arrive, greeting each one with a warm smile. "Welcome! Thank you for joining us this morning."

As the crowd grew, local reporters and photographers mingled with bird enthusiasts and families, all eager to explore the station. Janet, the nature reserve manager, approached Alex with a broad smile. "Alex, this is a wonderful addition to the reserve. You've really made something special here."

"Thank you, Janet. It's been a collaborative effort," Alex responded, his pride evident. "I hope it serves the community well and helps foster a deeper appreciation for our local wildlife."

"I'm sure it will," Janet agreed. "Shall we start the ceremony?"

"Yes, let's get everyone gathered," Alex suggested, and they both moved toward the small amphitheater.

"Ladies and gentlemen," Alex began, addressing the crowd once everyone had assembled. "Thank you for coming out to celebrate the opening of our new birdwatching station. This project is the result of many months of hard work and collaboration, and it stands as a testament to our community's commitment to conservation and education."

Elaine took the opportunity to speak next, her voice clear and enthusiastic. "This station will provide a unique opportunity for everyone, especially our younger visitors, to learn about and engage with nature in a direct and meaningful way. We have designed it to be a learning hub for birdwatching, a place where curiosity can flourish."

Michael followed, detailing the features of the station. "We've equipped this station with high-quality binoculars, informative displays, and interactive resources that make learning both fun and impactful. Whether you're a seasoned birdwatcher or a newcomer, there's something here for everyone."

The ribbon-cutting ceremony was filled with applause and cheers, as children rushed to be the first to use the binoculars and explore the interactive displays. Alex watched the joy and wonder on their faces, feeling a deep sense of accomplishment.

As the event continued, Alex mingled with the guests, answering questions and sharing insights about the station and its role in the community. "We plan to host regular workshops and guided walks," he explained to a group of interested parents. "It's important that we continue to educate and engage with all age groups."

Elaine, standing by one of the displays with a family, pointed out a particularly colorful bird poster. "See here, this chart helps you identify birds by their color and size. It's a great tool for beginners."

The morning passed in a blur of activity and positive feedback. As the crowd began to thin, Janet pulled Alex aside. "This has been a tremendous success, Alex. I've heard nothing but praise from everyone."

"I'm glad to hear that," Alex smiled, his eyes scanning the station, where a few children were still enthusiastically pointing out birds. "It feels good to see it all come together like this."

As the last of the guests departed, Alex, Elaine, and Michael gathered to reflect on the day's events. "We did it," Elaine said, a satisfied grin on her face. "It's been an incredible journey."

"It really has," Alex agreed. "And this is just the beginning. There's so much more we can do, so much more to explore."

"Here's to many more projects," Michael raised an imaginary glass, the others joining him in a laugh.

As they walked back to the library, the station stood quietly against the backdrop of the bustling nature reserve, ready to welcome its next visitors. Alex felt a profound connection to his work and the community, confident in the knowledge that they were making a real difference in the world, one bird song at a time.

Chapter 7
Unearthing Secrets

Summer had swept over Greenhaven with a warm embrace, the days stretching long and lazy under the benevolent sun. The birdwatching station, now a celebrated addition to the community, thrummed with life as families, students, and enthusiasts visited daily, drawn not only by the allure of the avian inhabitants but also by the engaging workshops that Alex and his team had organized.

One particularly warm afternoon, Alex stood at the entrance of the station, greeting a group of summer campers who bounded toward him with an energy that only the promise of a new adventure could sustain. He watched them with a contented smile, delighted by their enthusiasm.

"Alright, everyone, welcome to the Greenhaven Birdwatching Station!" Alex announced as the group circled around him, their faces upturned and eager. "Today, we're going to learn about the birds you can find right here in our reserve during the summer months."

A small hand shot up in the crowd, a young girl with bright, curious eyes. "Are we going to see any bluebirds?" she asked, her voice tinged with hope.

"Very possibly," Alex replied. "The Eastern Bluebird is quite common around here in the summer. We'll keep our eyes peeled for them and many others."

Elaine, who had been setting up a display of common bird feathers, joined Alex. "We've got a great activity planned for you today," she said to the group. "We'll start with a short walk where I'll show you how to spot nests and listen for bird calls. Then we'll come back here to make your own bird feeders to take home."

The children buzzed with excitement, their chatter rising as they discussed what birds they hoped to see. Alex and Elaine led them down a well-trodden path that wove through the lush greenery of the reserve, stopping occasionally to point out a flutter of wings or a distant chirp.

"Listen," Alex paused, holding up his hand for silence. The group immediately fell still, the forest around them alive with the sounds of nature. "That call you hear? That's a cardinal. A very distinctive sound."

The children listened intently, some with eyes closed, trying to isolate the sounds as Alex described them. After a few moments, they continued on, coming upon a small clearing that offered a perfect view of a hummingbird hovering near a patch of wildflowers.

Back at the station, the children gathered around tables laden with materials for making bird feeders. Elaine showed them how to use recycled materials—plastic bottles, wooden spoons, and string. "Birds are important for our environment," she explained as they worked. "By putting up feeders, we help them find food easily, especially during times when it might be scarce."

The workshop was a blend of learning and doing, with Alex and Elaine facilitating and answering questions. As the afternoon waned, the children's creations took shape, each feeder unique and brightly decorated.

As the campers prepared to leave, one of the counselors approached Alex. "This was really wonderful," she said. "The kids had a great time and learned a lot. We appreciate what you've set up here."

"It's our pleasure," Alex responded, watching the children clutch their homemade feeders with pride. "We love sharing our passion for birds and nature with the next generation. Hopefully, some of these kids will grow up to be stewards of the environment themselves."

The day closed with the laughter and excited voices of children recounting their experiences. Alex and Elaine tidied up the station, putting away unused materials and resetting the displays for the next group.

As the sun began to set, casting a golden glow over the landscape, Alex took a moment to reflect on the journey of the station from concept to reality, and now to a vital educational tool. It was more than just a place; it was a means to connect with and educate the community, fostering a love for the natural world.

With a deep sense of fulfillment, Alex locked up the station, the evening's chorus of crickets and frogs playing him off. The success of the day was a testament to the ongoing impact of their work, a reminder that each small effort contributed to a larger, enduring legacy.

As the summer season unfolded, the birdwatching station not only flourished as a hub of learning and activity but also became a catalyst for a larger discussion on local environmental issues. Alex found himself increasingly involved in community meetings, where he advocated for sustainable practices that would benefit not only the local wildlife but also the people of Greenhaven.

One warm evening, a town hall meeting was convened to address the growing concerns about a proposed development near the nature reserve. Alex, feeling a deep responsibility to protect the habitat that had become central to his life and work, prepared to speak against the proposal.

Gathering in the spacious, somewhat stark municipal building, community members filled the room, their murmurs reflecting a mixture of concern and curiosity. Alex, seated near the front with Elaine and Michael, reviewed his notes one last time before the meeting was called to order.

"Good evening, everyone," the town moderator began, her voice calm and clear. "Tonight, we are here to discuss several issues, key among them the proposed development on the east side of the nature reserve. We'll hear from various community members, and first, we have Alex Martin from the Greenhaven Birdwatching Station."

Standing, Alex approached the podium, his palms slightly sweaty but his resolve firm. "Thank you," he started, nodding to the crowd. "Many of you know me from the birdwatching station, a project that has grown significantly and positively impacted our community. The proposed development area is adjacent to habitats critical for many species we've come to love and learn about. These areas are not just patches of land; they are vital parts of our ecosystem."

A man in the crowd raised his hand, his expression one of polite skepticism. "Alex, while I appreciate your concerns, we also need to consider the economic benefits the development could bring. Can't we find a balance?"

Alex acknowledged the question with a respectful nod. "Absolutely, economic growth is important. However, it's crucial we achieve that growth without sacrificing the environmental health of our community. There are alternative sites for development that would have lesser impact on our natural surroundings."

Elaine chimed in, supporting Alex's point. "It's also worth mentioning the educational and recreational value these natural areas provide. Our children learn about science and ecology through direct experience. We risk losing these natural classrooms if we're not careful about how and where we build."

The discussion continued, with various community members voicing their opinions. Some spoke of the need for jobs and growth, while others, like Alex and Elaine, highlighted the potential long-term consequences of unchecked development.

As the meeting drew to a close, the town moderator summarized the points made. "It's clear we have much to consider. This decision impacts all of us, and it's essential that we proceed with a plan that respects both our community's economic needs and our environmental responsibilities."

Walking out of the town hall, Alex felt a mix of exhaustion and exhilaration. The issue was far from resolved, but he was pleased to have made a compelling case for conservation.

"Alex, you did well tonight," Michael said, clapping him on the back as they left the building. "It's important to stand up for what we believe in."

"Thanks, Michael. It's about more than just birds, isn't it?" Alex replied, his gaze drifting to the starlit sky. "It's about making sure there's a Greenhaven for future generations to enjoy, just as we do."

As they walked back to their cars, the air cool and filled with the scent of summer blooms, Alex felt a renewed commitment to his cause. The challenges were significant, but the value of preserving and respecting the natural world was immeasurable. With the community's engagement at the meeting, Alex saw a path forward—one that required patience, understanding, and continued advocacy.

As summer waned into a golden-lit autumn, the debate over the proposed development near the nature reserve continued to stir within the community of Greenhaven. Alex, who had become an unofficial spokesperson for the environmental cause, spent many of his days gathering data and speaking with experts to bolster the case for preserving the area as a natural habitat.

During one crisp morning, with the leaves beginning to show their fiery hues, Alex visited the site in question, accompanied by a local ecologist, Dr. Helen Barrett. Together, they walked the perimeter, taking notes and photographs, documenting the diverse species that called this small piece of wilderness home.

"This area is a crucial corridor for migratory birds," Dr. Barrett explained as they paused near a cluster of berry-laden bushes, a favorite stopover for many small songbirds. "Losing it could severely disrupt their migration patterns, which are already under pressure from environmental changes."

Alex, notebook in hand, documented her observations meticulously. "And it's not just the birds," he noted, "there are also several native plant species here that are vital for the local ecosystem."

"Yes, the interdependence of species here is delicate. Disruption could lead to unforeseen consequences," Dr. Barrett agreed, scanning the area with a practiced eye.

As they concluded their survey, Alex felt a renewed sense of urgency. The information they collected would be vital in the upcoming community meeting, intended to finalize the decision on the development project.

In the following weeks, Alex compiled the data into a comprehensive report, which he intended to present at the meeting. The evenings were spent in the library, organizing facts and figures into a compelling narrative that he hoped would sway the community and local policymakers to reconsider the development plans.

When the day of the meeting arrived, the library's community hall was packed with residents, a testament to the issue's importance in the town's collective conscience. Alex, feeling the weight of the moment, set up his presentation, the screen behind him displaying vivid images of the wildlife and lush landscapes that were at risk.

As he began to speak, his voice was steady, each word underscored by his deep commitment to the cause. "Thank you all for coming tonight. I want to share something important with you—why this land matters, not just to us, but to the flora and fauna that inhabit it," Alex began, clicking to a slide showing a map overlaid with migration routes and biodiversity hotspots.

"The data we've collected over the past weeks paints a clear picture. This isn't just a patch of land. It's a vital part of our environmental heritage," he continued, presenting graphs and photographs that illustrated the richness and vulnerability of the area.

The presentation included testimonials from other experts, like Dr. Barrett, and anecdotal evidence from local birdwatchers and naturalists who had observed the area's ecological dynamics for years.

As Alex concluded, the room was silent, the impact of his words hanging in the air. "We have a responsibility," he finished, "to protect and preserve these natural resources, ensuring that future generations can enjoy and learn from them as we have."

The discussion that followed was intense and thoughtful, with community members expressing their concerns and hopes. Alex answered questions, facilitated dialogue, and provided clarifications where needed.

After the meeting, as the crowd slowly dispersed, many stopped to thank Alex for his dedication and to express their support for the cause. The decision was yet to be made, but Alex felt that he had done everything in his power to advocate for the environment.

Walking home under the starry sky, the air crisp with the scent of approaching winter, Alex felt a complex blend of exhaustion and satisfaction. The path forward was uncertain, but he knew that whatever the outcome, he had ignited a conversation about conservation that would resonate within the community for a long time.

Reaching his home, Alex paused at the door, looking back at the quiet streets of Greenhaven. The night was peaceful, the only sounds the distant calls of an owl and the rustle of leaves in the gentle wind. Turning the key, he stepped inside, ready to face the future, whatever it might hold.

As the chill of early winter began to settle over Greenhaven, the fate of the nature reserve hung in the balance. The community's involvement had never been more crucial, and Alex found himself at the center of this burgeoning environmental movement. With the final decision on the proposed development looming, he doubled his efforts to rally support and solidify the case for conservation.

One cold, clear morning, Alex met with the town council members at the municipal building, a stately old structure with towering columns and expansive windows that looked out over the main street. With him, he carried a folder stuffed with petitions signed by hundreds of local residents, letters from environmental groups, and the comprehensive report he had compiled with Dr. Barrett.

"Good morning, council members," Alex greeted, his voice steady despite the flutter of nerves. "Thank you for meeting with me today. I'm here to discuss the proposed development near the nature reserve and to present some compelling reasons why we believe this project should be reconsidered."

Councilwoman Marjorie Lee, a middle-aged woman with a reputation for her commitment to community issues, nodded. "We appreciate you bringing this to us, Alex. We've heard a lot from the community on this, and we're eager to see your findings."

Alex opened his folder and distributed copies of the report to each council member. "What we have here are not just statistics and environmental data, but a community's expression of what matters to us. This land is more than just a potential site for development; it's a vital part of our environmental and social fabric."

Councilman Derek Sanderson, who had been a vocal supporter of the development for its potential economic benefits, leaned forward. "Alex, we understand the environmental concerns, but we also have to consider the long-term economic health of our town. How do you propose we balance these interests?"

"That's a fair question," Alex acknowledged. "But we believe that preserving this land can also be economically beneficial. Eco-tourism, educational programs, and community health—all are boosted by maintaining natural spaces. Furthermore, once a natural habitat is compromised, the cost of restoring it—if it's even possible—is often much higher than the economic benefits gained from development."

Councilwoman Lee looked thoughtful. "Your report mentions several species of birds that could be impacted by the development. Could you elaborate on that?"

"Absolutely," Alex said, turning to a section of the report. "Several migratory bird species use this area as a critical stopover. Disrupting their habitats could not only have local repercussions but also impact broader ecological networks. Our birdwatching station has recorded significant data on this, which has drawn interest from both educational institutions and wildlife enthusiasts."

As the discussion continued, Alex felt a cautious optimism. The council members seemed genuinely engaged by the arguments presented, asking insightful questions and discussing potential alternatives to the development plan.

After the meeting, Councilman Sanderson approached Alex. "I have to admit, you've given us a lot to think about. It's clear you're passionate about this, and you've done your homework."

"Thank you," Alex replied, hopeful. "It's about more than passion; it's about responsibility. We have a duty to future generations to keep Greenhaven green."

The days following the meeting were tense with anticipation as the community awaited the council's decision. Alex continued his advocacy, speaking at local events and engaging with the media to keep the issue at the forefront of public consciousness.

Finally, the day of the decision arrived. The council chambers were packed as the members prepared to vote, the air thick with tension. Alex sat among the residents, Elaine and Michael by his side, waiting silently for the outcome.

When the vote came, it was a relief: the council decided to halt the development project, opting instead to designate the land as a protected area. Cheers and applause broke out among the attendees, a wave of relief and triumph washing over the room.

As people filed out of the chambers, many stopped to thank Alex, shaking his hand or clapping him on the back. "You did it, Alex," Elaine said, her eyes bright. "You really made a difference."

Alex felt a profound sense of accomplishment and gratitude. "We did it," he corrected her gently, looking around at the faces of those who had supported the cause. "It was a team effort."

Walking out of the municipal building into the crisp winter air, Alex felt a renewed connection to Greenhaven. The town he loved had shown its commitment to preserving its natural beauty, and he knew that the real work—of continuing to protect and cherish these resources—was just beginning. As he walked home, the streets of Greenhaven seemed more vibrant than ever, the community's victory lending a certain magic to the winter landscape.

Chapter 8
The Confrontation

The winter's mantle eventually receded from Greenhaven, giving way to the tender buds of spring. With the nature reserve now officially protected, the community's spirits were high, and Alex was already planning a spring festival to celebrate the victory and to reinforce environmental awareness within Greenhaven.

On a bright, breezy Saturday morning, Alex met with Elaine and Michael at the library to organize the details of the festival. They gathered around a large table, spread with notes and a calendar, the sun streaming through the windows casting a warm glow on their plans.

"Okay, so we're thinking early May for the festival, right?" Alex began, marking the date on the calendar. "It gives us a month to get everything organized."

"That sounds perfect," Elaine agreed, flipping through a notebook. "We'll have plenty of time to set up booths, organize activities, and maybe even get some guest speakers."

Michael chimed in, "I spoke with a couple of local artisans who are interested in setting up stalls. They can sell environmentally friendly crafts and products. It'll add a nice touch to the festival."

"Great idea, Michael," Alex replied with a nod. "It'll help promote sustainable practices within the community. What about food vendors? We should encourage them to use biodegradable or recyclable containers."

"I'll handle that," Elaine offered. "I'll make sure everyone is on board with green practices. We want this festival to reflect our commitment to the environment in every aspect."

"Speaking of which, I was thinking we could use the festival as an opportunity to launch our new educational program for kids," Alex suggested, his eyes bright with enthusiasm. "We could have interactive workshops, maybe set up a mini birdwatching trail around the library with information stations."

"That's brilliant," Elaine responded, her expression animated. "Kids love getting involved, and it's a fantastic way to educate them about local wildlife and conservation efforts from a young age."

Michael leaned back in his chair, thoughtful. "We should also consider some activities for adults. Maybe a workshop on building birdhouses or a talk about native plants for gardening?"

"I love that," Alex agreed. "Let's make it educational for all ages. We could also organize a clean-up event the morning of the festival, around the reserve and the town. It would set a positive tone for the day."

Elaine jotted down notes as they spoke. "I'll get in touch with the local schools and the Scouts. They're always looking for community service projects, and it could really boost our turnout."

"As for funding," Michael added, pulling out a list, "I've reached out to some local businesses for sponsorships. Many are keen to support, especially after the success of saving the reserve. They see the value in being associated with our conservation efforts."

"That's fantastic news," Alex said, relief and satisfaction evident in his tone. "It shows that our community truly values the environment. We're not just talking about change; we're living it."

Elaine smiled, her enthusiasm infectious. "This is going to be one of our best events yet. I can feel it. It's not just a celebration; it's a statement about who we are as a community."

The meeting continued with the trio fine-tuning the details, assigning tasks, and discussing logistics. The atmosphere was buoyant, fueled by their shared commitment and the supportive buzz from the wider community.

As they wrapped up, Michael looked around at the piles of notes and plans. "We've got a busy month ahead of us," he remarked with a grin.

"We do," Alex agreed, standing and stretching. "But it's worth it. This festival isn't just a party; it's a showcase of our dedication to preserving what makes Greenhaven special."

With their plans set and roles assigned, Elaine, Alex, and Michael left the library, ready to put their plans into action. The work ahead was daunting but exciting, and as Alex locked the library doors, he felt a surge of pride for what they were about to achieve. The spring festival, much like the newly awakened earth, held the promise of renewal and continued growth, a fitting tribute to the community's love and respect for their natural environment.

The preparations for the spring festival were in full swing, with Alex, Elaine, and Michael coordinating a myriad of activities that promised to make the event a highlight of Greenhaven's social calendar. Each weekend leading up to the festival saw them, along with a team of dedicated volunteers, setting up the various stations and ensuring every detail was perfect.

Two days before the festival, Alex was at the reserve checking the setup of the main stage, which would host several speakers and presentations throughout the event. As he surveyed the area, Elaine arrived, her arms full of colorful banners and signs.

"How's it looking, Alex?" she called out as she approached, setting down her load with a satisfied grunt.

"It's coming together nicely," Alex replied, brushing his hands on his jeans. "The stage is almost ready, and the seating arrangements look good. How are the banners coming along?"

"Almost done," Elaine responded, beginning to unfurl one of the banners. "These will add some nice color to the place. Oh, and the local school's art club finished the wildlife murals. They look fantastic."

"That's great to hear," Alex said, helping her to secure a banner to a nearby post. "Those murals will really brighten up the space. And it's a wonderful way to involve the kids."

As they worked, Michael arrived, wheeling in a cart loaded with audio equipment. "Morning, you two. I've brought the sound system. We'll need to do a sound check soon to make sure everything's working for the big day."

"Good timing, Michael," Alex said, giving him a nod. "Let's set it up now. Elaine, could you give us a hand?"

Together, they installed and tested the sound system, ensuring that the speakers and microphones were perfectly positioned for optimal sound quality. As they adjusted the settings, Elaine spoke up.

"I've been thinking about the opening ceremony. Maybe we should have a few words from someone who's been directly involved in the reserve's conservation efforts—like Dr. Barrett. Her work has been instrumental."

"That's a good idea," Alex agreed. "I'll give her a call later today. It would be nice to have her share her experiences and the importance of the community's ongoing support."

"Speaking of support," Michael interjected, "the response from local businesses has been overwhelming. We've got donations ranging from refreshments to prizes for the contests. It's really encouraging to see so much community involvement."

"It's a testament to how much this festival means to everyone," Elaine added, checking off items on her clipboard. "People want to celebrate not just the arrival of spring, but also our achievements in conservation and community building."

As they finalized the setup, the trio reviewed the schedule for the day. The festival would feature guided nature walks, birdwatching sessions, children's craft tables, and educational booths alongside the main stage presentations.

"Do we have everything covered for the children's activities?" Alex asked, concern touching his features. "I want to make sure the little ones have plenty to keep them engaged."

"All set," Elaine assured him. "We've got face painting, storytelling, and even a small scavenger hunt planned around the murals. It should be a lot of fun for them."

Satisfied, Alex took a step back to look over the festival grounds. "This is going to be something special," he mused aloud. "A real celebration of what we can achieve when we come together as a community."

With the sun beginning to set, casting long shadows across the fields, the team decided to call it a day. As they gathered their things, Michael looked around at the nearly completed setup.

"Tomorrow's the big day," he said, a wide smile spreading across his face. "I can't wait to see it all come together."

"Me too," Alex replied, locking up the equipment. "After months of planning and hard work, it's finally happening. Let's make it a day to remember."

They left the site in the twilight, the air filled with the crisp scent of spring and the promise of a successful festival. As Alex drove home, the last light of the day fading in his rearview mirror, he felt a profound connection to Greenhaven and a deep gratitude for the community that had become his extended family.

The day of the spring festival dawned bright and clear, with a gentle breeze that promised to keep the day's warmth at a comfortable level. As the sun rose, its rays casting a golden glow over the nature reserve, Alex arrived early to oversee the final preparations. The grounds were abuzz with activity as volunteers bustled about, setting up the last of the booths and decorations.

Elaine was already there, directing a group of volunteers who were arranging the welcome table, laden with brochures and festival schedules. Michael was testing the microphone on the main stage, ensuring every word spoken would carry clearly across the gathering crowd.

The festival officially began with the cheerful sound of a local folk band, their music a lively backdrop as the first of the visitors arrived. Families, couples, and groups of friends streamed into the reserve, their faces bright with anticipation and curiosity. Children tugged at their parents' hands, eager to explore the various activities that awaited them.

Alex took a moment to stand back and watch as the community he had grown to love came together to celebrate the season and their collective efforts in conservation. The laughter of children at the craft tables, where they busily assembled bird feeders from recycled materials, the focused expressions of participants in the birdwatching workshops, and the lively discussions at the educational booths created a vibrant tapestry of engagement and learning.

Midway through the morning, Dr. Helen Barrett took the stage to give a talk on local wildlife habitats and the importance of community conservation efforts. Her words, passionate and informative, captivated the audience, drawing nods and murmurs of agreement.

"The preservation of our natural heritage is not just the responsibility of scientists and environmentalists," Dr. Barrett said, her voice carrying across the attentive crowd. "It is a duty shared by all of us, young and old, to participate in and advocate for the health of our environment."

As her talk concluded, the crowd dispersed to explore other parts of the festival. Alex walked among the booths, stopping to chat with volunteers and festival-goers, answering questions, and sharing in the joy of the day. At the birdwatching booth, he helped a group of teenagers use binoculars to spot a nesting pair of ospreys.

The afternoon brought a series of guided nature walks, led by local naturalists who explained the flora and fauna of the area. Alex joined one of the walks, his presence a reassuring sight to those who knew him as the steward of the birdwatching station. The path they followed wound through lush greenery, the air filled with the sounds of rustling leaves and distant bird calls.

Later, as the sun began its descent, casting long shadows and painting the sky in hues of orange and pink, the festival drew to a close. The folk band played their final set, a cheerful tune that had people tapping their feet and clapping along.

As the last of the guests left and the volunteers began to clean up, Alex felt a deep satisfaction in his heart. The festival had been a resounding success, not just in terms of turnout but in the palpable sense of community spirit it had fostered.

Walking through the now-quieting grounds with Elaine and Michael, they reviewed the day's events and began to discuss ideas for the next festival.

"It was a wonderful day," Elaine remarked, a smile of contentment on her face. "I think we've really managed to raise awareness and celebrate what makes Greenhaven so special."

"We did," Alex agreed, his eyes reflecting the colors of the sunset. "It's days like today that remind me of why we started all this in the first place."

As they finished packing up, the reserve was peaceful, the day's excitement settling into the tranquil evening. Alex locked up the equipment and took one last look around, feeling a kinship with the land and its creatures, a bond strengthened by the day's shared experiences.

With the festival over, he and his friends left the reserve, the fading light a soft cloak around their shoulders. The night was quiet, the successful day a memory to be cherished and built upon in the seasons to come. As Alex drove home, the sense of accomplishment and community connection stayed with him, a gentle reminder of the good that can be achieved when people come together for a common cause.

The aftermath of the spring festival left a buzz in the air throughout Greenhaven, reinforcing the community's commitment to conservation and the newfound pride in their local environment. The success of the event spurred Alex, Elaine, and Michael to hold a debriefing session at the library to discuss the outcomes and plan for future activities.

Gathered in the small meeting room surrounded by windows that showcased the blooming trees outside, they laid out their notes and feedback forms collected from the festival attendees.

"First off, I just want to say that was fantastic," Michael began, his voice enthusiastic. "The turnout was incredible, and the feedback has been overwhelmingly positive."

Elaine nodded in agreement, flipping through a stack of forms. "Absolutely, people loved the educational booths and the kids' activities were a hit. It's clear that involving the community in these hands-on experiences really resonates with them."

Alex, who had been quiet, reflecting on the event, finally spoke up. "It's more than just engagement; it's about building a legacy of conservation here. I think we're on the right track, but we need to keep the momentum going. What do you think about making the festival an annual event?"

"That's a great idea," Elaine responded immediately. "It could be our flagship event, something that people look forward to every year. Plus, it gives us a chance to showcase the progress of our projects and new initiatives."

Michael, jotting down notes, added, "We could tie it with Earth Day celebrations, make it a big environmental awareness week here in Greenhaven."

"I like that," Alex said, his mind already turning over the possibilities. "We could involve more schools, local businesses, even reach out to environmental experts to give talks or lead workshops."

"The potential for grants and sponsorships could increase as well," Elaine pointed out. "If we start planning now, we could secure more funding and possibly expand the festival's scope next year."

The conversation turned toward the logistics of making the festival an annual event, discussing potential dates, themes, and the resources they would need. Alex took detailed notes, his leadership and vision guiding the discussion.

"Another thing," Michael interjected, "the birdwatching station has been a fantastic addition. Maybe next year, we could unveil new additions or improvements to the station during the festival."

"That's a good point," Alex considered. "It would give us a chance to refresh interest in ongoing projects and unveil new research or conservation efforts."

Elaine looked up from her notes, her expression thoughtful. "Speaking of new projects, I've been thinking about starting a community garden with a focus on native plants. It could be a habitat for local wildlife and an educational resource."

"That sounds wonderful," Alex replied, genuinely excited by the idea. "It ties perfectly into our mission, and I can see it being a popular feature at the festival."

As they wrapped up their meeting, their excitement was palpable, each idea sparking another, building a comprehensive vision for the future.

"We've got our work cut out for us," Michael said, packing up his notes. "But I think we're up to the challenge."

Elaine stood, stretching slightly. "We always are. Let's get started on these plans sooner rather than later. I'll start reaching out to potential speakers and workshop leaders tomorrow."

"And I'll look into funding and grant opportunities," Alex added, closing his notebook. "We've started something special here, and I can't wait to see where it goes."

As they left the library, the setting sun cast long shadows across Greenhaven, the fading light seeming to underline the promise of continued growth and community effort. The streets were quiet as they walked, each lost in thoughts of future projects and possibilities, their conversation a testament to their dedication to making Greenhaven a beacon of environmental stewardship and community collaboration. The night settled softly around them, a gentle reminder of the quiet peace of nature they worked so hard to protect.

Chapter 9
The Apology

With the passing of each season, the roots of conservation within Greenhaven deepened, bolstered by the successful initiatives spearheaded by Alex and his team. The birdwatching station had become a beloved landmark, a testament to the community's dedication to preserving its natural heritage. As winter yielded to the promising warmth of spring, Alex and Elaine found themselves planning another significant project— an extension of the birdwatching station into a broader environmental education center.

One brisk morning, they met at the station to discuss the project, armed with blueprints and an array of documents outlining potential educational programs and expansions.

"As we've seen with the birdwatching station, there's a genuine interest in environmental education here," Alex began, unrolling a set of plans on the table between them. "I think it's time we expand on that. This center could serve as a hub for all sorts of activities—workshops, lectures, even hands-on science projects for kids and adults alike."

Elaine nodded, her eyes scanning the blueprints. "Absolutely, Alex. There's so much potential. We could have themed gardens that showcase native plants, a small wetland area, even a section dedicated to sustainable living practices."

"That's exactly what I was thinking," Alex agreed, pointing to a section of the blueprint. "Here's where we could set up the gardens. And over here, near the back, could be perfect for a classroom or workshop space."

"And don't forget about partnerships," Elaine added. "We could collaborate with local schools and universities. It would give students a chance to get involved in real-world environmental projects."

"That would also strengthen our grant applications," Alex noted, jotting down a note. "Real community involvement, especially with educational institutions, can be a huge boost."

Their discussion turned to funding and resource allocation. "We'll need to be strategic about it," Elaine said. "Grants, donations, maybe some fundraising events. It's ambitious, but definitely achievable."

"I've already started reaching out to potential donors," Alex revealed. "There's interest. People are eager to support projects that have a clear benefit to the community."

Elaine smiled, her enthusiasm growing. "I can start drafting a schedule for classes and workshops. We can offer everything from birdwatching to botany to eco-friendly home practices."

"Let's not forget about the kids," Alex reminded her. "Summer camps, after-school programs, weekend nature walks... there's a lot we can do to get them excited about the environment from a young age."

"Definitely," Elaine agreed. "Engaging them early is key. If we can instill a sense of stewardship and curiosity about the natural world, those lessons will stick with them for life."

As they continued to plan, the scope of their vision for the center expanded. "We could host an annual environmental fair," Alex suggested, inspired by the previous successes. "Local and regional environmental organizations could participate, making it a significant event that draws attention and resources."

"That's a brilliant idea," Elaine responded. "It could highlight not only what we're doing here but also bring in experts from various fields. A real community and learning experience."

Satisfied with their preliminary planning, Alex and Elaine decided to meet again soon with more detailed proposals and a potential timeline. As they packed up their materials, both felt a surge of excitement about the future.

"This could be something really special for Greenhaven," Alex said, locking the station as they prepared to leave. "Not just a center, but a movement."

"A movement," Elaine echoed, stepping out into the fresh spring air, filled with the promise of new growth. "Let's make it happen, Alex."

As they walked away from the station, their conversation continued, already planning the next steps, their commitment to the environment as enduring and vibrant as the landscape around them. With each step, they moved closer to realizing a vision that would educate and inspire their community for generations to come.

The momentum for the environmental education center grew as spring blossomed into full swing, with Alex and Elaine working tirelessly to bring their vision to life. Their days were filled with meetings, planning sessions, and community outreach, each task bringing them closer to breaking ground on the new facility.

One sunny afternoon, Alex found himself at the current birdwatching station, observing a group of local school children engaged in a bird identification workshop. The kids, equipped with binoculars and notepads, were a buzz of excitement, their youthful enthusiasm a vivid reminder of the project's importance.

As the children dispersed, a satisfied smile played on Alex's lips. "This is exactly why we're doing this," he murmured to himself, watching the kids chatter excitedly about the birds they'd spotted.

Later that day, he met with Elaine at a small café in town to review their progress and discuss the next steps. The café, with its rustic charm and views of the bustling main street, provided a perfect backdrop for their strategy sessions.

"We've got a solid lineup of classes and workshops planned," Elaine reported, flipping open her laptop to show Alex a detailed spreadsheet. "And I've been in touch with several experts who are eager to lead sessions on everything from water conservation to native plant gardening."

"That's fantastic, Elaine," Alex replied, taking a sip of his coffee. "How are we doing on the fundraising front?"

"We're about halfway to our goal," she said, her tone optimistic yet cautious. "The big donor event next week should help us close the gap.

I've prepared a presentation that I think will really drive home the value of what we're building."

Alex nodded, his mind already on the event. "I've seen your drafts; it's compelling stuff. This project isn't just about education; it's about creating a sustainable future for Greenhaven."

The conversation shifted to logistics, discussing construction timelines and potential challenges. "We need to make sure we're on track for a fall opening," Alex emphasized. "It's ambitious, but with the team we have, I'm confident we can do it."

"Agreed," Elaine said, her gaze firm. "I'll double-check with the contractors and the suppliers. We can't afford any delays."

As they wrapped up their meeting, they felt a renewed sense of purpose. The tasks ahead were daunting, but the impact of their work promised to resonate deeply within the community.

Returning to the station, Alex spent the rest of the afternoon finalizing the layout for the new center's interactive displays. Each exhibit was designed to be hands-on, encouraging visitors to engage directly with the information and connect more personally with the environment.

As the sun began to set, casting long shadows across the station grounds, Alex took a walk around the site where the new center would soon stand. The land was peaceful, with the occasional call of a distant bird cutting through the quiet. He envisioned the future: children and adults alike exploring the exhibits, learning, and growing together. This place would be a sanctuary not just for wildlife, but for curiosity, education, and community.

The day wound down, and as Alex locked up the station, he felt the weight of the responsibilities he carried. Yet, there was also an undeniable excitement about the future, about the difference they were making. This center would be his legacy—a testament to his love for Greenhaven and its natural treasures.

Driving home, the streets of Greenhaven were quiet, the twilight peace a contrast to the day's busy pace. Alex felt grounded, his dedication unwavering, as he looked forward to the challenges and triumphs the next day would bring.

As the day of the big donor event approached, tension and excitement built in equal measure. The event was critical for securing the remaining funds needed for the environmental education center, and both Alex and Elaine knew the success of their project hinged on this moment.

In the library's quiet back room, transformed for the day into a makeshift command center, Alex and Elaine reviewed every element of their presentation. Charts, graphs, and artist renderings of the center spread across the table, each detail scrutinized and polished.

"Are we sure about the flow of the presentation?" Alex asked, pointing to the layout on his laptop. "I want to make sure we're telling a compelling story. It needs to resonate emotionally, not just intellectually."

Elaine nodded, looking over the slides. "We start with the vision—what we're building and why it matters. Then we'll show them what we've achieved so far at the birdwatching station, the community engagement, and the educational programs that have already made an impact."

"And don't forget the testimonials," Alex added, clicking through to a slide showing quotes and pictures from local residents and program participants. "These personal stories really drive home the impact we're having. It makes the need for expansion clear."

"Exactly," Elaine agreed. "Then we'll wrap up with the specifics of what their contributions will enable us to do. We need to be clear about how their money will be used—down to the last penny."

"Speaking of money, do we have the updated budget breakdown to include?" Alex asked, his tone serious as he sifted through a stack of papers.

"Right here," Elaine said, handing him a sheet. "It's all itemized. I think it will reassure potential donors to see that we've thought through everything, even contingency funds."

"Good," Alex said, looking relieved. "Transparency is key."

As they put the final touches on the presentation, Michael arrived with a box of handouts and brochures. "How's it looking?" he asked, placing the box on a free corner of the table.

"We're just about ready," Alex replied, closing his laptop with a decisive snap. "How are things at the venue?"

"All set up," Michael confirmed. "The stage looks great, and the seating arrangement should work well for our audience. It feels intimate yet professional."

"Perfect," Elaine said, checking her watch. "We should head over soon. Give ourselves a little time to breathe before it all kicks off."

At the venue, a local community hall, the atmosphere was buzzing with last-minute preparations. As guests began to arrive, Alex, Elaine, and Michael greeted them, their expressions a mix of nervous anticipation and confidence.

The presentation began with Alex addressing the gathered crowd. "Thank you all for being here tonight," he started, his voice steady. "We're here to share something very close to our hearts—a project that extends beyond us and touches the future of our entire community."

Elaine took over, clicking through slides as she spoke about the existing programs and their success. "Our birdwatching station has become a cornerstone of environmental education in Greenhaven. But we want to do more. We want to expand our reach and deepen our impact."

As the slides showed images of smiling children and engaged adults at various programs, the room's energy shifted, the audience visibly moved by what they saw.

"And now, we need your help," Alex continued, stepping back up to the podium. "With your support, we can build an environmental education center that will serve as a beacon of learning and conservation. Not just for our generation, but for every generation to come."

The audience listened intently as Alex and Elaine outlined the financial goals and the specific uses for the funds. Each dollar was accounted for, from construction costs to educational materials.

As the presentation concluded, the floor opened for questions, and several hands went up. The inquiries were thoughtful, ranging from logistical aspects of the project to how the community could stay involved beyond financial contributions.

After the event, as the crowd slowly dispersed, many stayed behind to speak with Alex, Elaine, and Michael, offering words of support and, crucially, promising donations.

Driving home that evening, Alex felt a profound sense of accomplishment. They had not only presented their case well but had also ignited a shared passion among the attendees. The funds were almost secured, and the future of the environmental education center looked promising. As he parked his car and stepped out into the cool night air, the stars above seemed to shine a little brighter, reflecting the success of the evening and the hope for Greenhaven's future.

The donor event had been a resounding success, bringing the community closer to seeing the environmental education center become a reality. Now, with the necessary funds almost fully secured, Alex, Elaine, and Michael met at the library to plan the next crucial phase: construction and program development.

As they gathered around the library's conference table with cups of coffee in hand, the atmosphere was charged with excitement and anticipation.

"First of all," Alex began, looking around at his colleagues, "let's acknowledge what a fantastic job we did at the fundraiser. We've nearly hit our target, and it's all thanks to our combined efforts."

Elaine smiled, her eyes reflecting a mix of relief and pride. "It feels good, doesn't it? To see the community come together like this for the environment."

"It really does," Michael chimed in, flipping open his laptop. "So, what are our next steps? We need to start moving on the construction plans as soon as possible."

Alex nodded, pulling out a folder filled with documents. "Right. The first order of business is to finalize our contract with the construction company. They're ready to start as soon as we give them the green light."

"Do we have all the permits in order?" Elaine asked, concern evident in her tone.

"Yes, I checked with the city office last week. We're all set with permits," Alex confirmed. "No red tape is going to delay us this time."

"That's great to hear," Michael said. "And what about our program lineup? We should start getting those finalized so we can begin marketing as soon as the center opens."

Elaine opened her notebook, revealing a detailed list of potential programs and workshops. "I've outlined a preliminary schedule here. We've got everything from beginner birdwatching classes to advanced conservation workshops. I've also included weekend programs for families."

"Looks comprehensive," Alex observed, reviewing the list. "I think it's important that we launch with a strong variety of programs to attract a broad audience."

"Absolutely," Michael agreed. "We should also consider a few signature events for the opening week. Maybe a keynote speech from a well-known conservationist, or even a mini-symposium on local biodiversity."

"That could really set the tone for what the center is all about," Elaine said, nodding enthusiastically. "I'll reach out to some contacts who might be interested in participating or speaking."

"Good idea," Alex said. "And let's not forget about local schools. We should coordinate with them to ensure our educational programs align with their curricula where possible."

"I'll handle that," Michael volunteered. "I've already built a good rapport with the school district from our previous projects. They'll be keen to get involved."

"As for the construction timeline," Alex continued, shifting the focus back to the immediate tasks at hand, "we need to ensure that we're on track for a fall opening. It's aggressive, but with everything lined up, I think we can manage it."

"Do we have a contingency plan in case of delays?" Elaine asked, always the pragmatist.

"Yes, we've built in an extra month of buffer time," Alex reassured her. "And the contract with the builders includes penalties for significant delays. But let's hope it doesn't come to that."

"Right," Elaine said, closing her notebook. "Then I guess we're ready to move forward. It's going to be a busy few months, but I can't wait to see it all come together."

"Neither can I," Alex agreed, his voice filled with anticipation. "This center is going to be something special. Not just for Greenhaven, but as a model for what community-driven environmental education can look like."

With their plans robust and their spirits high, the trio wrapped up their meeting. As they left the library, their conversation continued, filled with ideas and plans, each step forward a stride toward realizing their vision. The community of Greenhaven, once just a backdrop to their individual lives, was now a canvas for their shared dreams, each brushstroke a testament to their dedication to the environment and each other.

Chapter 10
The Accuser

As the leaves began to change, signaling the arrival of fall, the construction of the environmental education center neared completion. The structure, designed to harmonize with its natural surroundings, rose elegantly from its foundation, a physical manifestation of the community's commitment to sustainability and education. The building was a palette of earth tones, with large windows that invited the outside in, and rooftops that would soon sprout green with vegetation.

Alex, who had poured so much of himself into this project, often visited the site to oversee the progress. Today, as he walked through the nearly finished classrooms and workshop areas, he could almost hear the buzz of eager minds that would soon fill these spaces. His heart swelled with a mixture of pride and anticipation. The center was more than just a building; it was a beacon for environmental stewardship—a place where knowledge and action would intertwine to foster a deeper respect for the natural world.

Outside, landscapers were busy planting native shrubs and flowers, creating a series of gardens that would serve both as learning tools and as habitats for local wildlife. The air was crisp, the rustle of leaves and the soft murmurs of the workers blending into a symphony of productivity.

Inside, Alex inspected the interactive displays being installed in the main exhibit hall. Each display was carefully crafted to engage visitors of all ages, with touchscreen panels, lifelike models, and sensory elements designed to mimic the sights and sounds of the regional ecosystem. He adjusted a panel slightly, ensuring it was perfectly level, then stepped back to admire the work.

"Looking good, isn't it?" Elaine's voice came from behind him, her footsteps light on the polished wooden floor.

"It's amazing," Alex replied, turning to her with a smile. "It's exactly how we envisioned it. I can't wait for the grand opening."

"Neither can I," Elaine said, joining him in front of the display. "This is going to change the way our community interacts with the environment. It's a real game-changer."

Their conversation was brief, as there was much to do. They discussed the upcoming training sessions for the volunteers who would staff the center, and Alex mentioned the first series of workshops that had already been scheduled. There was a palpable excitement about the launch, a sense that something significant was about to begin.

As the afternoon wore on, the sunlight began to wane, casting long shadows across the building. Alex took a moment to stand outside, watching as the sun dipped below the horizon. The sky turned a brilliant orange, mirrored by the fiery hues of the autumn leaves around him.

The center stood quiet and imposing against the twilight sky, its contours softly illuminated by the fading light. Alex felt a profound connection to this place, a sense of accomplishment and anticipation. This was the culmination of years of dreaming, planning, and hard work. It was a testament to the power of community and the unyielding human spirit that seeks to preserve and protect the beauty of the natural world.

As he locked up the site for the night, the chill of the evening air brushed against his skin, a reminder of the changing seasons and the cycles of life and growth. He walked to his car, the gravel crunching underfoot, his mind already on tomorrow's tasks. But for a moment, he paused, looking back at the center one last time, allowing himself a moment of quiet satisfaction.

The journey had been long, and the road had not always been smooth, but as Alex drove away, the center receding in his rearview mirror, he carried with him the certainty that what they had created would inspire and educate for many years to come. The night closed in, cool and silent, and Alex felt ready for whatever challenges and triumphs the next day would bring.

With the grand opening of the environmental education center just a week away, the atmosphere amongst the team was a mix of nervous excitement and bustling activity. Alex, Elaine, and Michael gathered in the center's main hall, surrounded by boxes of educational materials and equipment yet to be arranged.

"Okay, let's run through the event schedule one more time," Alex suggested, pulling out a printed itinerary from his folder. "We need to make sure everything flows smoothly on the day."

Elaine nodded, her eyes scanning the document as Alex held it out. "The ribbon-cutting is set for 10 AM, right? Who's confirmed from the town council to speak?"

"Mayor Johnson and Councilwoman Lee. Both have confirmed. They'll speak just after the ribbon-cutting," Alex replied, checking off names on his list. "After that, we'll move into the guided tours of the center."

Michael, who was checking the audio setup in the corner of the room, chimed in, "The sound system is all set for the speeches, and I've arranged for the local high school band to play during the tours. It should add a nice touch to the atmosphere."

"That sounds wonderful," Elaine said, smiling at the thought. "And the workshop stations? Are they all ready to go?"

"I've set up the first three—birdwatching basics, local flora and fauna, and the interactive digital map of the conservation area," Alex answered, gesturing toward the stations. "I still need to test the digital map's software, though, to make sure there are no glitches."

"Good idea," Elaine agreed. "We can't have anything going awry during the tours. What about the children's activities? Those are always a hit."

"They're all set," Michael responded, walking back from the audio console. "We've got the scavenger hunt mapped out, and the craft tables for making seed balls are ready to go. The volunteers running those stations are prepped and excited."

"Fantastic," Alex said with a nod. "Now, what about catering? We need to make sure there's enough food and drink for everyone."

Elaine pulled up her tablet, reviewing her notes. "The caterer is confirmed for light refreshments and beverages throughout the day. I've emphasized eco-friendly products and waste management, so everything should be in line with our sustainability theme."

"As for the evening program," Michael added, "the panel discussion on local environmental challenges should be a major draw. We've got some great speakers lined up."

"Right," Alex confirmed. "Dr. Barrett will moderate, and we've confirmed the other three panelists. They'll discuss everything from climate resilience to wildlife habitat preservation."

"Are we all set with the media coverage?" Elaine asked, her tone shifting to ensure no stone was left unturned.

"Yes, the local news has confirmed they'll cover the event, and I've prepared a press release to distribute afterward," Alex replied. "Plus, the community radio station will be broadcasting live for a couple of hours."

"That should generate some good publicity," Elaine noted, satisfied. "We want as much coverage as possible to boost visitor numbers after the opening."

"Absolutely," Alex agreed. "This center isn't just for today; it's a resource for the future. We need to keep the momentum going."

The three continued to work through their checklist, discussing each detail with precision and care. As the day wound down, they stood together in the center of the main hall, looking around at what they had accomplished.

"This is going to be more than just an opening day," Elaine said, her voice filled with a mix of pride and hope. "It's the start of a new chapter for our community."

"It is," Alex echoed, his gaze sweeping over the room. "And it's a testament to what we can achieve when we work together for something we believe in."

As they left the building, the setting sun cast a warm glow over the center, the golden light reflecting off the windows and bathing the building in a hopeful radiance. The night slowly took hold, enveloping Greenhaven in a peaceful quiet, but inside the center, the spark of tomorrow's promise kept the darkness at bay.

The morning of the grand opening dawned clear and crisp, a perfect day for celebration. As the sun rose, casting a gentle glow over the new environmental education center, Alex, Elaine, and Michael arrived early to oversee the final preparations. Volunteers bustled around, adding the last touches to make sure everything was perfect.

"Elaine, could you double-check the guest list and make sure everyone has their name badges?" Alex asked, surveying the setup with a critical eye.

"Already on it," Elaine replied, tapping on her tablet. "I've got the volunteers on the welcome table briefed and ready. They'll handle the registrations and guide our guests to their seats."

"Great. Michael, how are we doing with the setup outside?" Alex turned to Michael, who was coordinating the outdoor arrangements.

"All set up, Alex," Michael responded with a thumbs-up. "The chairs are arranged, the stage is set, and the sound system was tested again this morning. It's all good to go."

"Excellent," Alex nodded approvingly. "And the signage?"

"All in place," Michael confirmed. "Clear directions to each part of the event, plus emergency information. We're covered."

As they spoke, the first guests began to arrive, greeted by the gentle strains of music from the local high school band, which added a festive atmosphere to the morning air. Alex watched as community members, local dignitaries, and families started filling the seats, their faces bright with excitement.

"This is it," Elaine said, joining Alex as they watched the crowd gather. "It's really happening."

"It is," Alex agreed, a smile spreading across his face. "I can't believe we're finally here. Look at all these people coming together for this."

"It's more than I hoped for," Elaine admitted. "Do you think they'll love it as much as we do?"

"I'm sure they will," Alex assured her. "We've put everything into making this center a place for everyone. How can they not?"

Soon, Mayor Johnson approached them, his expression one of genuine delight. "Alex, Elaine, this is a fine day for Greenhaven! You've both done an outstanding job with this center."

"Thank you, Mayor Johnson," Alex responded warmly. "We appreciate all your support. It's a big day for all of us."

"Indeed, it is," the mayor agreed. "I'm looking forward to seeing the full tour. I've heard a lot about your interactive exhibits."

"They're ready for you to try out," Elaine chimed in. "We hope they'll be as educational as they are engaging."

As the time for the ribbon-cutting ceremony approached, Alex took his place on stage, alongside Elaine, Michael, and several town council members. The crowd quieted as he stepped up to the microphone.

"Ladies and gentlemen, thank you for joining us on this remarkable day," Alex began, his voice clear and steady. "Today isn't just about the opening of a building. It's about opening a gateway to understanding our environment and our role within it."

Elaine followed, adding, "This center represents our commitment to future generations. It's a place where we can learn about our world, and more importantly, how we can care for it."

Michael also spoke briefly, highlighting the community's involvement. "This project was made possible by your support, your enthusiasm, and your belief in a sustainable future. Thank you for making it a reality."

After the speeches, the ribbon was cut amid applause and cheers, marking the official opening of the center. Guests were then invited to explore the facilities, participate in the interactive exhibits, and attend the special workshops scheduled throughout the day.

As the event unfolded, Alex, Elaine, and Michael mingled with the guests, answering questions and sharing insights about the center's features and programs. The feedback was overwhelmingly positive, reinforcing their sense of accomplishment and the center's potential impact.

The day progressed smoothly, filled with laughter, learning, and a shared sense of purpose. As the crowd began to thin and the sun started to set, casting a warm, golden light over the center, Alex took a moment to stand back and take it all in.

"We did it," he said quietly to Elaine and Michael, who had joined him to watch the last of the guests depart.

"We really did," Elaine agreed, a touch of awe in her voice.

"And we're just getting started," Michael added, his eyes on the horizon where the last rays of the sun were disappearing. "Who knows what we'll achieve next?"

With the successful launch of the center, the evening wound down peacefully, leaving Alex, Elaine, and Michael with a deep, satisfying tiredness and the joy of a job well done. They locked up the center, already discussing plans for the next event, their conversation a testament to their ongoing commitment to environmental education and their community. As they left the center, the night settled around them, quiet and full of promise.

The environmental education center was alive with activity, reflecting the community's commitment to understanding and protecting their natural surroundings. In the weeks following the grand opening, the center hosted a variety of workshops and events, each designed to engage and educate attendees about different aspects of conservation and environmental science.

On a cool autumn morning, with leaves turning vibrant shades of orange and red outside, Alex walked through the center, observing a group of elementary school students as they engaged in a hands-on activity about local wildlife habitats. The children's laughter and eager voices filled the room, their excitement palpable as they learned how different animals adapted to their environments.

"This is really making a difference," Alex said to Elaine, who had joined him to observe the session. "Seeing the kids this engaged, it's exactly what we hoped for when we started this project."

Elaine nodded, her eyes bright with satisfaction. "It's wonderful to see. And it's not just the kids. We've had great turnout for all our events. The community really supports what we're doing here."

As the session ended, the children gathered their projects and lined up to leave, chattering about what they had learned. Alex and Elaine thanked the teacher, who expressed her gratitude for the center's resources and programs.

"We'll definitely be back," the teacher promised. "The kids have learned so much today. It's invaluable."

Watching the group depart, Alex and Elaine decided to walk through the center's native plant garden. The garden was designed not only as a beautiful space for relaxation but also as an educational tool to teach visitors about native flora and their importance to local ecosystems.

"The feedback has been overwhelmingly positive," Alex commented as they strolled along the garden paths. "I think we're really starting to see the impact of our work."

"It's more than I could have hoped for," Elaine admitted. "Do you remember when this was all just an idea? Now it's a thriving center of learning."

As they walked, they discussed plans for future programs and possible expansions. The success of the center had opened up new possibilities, and there was much they wanted to accomplish.

"We should consider partnering with more schools," Alex suggested. "Maybe even start a scholarship program for students interested in environmental sciences."

"That's a great idea," Elaine agreed. "Education is the key to long-term change. The more we can invest in these kids, the better."

Their conversation was interrupted by a call from Michael, who was managing a workshop on sustainable living practices at the other end of the center. "You both might want to see this," he said over the phone. "We've got a full house for the workshop, and the engagement is incredible."

Joining Michael, Alex and Elaine watched as participants, young and old, learned about reducing their environmental footprint. The workshop was interactive, with demonstrations on composting, recycling, and energy conservation.

"This is exactly the kind of impact we wanted to make," Michael said as they observed the session. "Educating people on how they can make a difference in their daily lives."

"It's all coming together," Alex responded, a sense of fulfillment evident in his voice. "It's proof that when a community pulls together, real change is possible."

The day wound down with a sense of accomplishment. As the last of the participants left, Alex, Elaine, and Michael gathered to close up the center.

"We've started something special here," Elaine said, locking the door behind them. "It's going to continue to grow, I can feel it."

As they left the building, the setting sun cast long shadows across the grounds, the fading light signaling the end of another successful day. They walked together, discussing plans for the next event, their shared vision for the center and its role in the community stronger than ever.

Driving home, the streets of Greenhaven were quiet, the peace of the evening reflecting the tranquility of the natural world they were working so hard to protect. Alex felt a deep connection to the town and its people, his drive home filled with contemplation and anticipation for the future, his heart full of hope.

Chapter 11
Planned Encounter

In the lush greenery of early spring, the Environmental Education Center buzzed with the energy of a community deeply engaged in its new season programs. Alex, Elaine, and Michael gathered in the center's main conference room, surrounded by the vibrant posters of flora and fauna native to Greenhaven, to plan a spring outreach initiative aimed at further embedding the center into the life of the community.

"Alright," Alex started, spreading a large calendar across the table, "we've got a great lineup of activities planned, but I think we can push a little harder to get more of the community involved. Especially the teenagers. They're the tricky group to engage."

Elaine nodded, tapping a pen against her notes. "You're right. We should think about something that appeals directly to them. Maybe something tech-oriented? Like an app development workshop where they can create something that helps track local wildlife or environmental changes?"

"That's a brilliant idea," Michael chimed in enthusiastically. "We could partner with the local tech club at the high school. They're always looking for real-world projects."

"I love that," Alex agreed. "Let's make sure we pitch it right. It needs to be hands-on and impactful. We could have the apps they develop be used by the center or the community for real data gathering."

"Let's set up a meeting with the high school tech teachers next week," Elaine suggested. "We'll need their buy-in and maybe some help facilitating the workshop."

"I'll handle that," Michael volunteered. "I've worked with them before on a smaller project last year. They're great and they'll jump at a chance like this."

"Perfect," Alex said, making a note. "What about reaching out to younger kids and families? Any ideas on how we can get them more involved?"

Elaine smiled, her mind racing with possibilities. "What about a 'Bioblitz' where families can come and help catalog as many species as they can find in a day? It's fun, educational, and really gets everyone looking closely at the environment around them."

"Another great idea," Alex approved. "We could make it a big event—have some guest speakers, some guides, turn it into a real community day."

"And maybe end with a picnic or a BBQ," Michael added. "Make it a real celebration of our natural heritage."

"Let's do it," Alex decided. "Elaine, can you take the lead on organizing the Bioblitz?"

"Absolutely," Elaine confirmed, already listing what she'd need to do. "I'll get started right away. We'll need to organize some volunteers, get some field guides, maybe set up some stations around the center where people can learn more about what they're finding."

"Sounds like we're going to have a busy spring," Michael noted, his tone a mixture of excitement and resolve. "I'll start putting together some promotional materials. We need to make sure the word gets out."

"And I'll work on the logistics for these events," Alex added, looking over the calendar again. "Make sure we have everything covered—permits, equipment, you name it."

As the meeting drew to a close, the trio felt energized by the plans taking shape. They stood together for a moment, looking out at the center's grounds, where early blooms added splashes of color to the landscape.

"We're really making a difference, aren't we?" Elaine remarked, a note of pride in her voice.

"We are," Alex affirmed, his gaze sweeping over the thriving center. "And we're just getting started. There's so much more we can do."

As they left the conference room, their conversation continued, each contributing ideas and building on the others' suggestions. The center was not just a place but a catalyst for broader change, driving the community towards a deeper understanding and respect for their environment. As they went about their tasks, the promise of the upcoming events filled them with a sense of purpose and anticipation. The center, once a dream, was now a vibrant hub of activity, echoing with the voices of those it had brought together.

The day of the Bioblitz arrived with a fresh spring breeze and a sky so clear it promised a perfect day for exploration and discovery. Early in the morning, Alex and Elaine met at the Environmental Education Center, already buzzing with the setup crew's activity and the early arrival of eager families equipped with binoculars, notepads, and cameras.

"This is turning out even better than I expected," Alex said as he watched a family of four receive their Bioblitz kit from a volunteer at the registration tent.

Elaine, checking off items on her clipboard, replied, "It's all coming together nicely. The station maps are in place, and the guides are ready at their posts. We just need to make sure everyone knows where to go and what to do."

"I'll make an announcement shortly," Alex offered, gesturing towards the makeshift stage set up near the main building.

As people continued to gather, Michael joined them, his face lit up with enthusiasm. "The local newspaper's here," he announced. "They're setting up by the oak grove to get some shots of the participants in action."

"Perfect," Elaine said, visibly pleased. "Let's make sure they get a chance to talk to some of the families and volunteers. It could make for great coverage."

Alex nodded in agreement, then walked over to the stage and picked up the microphone to address the crowd. "Good morning, everyone! Welcome to our first annual Bioblitz at the Greenhaven Environmental Education Center. Today, you're all going to be citizen scientists, helping us catalog the incredible biodiversity of our area."

Elaine then took the stage to explain the rules and goals. "You'll find stations set up around the center, each manned by expert guides. They'll help you identify the plants, birds, insects, and more that you find. Everything you record will help contribute to our understanding of this habitat."

"And don't forget," Michael added, joining them on stage, "we have a special prize for the team that records the most species today. So, make sure to check in at each station and record everything you see!"

The participants cheered, and the excitement was palpable as groups began dispersing towards different parts of the reserve, each led by a guide or following the detailed map provided.

As the day unfolded, Alex, Elaine, and Michael moved between stations, offering assistance and engaging with the participants. At the birdwatching station, Alex helped a group of teenagers spot a rare migratory bird, their excitement infectious as they noted it down.

"This is exactly why we do this," Alex said to Elaine as they watched the teenagers discuss their finding with the guide. "Seeing them so engaged, learning about the ecosystem firsthand—it's invaluable."

"It really is," Elaine agreed. "And seeing everyone from little kids to grandparents getting so involved is just fantastic. It shows how universal the appeal of nature is."

At noon, the participants gathered for a picnic in the large meadow, sharing stories of their morning discoveries. Alex took a moment to speak with several families, listening to their experiences and gathering feedback on the event.

One parent, a father of two young girls, shared, "We've never done anything like this before, but it's been an amazing learning experience for all of us. We'll definitely be back for more events."

"That's wonderful to hear," Alex responded warmly. "We're planning to make this an annual event, and we hope to see you again."

As the afternoon activities resumed, the groups became even more determined to add to their species count. The friendly competition added an extra layer of excitement to the day.

Finally, as the sun began to set, casting long shadows over the grounds, the Bioblitz drew to a close. Participants gathered for the closing ceremony, where the winners were announced and prizes awarded.

"Thank you all for coming out today and for making our first Bioblitz a resounding success," Elaine announced to the crowd. "Your enthusiasm and participation have not only contributed to our scientific understanding but have also helped foster a greater appreciation for our natural world."

As the crowd dispersed, Alex, Elaine, and Michael stayed behind to clean up, their conversation light and full of plans for the next event. The success of the day had surpassed their expectations, cementing the Bioblitz as a key feature in the center's calendar.

Driving home later, Alex reflected on the day's events, the community's enthusiasm echoing in his mind. The education center was truly living up to its potential as a catalyst for environmental awareness and engagement. With each new program and event, they were slowly but surely nurturing a community deeply connected to its environment.

As the Environmental Education Center continued to flourish under the growing involvement of the community, Alex found himself back at the drawing board with Elaine and Michael, planning a new series of seasonal events designed to bring even deeper engagement with Greenhaven's diverse ecosystems. They gathered in the center's cozy meeting room, surrounded by the lush greenery visible through the large windows, a testament to the vibrant life just beyond the glass.

"Okay, the Bioblitz was a huge success," Alex began, flipping open his notebook filled with ideas and observations. "What if we take that momentum and launch a series of seasonal workshops? Each one could focus on different aspects of the environment as it changes throughout the year."

"I love that idea," Elaine responded enthusiastically. "We could start with a winter wildlife tracking workshop. It's a great way to draw people outside and teach them about the animals active during the colder months."

"That would be fantastic," Michael agreed, jotting down the suggestion. "Especially if we could incorporate some night sessions. Winter is great for stargazing too, so we could easily tie that into learning about nocturnal wildlife."

Alex nodded thoughtfully. "Good points. And as we move into spring, we could shift the focus to plant life—maybe do something with wildflowers or tree identification. It would be a nice progression from the animal tracks."

"Spring is also perfect for starting a citizen science project," Elaine added. "Something like a phenology study where community members can help track when certain plants bloom or when animals are first sighted. It would give people a real sense of involvement in scientific research."

"That's brilliant," Alex said, clearly excited by the direction of the conversation. "And it ties back to our mission of making science accessible and engaging. What about summer and fall?"

"For summer, we could focus on water ecosystems," Michael suggested. "Kayaking tours to study aquatic plants and animals. It'd be both educational and a lot of fun."

"And fall is ideal for a workshop on migration and preparing gardens for wildlife in the winter," Elaine pointed out. "We could even include a community planting day where we add some native species to local gardens."

Alex smiled, pleased with the plans unfolding. "These are all great ideas. We'll need to start scheduling and marketing soon if we want to launch the winter workshop in time."

"Marketing is key," Elaine agreed. "We should definitely use social media to our advantage, maybe even create some teaser content to get the community excited about what's coming."

"I can handle the promotional materials," Michael offered. "I'll make sure they're eye-catching and informative. Plus, we can reach out to local schools and community groups directly."

"Perfect," Alex said, closing his notebook. "Let's aim to have a detailed plan for the first workshop by next week. We can review and finalize then."

As they wrapped up the meeting, each team member left with a clear list of tasks. Alex stayed behind for a moment, looking out at the fading light of the day. The center had become more than just a place for learning; it had grown into a vital part of the community, a hub where people of all ages could connect with and learn from the environment around them.

He finally stood, energized by the plans they had set in motion. As he locked up the center and walked to his car, the cool evening air reminded him of the upcoming changes in season. Each season brought its own beauty and teaching moments, and Alex was determined that the community would come to see and appreciate these through the center's programs. Driving home, he was already envisioning the next day's work, ready to continue forging a path that bridged humanity with the natural world around them.

As winter approached, bringing with it a crisp chill in the air, the Environmental Education Center buzzed with preparation for the upcoming Winter Wildlife Tracking Workshop. Alex, Elaine, and Michael convened in the newly installed conference room that overlooked the frosted expanse of the reserve. They were surrounded by a landscape slowly turning white, which provided the perfect backdrop for their discussion on the final details of the event.

"Okay, we're nearly set for the workshop next Saturday," Alex began, spreading a checklist on the table. "Elaine, have all the instructors confirmed their availability?"

"Yes, they've all confirmed," Elaine replied, scrolling through her emails on her tablet. "Each one is prepped and ready. We have the forest ranger, Mr. Thompson, leading the mammal tracks session, and Ms. Carter, our local ornithologist, will handle the bird tracking and identification."

"Excellent," Alex nodded with satisfaction. "And Michael, what's the status on the equipment? Do we have enough snowshoes and tracking guides for everyone?"

"All ordered and set to be delivered by Wednesday," Michael assured him. "I've also checked the weather forecast, and it looks like we'll have a light snowfall the day before, which should be perfect for fresh tracks."

"That's ideal," Alex remarked, pleased with how things were shaping up. "Now, let's talk about logistics. How are we handling registration and group organization?"

Elaine answered, "We're capping each group at ten participants to ensure everyone gets a personal learning experience. Registration is online, and it's filling up fast. I'll send a reminder email to all registrants with what to expect and what to bring."

"Good thinking," Alex said. "Let's make sure to emphasize the need for appropriate winter clothing. Last thing we need is someone getting cold feet—literally."

Michael chuckled, then added, "I'll set up a welcome station with hot cocoa and tea. It should keep everyone warm before they head out. Also, I thought about setting up a small photo exhibit of the wildlife they might encounter. It could be a nice touch to the registration area."

"That's a fantastic idea," Elaine responded enthusiastically. "Visuals always help in sparking interest and setting the scene."

"Okay, next on the agenda," Alex continued, "is safety. Let's ensure all guides are equipped with first aid kits and walkie-talkies. And, given the season, let's have a quick refresher with them about handling any potential wildlife encounters."

"Will do," Elaine noted. "I'll arrange a brief training session for them on Friday. Better safe than sorry."

"And finally," Alex concluded, looking at both of his colleagues, "let's talk about promotion. Are we all set with the press release and social media announcements?"

"Press release goes out tomorrow morning, and social media posts are scheduled throughout the week," Michael confirmed, tapping away on his laptop. "I've also reached out to the local community cable channel.

They're interested in doing a segment on the workshop, which could really boost our visibility."

"Fantastic work, Michael," Alex commended. "It looks like we're on track for a successful event. This workshop is going to be a great way to engage the community and educate them about the wildlife in their own backyard."

As the meeting wrapped up, they all felt a sense of anticipation for the event. The winter workshop was not just an educational opportunity but a chance to strengthen the community's connection to their environment.

"Alright, team," Alex said, standing up and stretching slightly, "let's make this a winter to remember."

As they left the conference room, the setting sun cast a golden glow across the snowy landscape, painting a serene and beautiful picture of the reserve. The coming days promised to be busy but rewarding as they worked together to bring another enriching experience to the people of Greenhaven. As they walked through the crisp evening air back to their cars, their conversation continued, filled with ideas and plans, each step echoing their commitment to the environment and their community.

Chapter 12
Public Revelations

The Winter Wildlife Tracking Workshop proved to be a resounding success, leaving the community of Greenhaven buzzing with renewed enthusiasm for local wildlife and conservation efforts. As winter waned and the first signs of spring began to show, Alex, Elaine, and Michael gathered at the Environmental Education Center to discuss the impact of the workshop and to plan for the upcoming season.

"I've been looking over the feedback from the workshop," Alex began, spreading several sheets of summarized responses on the table in front of them. "It's overwhelmingly positive. People really appreciated the hands-on learning experience."

"That's fantastic to hear," Elaine replied, sipping her coffee. "I think it really helped to have the experts on hand to guide them. The personal touch makes a difference."

Michael nodded, scrolling through data on his laptop. "The social media engagement was off the charts as well. We had participants posting pictures and sharing their experiences. It's done a great job of raising awareness."

"Let's capitalize on this momentum," Alex suggested. "Spring is just around the corner, and it's a perfect time to introduce new programs. Any thoughts?"

"Well, considering the interest in the tracking workshop, why not continue with a similar theme?" Elaine proposed. "Perhaps a series on bird migration could be timely. We could tie it in with global birdwatching days and even involve some citizen science projects."

"That sounds great," Michael chimed in. "And bird migration is a topic that could attract a broader audience. We could set up some live streaming of nest cams, have interactive migration maps, and maybe even host some talks from ornithologists."

"I like where this is heading," Alex said, his mind racing with possibilities. "Let's not forget the educational aspect for schools. We could develop a curriculum module that teachers can use alongside the events."

"We should also consider expanding our volunteer base," Elaine added. "With more programs, we'll need more hands on deck. Maybe a volunteer recruitment day? We could pair it with an open house or a nature walk."

"Good idea," Alex agreed, making a note. "Let's schedule that early in the season. It would give new volunteers a chance to get involved right from the start."

"As for logistics," Michael said, shifting topics, "we'll need to ensure that our facilities can handle increased visitor numbers, especially if we're planning more live events. Maybe we should think about adding some temporary structures or enhancing our existing spaces."

"That's a valid point," Elaine acknowledged. "Especially with unpredictable spring weather. Let's look into some options for that. Perhaps some weather-resistant pavilions or even expand the indoor lecture halls."

"Alright," Alex concluded, gathering up the feedback sheets. "Let's start putting these ideas into action. Elaine, can you take the lead on the bird migration series? And Michael, look into the logistics for the volunteer day and additional infrastructure."

"Will do," they both responded, energized by the plan.

As the meeting wrapped up, the trio looked out over the grounds of the center, where the snow was slowly melting away, revealing the dormant life beneath. The promise of spring was in the air, a season of growth not just for the natural world outside but also for their burgeoning initiatives at the center.

Walking back to their respective offices, their conversation continued, each exchange brimming with ideas and strategies. The center was more than just a place; it had become a catalyst for community engagement and environmental stewardship. As they parted ways, Alex felt a deep sense of gratitude and purpose, energized by the path they were paving together.

As spring unfurled its verdant leaves and colorful blossoms, the Environmental Education Center was abuzz with preparations for the upcoming bird migration series. Alex, Elaine, and Michael convened in the newly expanded lecture hall, surrounded by promotional materials and ornithological guides, to finalize the details of the event.

"Elaine, how's the schedule looking for the migration talks?" Alex asked, peering over a stack of flyers designed to attract local bird enthusiasts.

"It's shaping up nicely," Elaine replied, flipping through her planner. "We've got three confirmed speakers so far, including Dr. Aimes, who's an expert on migratory patterns in our region. Each talk will focus on a different aspect of migration, from navigational strategies to the impact of climate change."

"That sounds incredibly insightful," Michael interjected, arranging the seating chart for the hall. "Have we sorted out the tech setup for live streaming the nest cams? I know that's going to be a huge draw."

"Yes, the IT team finalized the installation yesterday," Elaine confirmed. "We'll have live feeds from three local nests, which we'll project onto screens here and in the main foyer. Viewers can watch the birds in real time, which will be a fantastic educational tool."

"Great work, Elaine," Alex said, clearly pleased. "Now, regarding the citizen science project, Michael, where do we stand with the online platform for data collection?"

"We're all set up," Michael replied, tapping on his laptop to bring up the website. "Participants can log their own sightings and upload photos. We've made it very user-friendly, and there's a section for kids to participate with their schools."

"Perfect," Alex nodded. "Engaging families and schools is key. Speaking of which, have we reached out to the local schools to encourage participation?"

"Yes, I've sent packages to all the schools in our district," Elaine answered, checking off another item on her list. "The packages include lesson plans, identification guides, and information on how to access the online platform. We've also invited them to a special educational day at the center."

"That's excellent," Alex said. "We want to make sure the educational impact of this series is as broad and deep as possible."

"And what about our volunteers?" Michael asked, looking over a list of names. "We'll need plenty of help during the event, especially with guiding visitors and managing the interactive stations."

"I've scheduled a training session for all new volunteers next week," Elaine responded. "They'll learn about bird identification, use of the digital tools, and customer service. I want everyone to feel confident and knowledgeable."

"Sounds like we're almost ready to go," Alex said with a smile. "Just one last thing—how are we handling promotions for the rest of the community?"

"We've planned a community day right before the series starts," Michael answered. "It'll include a mini-expo with booths from local conservation groups, a guided nature walk, and some fun activities for kids. It should be a good way to drum up excitement and attendance for the series."

"That's a great way to kick things off," Alex agreed. "Let's make sure we have enough promotional materials ready for that day. Flyers, posters, and maybe some freebies to give away."

"I'll take care of that," Elaine said, making a note. "I think we're in good shape to make this series a major success."

As they wrapped up their meeting, the three stood together, looking around the lecture hall, now ready to welcome crowds eager to learn about the wonders of bird migration. Their collaborative spirit had transformed the center into a vibrant hub of learning and community engagement.

Walking out of the hall, their conversation lingered on the exciting weeks ahead, each detail meticulously planned to ensure that the bird migration series not only educated but also inspired. They parted ways, each to attend to their final tasks, the center buzzing with the same vibrant energy that spring brought to the world outside.

The bird migration series, titled "Wings of Spring," finally commenced, drawing an enthusiastic crowd eager to delve into the mysteries of avian journeys. The Environmental Education Center was alive with visitors of all ages, their faces bright with anticipation as they gathered in the newly enhanced lecture hall. Alex, Elaine, and Michael were at the forefront, ensuring the inaugural session ran smoothly.

As the crowd settled, Alex stepped up to the podium to introduce the first speaker, Dr. Aimes, a renowned ornithologist known for her research on migratory patterns. "Good morning, everyone! Thank you for joining us at the start of our 'Wings of Spring' series," Alex began, his voice filled with genuine enthusiasm. "Today, we have the pleasure of hearing from Dr. Aimes, who will share fascinating insights into how birds navigate across continents."

Dr. Aimes took the stage amid applause, her presence commanding attention. "Thank you, Alex, and thanks to all of you for being here. It's truly inspiring to see so many faces, young and old, eager to learn about our feathered friends. Migration is one of nature's most remarkable phenomena, and it offers us critical insights into the health of our planet."

As Dr. Aimes continued with her presentation, Elaine leaned over to Michael, whispering, "The live feeds from the nest cams are ready to go. We should transition to that after Dr. Aimes discusses the challenges birds face during migration."

"Perfect timing," Michael whispered back. "It'll give everyone a real-time look at what she's been describing. I'll cue up the tech team."

Dr. Aimes wrapped up her talk with a powerful call to action, emphasizing the role everyone plays in conserving migratory pathways. "And now," she concluded, "let's take a live look at some of our local nests, where you can see the culmination of incredible migratory journeys happening right in our backyard."

Michael signaled to the tech team, and the screens around the hall lit up with images of nesting birds, some feeding chicks, others tending to their nests. Murmurs of awe filled the room as attendees experienced the intimate lives of birds through the cameras.

"This is incredible," a young boy exclaimed, his eyes wide as he pointed at the screen showing a hawk delicately maneuvering in its nest.

"It really is," Elaine responded, joining the boy and his family. "These cameras help us study and protect these birds by understanding their needs and behaviors."

The session transitioned into interactive Q&A, where audience members asked Dr. Aimes and the center's experts various questions. "How can we help protect these birds during migration?" one attendee asked.

"Great question," Dr. Aimes answered. "Preserving natural habitats is key. Also, participating in local conservation efforts and being mindful of how our actions impact the environment can make a big difference."

As the day progressed, attendees moved between different stations set up around the center, including hands-on workshops on building birdhouses and crafting bird feeders from recycled materials. Michael oversaw these activities, offering guidance and sharing tidbits of bird lore with participants.

"Did you know that some birds can travel thousands of miles back to the exact same nesting spot each year?" he told a group of wide-eyed children hammering away at their birdhouses.

"No way! That's so cool!" one of the children responded, clearly impressed.

"Yes, it is," Michael agreed, smiling. "Birds are amazing navigators, which is why we need to ensure their travel routes are safe and undisturbed."

As the event drew to a close, Alex, Elaine, and Michael gathered briefly to debrief. "Today was a great start," Alex said, looking around at the still-buzzing crowd. "I think we've sparked a lot of interest and, hopefully, a lot of future conservationists."

"I agree," Elaine nodded. "It's about building a community that cares deeply about these issues. Days like today go a long way towards that goal."

"Here's to many more successful days," Michael added, his gaze sweeping across the hall where families were still engaged in activities, talking and laughing.

As they parted ways to tend to the final activities of the day, the center buzzed with the vibrant energy of shared learning and community spirit. The success of the day was a testament to the enduring commitment of the center's staff and the community's growing passion for environmental stewardship. As the visitors eventually trickled out, Alex took a moment to appreciate the impact of their efforts, feeling a profound connection to both the people and the purpose they served.

As the "Wings of Spring" series progressed, it became a highlight of the community calendar in Greenhaven. The environmental education center, bustling with activity, prepared for the closing ceremony of the series, which promised to be as enlightening as it was celebratory. Alex, Elaine, and Michael gathered in the center's main hall, surrounded by displays of photos and data collected by participants over the weeks.

"Today's been an incredible journey, hasn't it?" Alex remarked, adjusting the placement of a display board showcasing migration patterns. "I think we've really managed to raise awareness about the importance of bird conservation."

"It really has," Elaine agreed, arranging pamphlets and interactive materials on a table. "We've seen a lot of new faces. It's great to see the community so engaged."

Michael, checking the sound system for the evening's presentations, chimed in, "The feedback has been overwhelmingly positive. I think the hands-on activities really made an impact. It's one thing to hear about migration, but it's another to see it and participate in tracking it."

"That's the goal," Alex said with a nod. "To turn information into action. Speaking of which, how are we doing on the schedule for tonight?"

Elaine glanced at her clipboard. "We're on track. Dr. Aimes will do a wrap-up talk, then we'll have a session where participants can share their experiences. After that, we'll present certificates to our citizen scientists who've completed the series."

"Perfect," Michael responded, giving a thumbs up. "I've also set up a slideshow of the images captured by the nest cams and some of the best participant photos. It should be a nice touch for the evening."

As the guests began to arrive, Alex took a moment to greet them at the door, welcoming them back with a smile. "Thank you for joining us again," he would say. "Tonight is a celebration of all we've learned and observed together."

Once everyone had settled, Dr. Aimes took the stage, her presence commanding attention as always. "Good evening, everyone," she began, her voice clear and resonant. "These past weeks have been an extraordinary glimpse into the world of our migratory birds. Your participation has not only contributed to our knowledge but has helped foster a greater appreciation for the incredible journeys these animals undertake."

The audience listened intently, many nodding in agreement as Dr. Aimes continued to describe some of the remarkable findings from the series, including unusual migration patterns that were documented and the surprising diversity of species observed.

"As we close this series," Dr. Aimes concluded, "let's remember that our role as stewards of these creatures continues. Every bit of habitat we preserve, every effort we make to reduce our environmental impact, adds up to a safer journey for them."

After her talk, participants were invited to share their experiences. One young girl, no older than ten, stepped up, her voice shaky but excited. "I never knew birds could travel so far! I told my dad, and now we're going to build birdhouses this summer to help them."

Her enthusiasm sparked smiles and even a few cheers from the crowd. It was clear that the series had touched more than just a curiosity about birds; it had sparked a commitment to protecting them.

Elaine then took the stage to distribute certificates. "Each of you has been a vital part of this series," she said. "These certificates are just a small token of our appreciation for your dedication and curiosity."

As the evening wound down, Michael played the slideshow he had prepared. Images of birds in flight, participants peering through binoculars, and children laughing as they learned about wildlife filled the screen, each image a story of connection and discovery.

"Looks like we've started something wonderful here," Alex commented quietly to Elaine and Michael as they watched the crowd.

"We really have," Elaine replied. "It's about more than just birds. It's about community, about understanding our place in the natural world."

"And taking responsibility for it," Michael added.

As the last of the guests departed, the team felt a collective sense of accomplishment and anticipation for future programs. They began to tidy up the space, already discussing ideas for the next series, their conversation filled with possibilities.

Leaving the center that evening, the trio looked back at the building, its windows aglow in the twilight. The successful series had not only brought the community together but had reinforced the center's role as a beacon of learning and conservation in Greenhaven. The night closed gently around them, a fitting end to a day of celebration and a season of meaningful engagement.

Chapter 13
Aftermath

With the successful wrap-up of the "Wings of Spring" series, the Environmental Education Center was now a well-established hub for community learning and engagement in Greenhaven. Alex, Elaine, and Michael met early one summer morning to discuss the future of the center, particularly focusing on new educational programs and the sustainability of their initiatives.

As they sat around the polished wooden table in the center's main conference room, surrounded by windows that framed the lush greenery outside, Alex looked at his colleagues with a mixture of pride and determination.

"We've built something incredible here," Alex started, spreading out a new proposal document on the table. "But I want to ensure we keep moving forward, keep innovating. What are your thoughts on introducing a series focused on climate change? It's a pressing issue, and I think we have the platform to really make an impact."

Elaine nodded in agreement, her eyes scanning the proposal. "I think it's essential. Climate change affects everything we do here. We could integrate it with hands-on workshops that show not just the challenges but also what individuals can do locally to make a difference."

"That's a solid plan," Michael added, sipping his coffee. "We could partner with local green businesses and maybe even get some grants for renewable energy projects on-site. Solar panels, rainwater collection systems—things that make the center a living example of sustainability."

Alex leaned back, pleased with their brainstorming. "I like where this is going. Let's sketch out some potential workshops and maybe a speaker series. I'd like to bring in experts not just from the environmental field but also from policy, technology, even economics."

As they discussed, a light breeze fluttered in through an open window, carrying the scent of blooming flowers—the same wildflowers they had planted around the center to promote local biodiversity. It was a subtle reminder of the interconnectedness of their work with the world outside.

Elaine, pulling up a calendar on her laptop, suggested, "We should aim to launch this new series in the fall. It gives us enough time to plan and promote. Plus, the timing could align with international climate events for broader engagement."

"Great idea," Alex agreed. "Michael, could you handle the outreach? Maybe set up some preliminary meetings with potential partners?"

"Absolutely," Michael responded, already making notes. "I'll start reaching out this week. There's a lot of potential for collaboration."

The meeting continued with discussions on funding sources, potential challenges, and the logistical needs of the new programs. They each brought their strengths to the table, weaving together ideas that balanced ambition with the practical needs of their community.

As the meeting drew to a close, Alex, Elaine, and Michael reviewed their action items, each person clear on their next steps. They stood up, stretching and taking one last look at the plans laid out before them.

"We're doing good work here," Elaine remarked as they began to gather their papers. "It's exciting to see how far we can take this."

"It really is," Alex replied, a smile tugging at the corner of his mouth. "Thanks for all your hard work, both of you. Let's keep pushing the boundaries of what we can achieve."

As they left the room, the sun had climbed higher, casting a warm glow through the corridors of the center. Outside, the buzz of insects and the gentle rustling of leaves filled the air, a natural symphony that underscored the vitality of their mission. The day ahead was full of promise, and as they parted ways, each felt a renewed sense of purpose, driven by the knowledge that their efforts were a vital part of fostering a more informed and engaged community.

As the fall approached, the planning for the climate change series gained momentum. Alex, Elaine, and Michael found themselves in the midst of a particularly productive meeting in the Environmental Education Center's library, a room lined with books on every aspect of the natural world. They were joined by Jenna, a local expert in sustainable technologies, who had come to offer her insights on integrating practical green solutions into the upcoming series.

"So, Jenna, we're thinking about showcasing real-life applications of sustainable practices during these sessions," Alex began, gesturing towards the array of brochures and notes spread out on the table. "Things like home energy efficiency, water conservation, and sustainable gardening. How do you see your involvement?"

Jenna adjusted her glasses, her eyes scanning the documents. "I think it's a great initiative. I can provide workshops on solar panel installation and the benefits of smart home systems that help reduce energy usage. We could also set up a demo area here at the center to give visitors a hands-on experience."

"That sounds excellent," Elaine responded, her tone enthusiastic. "We could use the demo as an ongoing educational tool, not just for the series. It would be a tangible way to see the impact of these technologies."

Michael chimed in, "And it ties perfectly into our goal of making the center a model for sustainability. We could track the center's energy usage and water conservation stats and display them to show the real-time benefits of the installations."

Jenna nodded, "Absolutely. It's all about making it relevant to people's everyday lives. If they see the immediate benefits, they're more likely to consider these options for their own homes."

Alex took notes diligently, then looked up, "Let's talk about the speaker series. We want to cover not just the 'how' but also the 'why'—the bigger picture of climate change."

Elaine, pulling up a list on her laptop, added, "I've reached out to several potential speakers, including climatologists, wildlife biologists, and even economists who specialize in environmental impact. We're lining up some strong voices to discuss the global effects of climate actions."

"That will provide a good balance," Michael noted. "By covering a wide range of topics, we ensure there's something that resonates with everyone in the community, regardless of their background or interests."

Jenna suggested, "You might also want to include local farmers or gardeners who practice sustainable agriculture. They can speak about soil health, permaculture, and other techniques that benefit the environment."

"That's a fantastic idea," Alex agreed. "Local impact stories can be very powerful. They show that effective climate action isn't just something happening on a global scale—it's also about local communities adapting and innovating."

Elaine smiled, pleased with the progress. "I'll start setting up a schedule for these talks and workshops. We'll need to coordinate closely to make sure everything runs smoothly."

"As for promotion," Michael added, "we should start ramping up our efforts. Social media campaigns, local radio spots, and maybe an article in the community newsletter. We need to get the word out as broadly as possible."

Jenna gathered her things, ready to leave. "Let me know how I can assist with the preparations. I'm excited to see how this all turns out."

"Thank you, Jenna, for your insights and for joining us today," Alex said, standing to shake her hand. "Your expertise will certainly enrich our series."

After Jenna's departure, the trio lingered for a moment, reviewing their action items. The library's quiet, surrounded by reminders of the natural world they were working so hard to protect, was a perfect backdrop for their mission. They left the meeting with a clear vision of the next steps, each ready to tackle the challenges ahead with renewed vigor.

As they stepped out of the library, the center was quiet, the late afternoon sun casting long shadows across the foyer. The peacefulness was a stark contrast to the urgency of their task, but they were undeterred. The path forward was clear, and each step they took was a move towards a more informed and proactive community.

As autumn deepened, the leaves shifted to a tapestry of fiery hues, mirroring the vibrant energy at the Environmental Education Center. The climate change series, meticulously planned over the previous weeks, was now in full swing, drawing attention from across Greenhaven and beyond. With each session, the center buzzed with attendees eager to learn about sustainable practices and the science of climate change.

One particular morning found Alex walking through the center, his steps resonant against the polished wood floors, as he made his way to the newly installed demonstration area for sustainable home technologies. Here, attendees were interacting with the latest in energy-efficient appliances and smart home systems, their expressions a mix of curiosity and intrigue. The demonstration area, a brainchild of the recent planning sessions, served as a practical example of the series' themes, illustrating how individual actions could lead to significant environmental impacts.

In the background, Elaine was overseeing the setup for the day's key lecture on the global impact of renewable energy. The lecture hall was filling steadily, with every seat soon to be occupied by community members ranging from students to retirees, all united by a common interest in environmental stewardship.

Outside, Michael was coordinating a small group of volunteers who were preparing for an afternoon workshop on rainwater harvesting systems. The outdoor setup included various models of rain barrels and water collection systems, demonstrating the ease and efficiency of implementing such systems in a residential setting.

Throughout the day, the series facilitated rich interactions, with experts answering questions and guiding discussions that ranged from the basics of composting to the complexities of global warming. Each session not only educated but also inspired, pushing attendees to consider how they might contribute to a more sustainable world.

As the sun began to set, casting long shadows over the grounds of the center, the final session of the day concluded with a panel discussion featuring local farmers who practiced sustainable agriculture. They shared insights into organic farming techniques and the benefits of crop rotation and natural pest control, further emphasizing the practical applications of the knowledge being shared throughout the series.

The day wound down with participants lingering to chat with the experts and speakers, exchanging ideas and contact information. Alex, Elaine, and Michael gathered briefly to debrief, reviewing the day's successes and noting any areas for improvement.

"Today was a testament to what we envisioned when we first planned this series," Alex commented, his voice filled with a mixture of fatigue and satisfaction as they watched the last of the attendees depart.

"It's seeing the community come together like this that really makes it all worthwhile," Elaine added, tucking away some brochures and notes. "The questions today were particularly insightful. It shows that people are really thinking about what they can do personally."

"And the interest in the demonstration models has been incredible," Michael pointed out. "I think we should consider making some of these features permanent here at the center."

As they turned off the lights and locked up the building, the cool evening air greeted them, a reminder of the changing seasons and the ongoing passage of time. The center was quiet now, but the ideas and conversations sparked within its walls promised ongoing ripples throughout the community.

Driving home, Alex reflected on the day, the weeks of planning, and the years of effort that had brought them to this point. The road had been long, and the work often challenging, but the impact was undeniable. Greenhaven was changing, slowly but surely, its community more aware and engaged with each passing season. As he parked his car and stepped out into the crisp night air, the stars overhead shone brightly, a serene end to a day full of promise and purpose.

As the climate change series drew to a close, the Environmental Education Center prepared to host its final event—a symposium focused on innovative environmental solutions. This event was intended to capstone the series with discussions on cutting-edge sustainability practices that could be implemented at both local and global levels. Alex, Elaine, and Michael met in the early morning light filtering through the high windows of the center, discussing the setup and flow of the day.

"Everything looks good in the main hall. The tech team has the video links tested for our international speakers," Alex noted, checking items off on his digital tablet. "It's important that there are no hitches today."

"Agreed," Elaine replied, reviewing the schedule. "We have a good mix today—local experts and some from abroad who will provide a broader perspective on environmental innovation."

Michael, arranging the last of the chairs, added, "The panel on urban sustainability should be particularly interesting. We've got architects and city planners discussing green buildings and eco-friendly urban planning."

As the guests began to arrive, the trio greeted them, ensuring everyone received a program and knew where to find the various sessions. The symposium began with a keynote address from a renowned climate scientist, who discussed the impact of renewable energy adoption on global warming. Her presentation set an optimistic tone for the day, emphasizing solutions and collective action.

Throughout the morning, breakout sessions ran concurrently. Topics ranged from advancements in biodegradable materials to the latest in conservation technology. In one packed room, a local entrepreneur demonstrated his company's new water purification system, which had potential applications in developing countries.

In the main hall during a break, Alex and Elaine chatted briefly with some attendees. "It's encouraging to see the enthusiasm," Alex observed, watching a group of university students deep in conversation. "These discussions are exactly what we hoped for—engaging and forward-thinking."

Elaine smiled, replying, "Absolutely. And the feedback has been overwhelmingly positive. People appreciate the practical focus, the real-world applications of what they're learning here."

The afternoon culminated in a panel discussion that brought together different experts to discuss the role of policy in supporting environmental innovation. The discussion was lively, with panelists debating and the audience asking probing questions.

"As policymakers, it's our job to pave the way for these technologies to be adopted more widely," one panelist, a local government official, stated. "We need to ensure that regulations and incentives align with our environmental goals."

Another expert, a technology developer, added, "And from a tech perspective, we need clarity and consistency in these policies to invest confidently in new developments. It's a partnership."

As the symposium neared its end, Alex took the stage to offer closing remarks. "Today has been about envisioning a sustainable future together. Each speaker, each discussion has highlighted not only the challenges we face but also the many pathways to overcoming them."

He continued, "Let's take what we've learned, the connections we've made, and translate them into action. Whether in our local communities, our businesses, or through policy advocacy, we all have a role to play."

With a final round of applause, the event concluded. Attendees lingered, exchanging contact information and discussing collaborations. Alex, Elaine, and Michael watched with satisfaction, their efforts having fostered a forum not only for learning but for active engagement and networking.

As the last of the guests departed and the center's lights dimmed, the team gathered their belongings. The night was settling in, a gentle reminder of the passing time and the ongoing efforts needed to address the global challenge of climate change.

Walking to their cars, they reflected on the day's successes and the work ahead. "This is just the beginning," Michael said, a determined look in his eyes.

"Yes, it is," Elaine agreed, her voice resolute. "But it's a good beginning."

They parted ways, each inspired by the day's outcomes, ready to continue the work that lay ahead, their dedication unwavering in the face of the monumental task of nurturing an environmentally conscious community.

Chapter 14
Healing Together

The brisk winds of early winter brought a palpable shift to Greenhaven, mirroring the transformative strides at the Environmental Education Center. With the recent conclusion of the successful climate change series, Alex, Elaine, and Michael convened to discuss the implementation of the innovative ideas that had sprung from the symposium. The meeting took place in Alex's office, where the morning light filtered softly through frosted glass, casting a serene glow over their planning documents.

"Looking at the feedback from the symposium, it's clear that one of the most pressing interests was in sustainable living practices at the household level," Alex observed, shuffling through a stack of feedback forms. "I think we should launch a series that focuses specifically on that—how individuals can make their homes more environmentally friendly."

Elaine, who had been flipping through a digital presentation, nodded in agreement. "I agree, and I think we could partner with local businesses for this. There's a lot of potential for workshops on energy efficiency, waste reduction, and even sustainable food practices."

"That's a solid approach," Michael added, leaning back in his chair. "We could showcase real case studies from within the community. People who have already made these changes to their homes and lifestyles could share their experiences and benefits."

As they discussed, the gentle hum of the heating system provided a comforting background noise, reinforcing the center's commitment to using renewable energy sources.

"We should also consider adding a new exhibit to the center," Alex suggested. "Something interactive that demonstrates these sustainable practices in real-time. Like a model eco-friendly home that visitors can walk through and interact with."

Elaine looked thoughtful. "That's an excellent idea. It could really help visualize the changes people can make. Plus, it would be a permanent addition to our offerings, something that could attract visitors year-round."

"I'll start reaching out to potential sponsors and partners for this project," Michael offered, already drafting a list of local businesses that might be interested in collaborating. "There's a lot of enthusiasm around green technologies now, especially after the symposium."

"Good," Alex replied, satisfied with their direction. "Let's aim to have a detailed proposal by the end of the month. We'll need a budget, a project timeline, and a marketing plan. Elaine, could you take the lead on the exhibit design?"

"Of course," Elaine responded, her tone decisive. "I'll sketch out some preliminary ideas and get in touch with some eco-design consultants. We need to make sure whatever we build is both educational and inspiring."

The meeting continued with a sense of urgency and purpose, as they outlined the steps needed to bring their new initiatives to life. Each task was assigned with care, ensuring that all bases were covered, from educational content to visitor engagement.

As they wrapped up, the room was filled with a sense of accomplishment and anticipation for the projects ahead. They stood, stretching and gathering their notes, the winter light now stretching longer across the floor.

"We're really making strides in turning this center into not just a place of learning, but a place of action," Alex remarked as they prepared to leave the room.

"That's the goal," Elaine agreed, a smile playing at the corners of her mouth. "Education is the foundation, but it's what people do with that knowledge that really counts."

With a final nod to each other, they stepped out of the office, the echo of their determined steps mingling with the sounds of the center coming to life for the day. Outside, the crisp air was a reminder of the seasonal cycles of nature, a parallel to the cycles of learning and growth happening within the center's walls. Each initiative, each project they embarked on, was a step towards a more informed and proactive community, ready to face the environmental challenges of the future.

In the following weeks, as the plan for the model eco-friendly home exhibit took shape, Elaine found herself deep in discussion with Jasper, a renowned eco-design consultant. They sat in a small, sunlit conference room within the Environmental Education Center, surrounded by blueprints and digital renderings of the proposed exhibit. Outside, a light snow began to fall, dusting the bare branches of the trees visible through the window.

"So, Jasper, based on your experience, what are the most crucial elements we need to include in this model home to truly resonate with our visitors?" Elaine asked, her eyes scanning the detailed plans laid out before them.

Jasper, adjusting his glasses, leaned over the table, pointing at various sections of the blueprint. "Energy efficiency is key. I'd suggest we focus on integrating solar panels and maybe even a small wind turbine if the budget allows. Also, incorporating smart home technology can really appeal to visitors—it not only saves energy but also modernizes the entire concept of living sustainably."

Elaine nodded thoughtfully. "I like that. And what about materials? We should showcase sustainable building materials, right?"

"Absolutely," Jasper agreed. "Bamboo flooring, recycled insulation, and perhaps walls made from reclaimed wood. It's all about showing sustainable options that are both practical and visually appealing. Also, a green roof could be a fantastic feature, both for insulation and biodiversity."

"That's a fantastic idea," Elaine said, making notes on her tablet. "A green roof would really illustrate the dual benefits of aesthetic appeal and functionality. Plus, it ties directly into our broader message about biodiversity and local ecosystems."

As they continued to discuss, Michael entered the room, a folder of potential sponsorships and partnerships under his arm. "I just had a very promising meeting with a local business that's interested in sponsoring part of the exhibit. They're particularly keen on the smart home technology aspect."

"That's great news, Michael," Elaine responded, her face brightening. "Having business backing could really help push the project forward and make it a standout feature of the center."

Jasper added, "Business partnerships can also lend credibility to the exhibit. It shows that these technologies and materials are not just theoretical but are being embraced by the market."

Elaine looked between the two, her mind working swiftly. "Let's make sure we highlight those partnerships in the exhibit information. It could encourage other local businesses to think about sustainability in their operations."

"Definitely," Michael agreed. "I'll work on a display that outlines our sponsors and their contributions to sustainability. It could serve as an inspiration for others."

As they wrapped up their meeting, the snow outside had thickened, blanketing the landscape in white. The three of them stood for a moment at the window, appreciating the quiet beauty of the scene.

"This exhibit is going to be something special," Elaine mused, watching the snowflakes gently fall. "Not just as an educational tool, but as a demonstration of what's possible."

"Absolutely," Jasper concurred. "It's projects like these that push the envelope and really make people think about the choices they make in their own lives."

With a final review of their tasks and timelines, Jasper packed up his materials, and Michael prepared to head back to his office. Elaine lingered a moment longer, her gaze fixed on the serene winter tableau outside. This project, like the falling snow, had the potential to transform the landscape of Greenhaven, encouraging its residents to embrace a more sustainable way of life.

Leaving the conference room, Elaine felt a renewed sense of purpose. Each step in the planning of this exhibit was a step toward a greener, more conscientious community, echoing the center's mission to educate and inspire. As she walked down the hallway, her thoughts already on the next steps, the quiet hum of the center around her was a reminder of the ongoing journey of environmental education.

As the days shortened and the chill of late autumn settled over Greenhaven, the Environmental Education Center was a hive of activity, brimming with anticipation for the unveiling of the model eco-friendly home. Elaine, Alex, and Michael had worked tirelessly, coordinating with contractors, sponsors, and experts to ensure every detail was perfect. The exhibit was designed not just to educate but to inspire action, showcasing sustainable living practices that could be adopted by anyone.

The construction of the model home was an exercise in sustainability itself. Materials sourced were either recycled or sustainably produced, and local labor was employed to both support the community and reduce the carbon footprint associated with long-distance transportation. Solar panels were installed on the roof, sleek and efficient, designed to harness the weak winter sun to its maximum potential. Inside, the house featured bamboo flooring and walls lined with reclaimed wood, giving it a warm, inviting atmosphere that contrasted with the cold outside.

Days before the opening, Elaine toured the nearly completed exhibit, her critical eye scanning every corner. Energy-efficient LED lighting illuminated the space, casting a soft glow on the informative plaques that explained each feature's environmental impact. A smart thermostat adjusted the temperature automatically, a small digital display explaining the energy savings compared to traditional models.

In one corner of the house, a cut-away display showed the layers of recycled insulation, a touchscreen panel beside it allowing visitors to simulate how different insulation levels affected heat retention and energy use. Nearby, a rainwater collection system was connected to a small garden in the back, demonstrating how collected water could be used for irrigation.

Throughout the exhibit, interactive displays were set up to engage visitors more deeply. One station allowed guests to calculate their household's carbon footprint and see how implementing various features of the model home could reduce it. Another display provided a virtual tour of the house, highlighting less visible technologies like the heat-recovery ventilation system.

As Elaine moved through the house, she adjusted a few displays, ensuring that everything was accessible and informative. Her phone buzzed with a message from Michael, confirming that the final promotional materials had been distributed around town and posted online. Everything was in place, and the buzz in the community was growing.

On the eve of the opening, Alex joined Elaine for a final walk-through of the exhibit. "It really has come together beautifully," he remarked, admiration clear in his voice as he examined the solar panel display. "This is going to change the way people think about their homes and their impact on the environment."

Elaine nodded, her eyes reflecting a mixture of pride and a hint of nerves for the opening day. "I hope so. It's one thing to tell people about sustainability; it's another to show them what it can actually look like."

The opening day dawned clear and cold, the first hint of winter in the air. The center opened its doors to a line of visitors, their breath visible in the chilly air as they talked excitedly about the exhibit. Families, students, and local dignitaries all stepped into the warmth of the model home, greeted by the sight of the future of sustainable living.

As the day progressed, the house was filled with the murmur of impressed and curious visitors. Children's laughter rang out from the interactive carbon footprint calculator, and adults discussed the insulation materials with keen interest. Outside, a group gathered around the rainwater collection system, pointing and asking questions about its capacity and installation.

Elaine, Alex, and Michael circulated among the guests, answering questions and sharing insights. The feedback was overwhelmingly positive, the community enthusiastic about the practical applications they could see and touch.

As the sun set, casting long shadows through the large windows of the model home, the first day of the exhibit closed with a sense of accomplishment. The team gathered briefly to celebrate the successful launch, already discussing plans to host workshops and events centered around the features of the model home.

Walking out of the center, Elaine felt a chill from the evening air, a stark reminder of the season's change. But inside, the warmth of their success and the brighter future they were helping to build kept the cold at bay. As she drove home, the lights of the center faded in her rearview mirror, but the impact of their work illuminated the path ahead.

The success of the model eco-friendly home exhibit had sparked a surge of interest in sustainable living within the Greenhaven community. To build on this momentum, Alex, Elaine, and Michael organized a series of weekend workshops focused on specific aspects of sustainability highlighted within the exhibit. Today, they were preparing for a workshop on solar energy applications in residential settings, a topic that had garnered significant attention.

As they set up in the main hall of the Environmental Education Center, Elaine checked the registration list on her tablet. "We've got a full house today," she announced, looking up at Alex who was arranging chairs in a semi-circle. "It seems like the solar panel display really captured everyone's interest."

"That's great to hear," Alex replied, aligning the last chair before stepping back to survey the arrangement. "Do you think we should consider expanding this section of the exhibit based on the feedback?"

"It might be worth exploring," Michael added as he organized the informational brochures on a side table. "Especially if we can show the long-term financial benefits more clearly. It could really drive the point home."

Elaine nodded, tapping on her tablet to pull up some notes. "I've been talking to a few solar installation companies about potential partnerships. They're interested in doing live demos here, which could be a fantastic interactive element for the exhibit."

"That's an excellent idea," Alex said, pleased. "Live demos could make the technology more tangible for people. It demystifies the process, showing it's not as complex as one might think."

As the attendees began to arrive, Michael greeted each one at the door with a brochure and a warm smile. "Welcome! We're just about to get started. Please, take a seat anywhere you like."

Once everyone was seated, Elaine began the workshop with a brief introduction. "Thank you all for coming out today. This workshop is designed to give you a closer look at how solar energy can be implemented in your homes, the benefits, and what you should consider before installing a solar system."

Alex took over to delve deeper into the technical aspects. "Let's start with the basics of how solar panels work. Solar energy is a clean, renewable resource that can significantly reduce your electricity bills and decrease your carbon footprint."

A hand shot up in the middle of the crowd. "How much maintenance do solar panels require?" asked an elderly man with a note of curiosity in his voice.

"That's a great question," Alex responded. "Solar panels require very little maintenance. You'll need to keep them relatively clean and check for any debris or damage occasionally, but generally, they're designed to withstand the elements and operate smoothly for years."

Another attendee, a young woman with a notebook in hand, asked, "What about the cost? Isn't the initial investment pretty high?"

Elaine answered, "Yes, the upfront cost can be significant. However, many states offer rebates and incentives to offset some of these costs. Plus, the reduction in your monthly energy bills can make up for the initial investment over time."

The discussion continued with high engagement, attendees asking detailed questions and Elaine, Alex, and Michael providing answers, backed by data and examples. The atmosphere was lively, with participants eager to learn and discuss.

As the workshop wrapped up, Michael concluded, "We hope this session has been informative and has perhaps even inspired you to consider how you might use solar energy in your own homes."

Attendees began to disperse, many staying back to thank the team or ask a few more questions. Alex, Elaine, and Michael exchanged satisfied glances, pleased with the workshop's success and the community's enthusiasm.

"Seeing this kind of turnout and engagement, it really feels like we're making a difference," Elaine said as they began to tidy up the room.

"It does," Alex agreed, stacking chairs. "Let's keep this momentum going. Sustainability isn't just a concept—it's a practical, achievable lifestyle, and we're showing that here."

As they locked up the center, the sun set, casting a soft glow over Greenhaven. The day's success was a testament to the community's growing commitment to sustainability, each workshop adding another layer to their understanding and involvement.

Chapter 15
A New Threat

As winter relinquished its hold, allowing the first signs of spring to emerge, the Environmental Education Center in Greenhaven prepared for an ambitious new initiative: a community-wide sustainability challenge. The challenge was designed to engage residents in a series of activities aimed at reducing their environmental impact, from waste reduction and energy conservation to sustainable gardening and water use.

Alex, Elaine, and Michael met to discuss the logistics of this large-scale project, aiming to harness the enthusiasm generated by previous workshops and the eco-friendly home exhibit. They gathered in the center's main hall, which was lined with posters and informational displays about the upcoming events.

Under the bright, airy skylights of the hall, Elaine laid out the newly printed brochures across a long table. Each brochure outlined the challenge's objectives, detailed the activities included, and provided tips on how residents could participate and track their progress.

"The challenge will kick off with a community fair right here," Alex said, gesturing to the space around them. "We'll have booths set up for each activity category, where participants can sign up and get their starter kits."

Michael added, "We've also developed an app to help participants track their activities and see their impact in real time. It should make the experience more interactive and give us a way to measure the overall success of the challenge."

The fair would not only serve as the launching point but also as an educational hub, where community members could learn more about the issues at the heart of the challenge. Local experts and enthusiasts would man the booths, providing hands-on demonstrations and answering questions.

As they continued to plan, the center buzzed with the usual pre-event energy, but there was a palpable sense of anticipation for what was to come. This challenge represented a significant step forward in their mission to not only educate but actively involve the community in environmental stewardship.

In the days leading up to the fair, Alex, Elaine, and Michael distributed flyers and visited local schools, businesses, and community groups to drum up interest. They spoke about the tangible benefits of adopting more sustainable practices, not just for the environment but for residents' own lives and wallets.

The community's response was enthusiastic. Many Greenhaven residents were already aware of environmental issues, but the challenge presented them with a structured, supportive way to take action. Families discussed which activities they might engage in together, from starting a vegetable garden to implementing a home energy audit.

On the eve of the fair, the team met one last time to go over everything. "Let's make sure we're all clear on what we're doing tomorrow," Elaine said, checking off items on her list. "We need to be ready to inspire and guide our community through this challenge."

"Yes," Alex agreed. "This is more than just an event; it's the start of a significant change in how our community relates to the environment. We're fostering a shift towards a sustainable lifestyle that hopefully, will last well beyond this challenge."

As they finished their preparations, the setting sun cast a warm glow through the hall's large windows. Outside, the trees were beginning to bud, a reminder of the renewal that spring brought with it.

The next morning, as they opened the doors to the community fair, the first participants arrived, their faces bright with curiosity and determination. The challenge was officially underway, and as the hall filled with people, the team watched as their months of planning came to fruition.

Throughout the day, Alex, Elaine, and Michael circulated among the booths, offering encouragement and seeing firsthand the community's commitment to the challenge. It was a day of meaningful conversations and shared discoveries, laying the groundwork for what they hoped would be a transformative experience for Greenhaven.

As the fair ended and the participants left, armed with information and new ideas, the team felt a profound sense of accomplishment. They had not only shared knowledge but had catalyzed action. The center closed for the day, but the challenge had just begun, its impact set to unfold in the weeks and months ahead.

Several weeks into the community-wide sustainability challenge, the Environmental Education Center buzzed with activity and enthusiasm. The initial momentum from the kickoff event had not waned but rather intensified as residents of Greenhaven actively participated in various sustainability activities. Alex, Elaine, and Michael now found themselves reviewing the mid-challenge data, assessing the community's engagement and environmental impact.

In the center's conference room, surrounded by charts and graphs depicting energy savings, waste reduction, and water conservation metrics, the team was deep in discussion.

"We're seeing some impressive numbers here," Michael noted, pointing to a graph on his laptop. "Look at the energy savings from those who've implemented the recommended changes in insulation and smart thermostats. It's significant."

Elaine leaned over to look closer, nodding in approval. "It's fantastic, and the feedback has been overwhelmingly positive. People really enjoy seeing the tangible results of their efforts. It's empowering."

Alex, who had been flipping through feedback forms, chimed in. "And it's not just about the numbers. Participants are sharing stories about how these changes are improving their daily lives. There's a real sense of community forming around these efforts."

"As we move into the next phase of the challenge, we should consider how we can further support these community connections," Elaine suggested. "Maybe facilitate more group activities or workshops where participants can share their experiences and tips."

"That's a great idea," Michael agreed. "Perhaps a monthly meet-up where people can bring questions, share successes, and even swap items like books on sustainability or energy-efficient appliances."

The conversation was interrupted by a knock on the door, and Jenna, the eco-design consultant, entered with a folder in hand. "I've compiled some additional data on the rainwater collection systems we installed," she announced, spreading out some sheets on the table. "Homes that have started using these systems have cut down their municipal water use by up to 30%."

"That's incredible," Alex responded, examining the sheets. "Jenna, your expertise has been invaluable in this challenge. We're seeing real, positive changes."

Jenna smiled, pleased. "I'm thrilled to hear that. It shows that with the right tools and information, people are ready and willing to make significant changes."

Elaine looked thoughtful. "These results could be a powerful tool in encouraging more residents to join the challenge. We could use these success stories in our next newsletter and on social media to highlight what's possible."

"Absolutely," Michael said, picking up on the idea. "And maybe we could create a short video series featuring some of our participants. They could talk about their projects and the impact they've noticed."

"Let's do it," Alex decided. "We'll need to keep the momentum going and ensure that the challenge's impact extends beyond just those who are currently participating."

As the meeting drew to a close, the team felt a renewed sense of purpose. They organized their next steps, assigning tasks to expand the challenge's reach and deepen its impact.

The meeting ended with a round of congratulatory remarks for the progress made, and the trio left the conference room energized. The sun was setting outside, casting a golden glow over the bustling center. Families and individuals continued to arrive, some to attend a workshop, others to check in with their progress on the challenge.

Alex, Elaine, and Michael separated to attend to their evening responsibilities, each moving through the crowds, engaging with participants, and sharing in the communal spirit that the challenge had fostered. The center, once a quiet place of learning, had transformed into a vibrant hub of action and interaction, a testament to the community's commitment to sustainability. As they worked through the evening, the sense of accomplishment was palpable, and the impact of their efforts was visible in every interaction and every saved statistic on their charts.

As the community-wide sustainability challenge neared its conclusion, the atmosphere around the Environmental Education Center was one of excited anticipation. The initiative had deeply resonated within the Greenhaven community, bringing together families, local businesses, and individual residents in a shared commitment to environmental stewardship. Alex, Elaine, and Michael were busy preparing for the final event of the challenge—a celebration and award ceremony to recognize the participants' efforts and achievements.

The center was festooned with green and blue decorations, symbolizing the earth and water, reflecting the environmental focus of the event. Tables were arranged with displays of participant projects and information panels showcasing the quantifiable impact of the community's efforts over the past months.

Alex reviewed the final details with Elaine and Michael in the center's main hall, which had been transformed into a vibrant venue for the evening's activities. "I think everything's just about set," Alex observed, scanning the room with a satisfied nod. "The data displays are up, and the award certificates are ready."

Elaine, double-checking the list of awardees, added, "It's incredible to see how much has been achieved. We've got families who've reduced their household energy consumption by 20%, and several local businesses have completely revamped their waste management systems."

"That's fantastic," Michael chimed in, arranging the certificates on a table. "Tonight isn't just a celebration; it's a testament to what we can accomplish when we come together for a common goal. I'm really proud of what everyone's achieved."

As they spoke, early attendees began to arrive, their faces bright with curiosity and pride. Among them were families with children, local business owners, and even representatives from other communities interested in learning from Greenhaven's initiative.

"Looks like we're about to start," Elaine said, gesturing toward the growing crowd. "Let's make sure to engage with as many participants as we can tonight. Their feedback will be invaluable for planning future initiatives."

Throughout the evening, Alex, Elaine, and Michael mingled with the attendees, discussing the projects and sharing insights about the challenges and successes. The community's enthusiasm was palpable, with many expressing their hopes for continued efforts and new sustainability challenges.

As the award ceremony began, Alex took the stage to address the crowd. "This evening, we celebrate not just the conclusion of a challenge but the beginning of a continued journey toward sustainability," he began, his voice carrying across the attentive audience. "Each certificate we hand out tonight is a recognition of commitment and change—a sign that together, we are making a real difference."

One by one, families and businesses were called to the stage to receive their certificates and share a brief word about their experiences. A local café owner spoke about the improvements they made to minimize food waste, while a middle school student described her family's efforts to reduce water use at home.

The ceremony was more than a mere formality; it was a communal affirmation of Greenhaven's dedication to a healthier, more sustainable way of living. The evening concluded with a community pledge, led by Elaine, where everyone committed to maintaining and building upon the changes they had implemented.

As the crowd dispersed, many lingered to talk with Alex, Elaine, and Michael, thanking them for their guidance and expressing excitement about future projects. The team felt a profound sense of fulfillment as they saw firsthand the impact of their work.

Cleaning up after the event, the trio shared a quiet moment of reflection. "Tonight was a reminder of why we do what we do," Michael said, stacking chairs. "Seeing the community come together like this—it's really something special."

"It is," Elaine agreed, turning off the hall lights. "And it's just the beginning. We've sparked something here that has the potential to grow even bigger."

They left the center together, the night quiet around them but alive with the promise of future endeavors. The success of the sustainability challenge had sown seeds of environmental awareness and action that would continue to grow, driven by the community's shared commitment and the continued support of the Environmental Education Center. As they locked the door behind them, they were already discussing plans for the next project, their conversation filled with ideas and optimism for what lay ahead.

Winter returned to Greenhaven, cloaking the town in a serene blanket of white. Inside the Environmental Education Center, the warmth of recent victories against the cold reality of the outside world made the space a sanctuary for those committed to sustainability. Reflecting on the success of the community-wide sustainability challenge, Alex, Elaine, and Michael planned their next step—a symposium to discuss the impact of the challenge and to explore new environmental initiatives.

The meeting room was cozy, with a gentle hum of conversation as community members filed in, greeted by the familiar faces of the center's staff. A large display at the front of the room highlighted key achievements from the sustainability challenge, including impressive statistics on waste reduction and energy savings achieved by the participants.

Elaine, standing beside the display, addressed a small group gathered around her. "We've seen real, measurable change from the challenge, and it's all thanks to the commitment from everyone in this room. Today, we want to build on that momentum and brainstorm how we can extend these efforts even further."

Alex joined her, his presence commanding the room's attention. "Thank you, Elaine. As we move forward, it's important that we think big but also focus on what can realistically be achieved here in Greenhaven. We're here to find those opportunities and figure out how to make them happen."

The room filled with nods of agreement as Michael distributed handouts with potential project ideas. "We're considering several initiatives," he explained, "including a proposal to enhance local green spaces, a plan for community-supported agriculture, and perhaps even a green tech startup incubator."

As the discussions unfolded, the attendees split into smaller groups, each tackling a different topic. Ideas flew, punctuated by the scribble of markers on whiteboards and the tapping of laptops as notes were taken.

In one corner, a lively debate about the potential for a green tech incubator took place. "We have so many talented individuals in Greenhaven who could benefit from such a platform," one community member argued. "It could really put our town on the map as a leader in sustainable technology."

Another group focused on enhancing green spaces. "If we integrate more native plants and create more pollinator-friendly areas, it could significantly impact our local biodiversity," a local botanist suggested, drawing nods from her group members.

Throughout these discussions, Alex, Elaine, and Michael circulated, offering insights and helping to steer the conversations toward actionable plans. They were deeply involved, their passion for the environment evident in their enthusiastic engagement with every topic.

As the symposium drew to a close, Elaine gathered everyone's attention once more. "The ideas we've discussed today are not just inspiring—they're necessary. We'll be compiling all the suggestions and creating a roadmap for the coming year. This is an exciting time for Greenhaven, and it's all possible because of your hard work and dedication."

After the meeting, as the community members left, the center's team stayed behind to debrief. "I think we've got a lot to work with here," Michael said, collecting the last of the handouts. "The enthusiasm is there, and the ideas are solid. We just need to prioritize and start the planning process."

Alex, looking out at the snow gently falling outside, felt a profound sense of purpose. "This town has the potential to become a model of sustainability. We've started something special, and we're going to keep pushing forward."

Elaine smiled, her optimism undimmed by the challenges ahead. "Let's get to work then. We have a busy year ahead."

As they turned off the lights and locked up the center, the quiet of the evening was a sharp contrast to the day's vibrancy. But the silence was merely a backdrop to their thoughts, busy with plans for the future. The drive home was reflective, with each member of the team considering the steps ahead, their commitment to the environment as steadfast as ever.

Chapter 16
Old Allies

Spring brought a vibrant renewal to Greenhaven, mirroring the budding enthusiasm at the Environmental Education Center where Alex, Elaine, and Michael were planning an ambitious Earth Day event aimed to consolidate the community's growing commitment to sustainability. The event was to be a festival of sorts, featuring educational booths, interactive workshops, and guest speakers.

In the meeting room adorned with posters of past events and charts of environmental impacts from the community's efforts, the team sat around a cluttered table, bustling with plans and promotional materials.

"Okay, let's focus on the logistics for the Earth Day festival," Alex began, tapping a pen against his notepad. "We need to ensure that the setup is as eco-friendly as possible. Everything from biodegradable utensils to solar-powered lights."

Elaine nodded, scanning her laptop screen. "I've contacted several local vendors who specialize in sustainable products. They're excited to participate and showcase their goods. We'll have organic food stalls, recycled crafts, and even a booth for trading used books and toys."

"That sounds fantastic," Michael chimed in. "What about the workshops? Last year's composting demo was a huge hit. We should consider adding more hands-on activities like that."

Elaine perked up at the suggestion. "I love that idea. We could do a rain barrel workshop this time—teach people how to set up their own systems at home. It's practical and ties directly into our water conservation efforts."

Alex made a note. "Good, let's do that. Also, I think we should have a series of short talks throughout the day. Maybe 15-minute segments where experts can discuss important topics like renewable energy, wildlife conservation, and sustainable gardening."

Michael pulled up a document on his tablet. "I've drafted a schedule. We could have these mini-talks at the top of every hour, giving people plenty of opportunities to catch at least a couple throughout the day."

Elaine looked over his shoulder. "That's well-organized. Let's make sure we have a diverse group of speakers. Perhaps even include some of our local high school students who've been involved in our programs. It could be empowering for them and inspirational for the younger attendees."

"Absolutely," Alex agreed. "Involving the youth is key. They bring energy and a fresh perspective that can really resonate with other kids and their families."

Michael added, "And let's not forget about proper signage and information dissemination. We need clear, informative signs not only directing people to various stations and booths but also explaining the purpose behind each activity and its environmental benefits."

"That's crucial," Elaine said. "Educational impact is just as important as the fun factor. We want everyone to leave with new knowledge and practical tips they can apply in their own lives."

As they wrapped up the meeting, the trio reviewed their checklist: confirm speakers, finalize workshop materials, organize volunteer schedules, and promote the event in local media and online.

"We've got a busy few weeks ahead," Alex concluded, standing and stretching. "But this is going to be our best Earth Day event yet. Let's make sure it's not only enjoyable but also impactful."

Elaine and Michael nodded in agreement, their faces a mix of determination and excitement. As they left the room, the energy between them was palpable, each step they took imbued with purpose. They split up to start on their respective tasks, the center abuzz with the usual pre-event energy but amplified by the community's heightened engagement and the team's seasoned coordination.

The Environmental Education Center was a flurry of activity as the Earth Day event approached. Banners and signs advocating sustainability adorned the walls and outdoor spaces, and Elaine, Alex, and Michael were finalizing the details in a last-minute meeting in Alex's office, surrounded by plans and promotional materials.

"Elaine, have all the vendors confirmed their spots for the festival?" Alex asked, reviewing the list of participants on his digital tablet.

"Yes, they've all confirmed," Elaine responded, checking off her list. "Each one is prepared to showcase eco-friendly products and practices. We've got everything from organic food vendors to sustainable fashion."

"That's great to hear," Michael interjected. "What about the setup for the workshops? The rain barrel installation and the composting workshops need to be strategically placed so that they're easily accessible but also close enough to related displays for educational continuity."

Elaine nodded, pulling up a map of the event layout on her laptop. "I've placed the composting workshop near the organic gardening booth. It should help link the ideas of waste reduction and sustainable gardening practices. The rain barrel workshop will be near the entrance where we'll also have information on water conservation."

Alex smiled, satisfied with the arrangement. "Perfect. And how are we handling the mini-talks? I want to make sure we have a good flow and that none of the talks overlap with key activities."

Michael scrolled through the event schedule on his tablet. "I've spaced them out every hour, starting from thirty minutes after the festival opens. This way, attendees can visit booths or participate in a workshop, then head over to a talk without feeling rushed."

"Have we finalized the speakers for each talk?" Alex asked, glancing at Elaine, who was coordinating the speaker lineup.

"Yes, we have a solid lineup," Elaine confirmed. "We're covering topics from the basics of solar energy to advanced sustainable agricultural practices. I've also included a segment from some of our youth ambassadors who will talk about their projects on reducing plastic use in schools."

"That will definitely resonate well, especially with the younger attendees," Alex said. "Are we prepared for any media coverage? This event could provide good exposure for the center and our initiatives."

Michael nodded. "I've already sent out press releases and invited local news outlets. We have confirmed that at least two stations will be covering the event live, which should help increase visibility."

"That's excellent," Elaine chimed in. "I think it's also important we capture testimonials during the event. Getting feedback from participants could be really valuable for future grants and sponsorships."

"Absolutely," Alex agreed. "Let's make sure we have volunteers ready with cameras and questionnaires. We need to document everything, from general attendance to reactions at specific workshops and talks."

"As for the volunteers," Michael added, "I've organized a briefing session for them first thing in the morning on the event day. They'll get all the information they need to help guide attendees and answer any questions."

"Sounds like we've covered almost everything," Alex said, looking around the room at his team. "Let's keep the energy up and ensure everything runs smoothly. This is more than just an event; it's a showcase of what our community is about—innovation, education, and commitment to sustainability."

With a collective nod, the trio stood up, their meeting adjourned. They moved toward the door, their conversation already turning to the final tasks ahead. The center buzzed with the shared anticipation of the event, and as they stepped out into the hall, the buzz of activity from the rest of the team was a reminder of the importance of the day to come. Each discussion, each decision taken, was another step toward a successful Earth Day that would not only celebrate but actively advance their mission of environmental stewardship.

On the morning of the Earth Day event, the Environmental Education Center was abuzz with last-minute preparations. Elaine, Alex, and Michael walked through the festival grounds, ensuring everything was in place for the day's activities. Vendors were setting up their eco-friendly products at their booths, volunteers were distributing program schedules at the entrance, and the workshop areas were being outfitted with the necessary equipment for hands-on learning.

"This is coming together nicely," Alex observed, glancing around at the bustling activity. "How are we looking on the volunteer front, Michael? Is everyone briefed and ready to go?"

"Absolutely," Michael replied, checking off items on his clipboard. "I had a final meeting with them this morning. Everyone is clear on their responsibilities, from managing the workshops to guiding the visitors through the exhibits."

Elaine, arranging some signage near the main stage, chimed in, "I just checked in with the speakers for our mini-talks. They're all here and getting acquainted with the stage setup. I think we're going to see some really engaging presentations today."

"That's great to hear," Alex said, his tone upbeat. "And the media? Are they set up yet?"

"Yes, they've got their area near the main stage," Michael confirmed, pointing towards a corner of the grounds where a local news crew was setting up their equipment. "They're planning to broadcast live segments throughout the day, highlighting different parts of the event."

"Perfect. And the interactive displays, Elaine?" Alex inquired, his eyes scanning the various stations set up around the venue.

"They're all up and running," Elaine assured him, her voice filled with excitement. "I just did a final walk-through. The solar energy setup is particularly impressive this year, and I think it's going to draw a lot of attention."

As they walked towards the main stage, a local business owner approached them, a broad smile on his face. "Alex, Elaine, Michael, this is fantastic. What a turnout already!" he exclaimed, gesturing towards the growing crowd. "Our booth is already getting queries about sustainable packaging. This event is just what we needed to showcase our new line."

"That's wonderful to hear," Elaine responded warmly. "It's exactly the kind of community engagement we hoped for. Your participation really adds value to the event."

"Absolutely," Alex agreed, shaking the business owner's hand. "It's partnerships like these that make our efforts worthwhile. We're not just spreading knowledge; we're facilitating practical solutions and business opportunities."

The business owner nodded appreciatively before heading back to his booth. As the team continued their inspection, they stopped by the children's activity area, where a group of young volunteers was setting up an educational game about recycling.

"How's it going over here?" Michael asked, watching as the volunteers arranged various bins labeled with different types of recyclable materials.

"It's going great," one of the volunteers replied enthusiastically. "We've set up a sorting game where kids can learn which materials go into which recycling bins. They even get a small plantable seed paper as a prize for participating."

"That's a fantastic way to make learning fun," Elaine commented, her eyes twinkling with approval. "Keep up the great work, everyone. These activities are crucial for educating the next generation about sustainability."

As the event officially began, Alex took a moment to address the crowd from the main stage. "Welcome, everyone, to our Earth Day celebration! Today is about coming together as a community to learn, share, and commit to a more sustainable future. We have a full schedule of workshops, talks, and activities designed to inspire and inform. So please, explore, ask questions, and enjoy the day!"

With that, the day was in full swing, with attendees moving between workshops, talks, and booths, their faces alight with curiosity and enthusiasm. Alex, Elaine, and Michael circulated among the visitors, facilitating discussions and ensuring everything ran smoothly.

As they converged near a booth showcasing water conservation techniques, Michael commented, "Seeing all this in action, it really feels like we're making a difference, doesn't it?"

"It does," Alex replied, his voice filled with pride. "And it's all thanks to the hard work and dedication of everyone involved, especially our community. This is what makes it all worthwhile."

The day continued with a vibrant energy, a testament to the community's commitment to sustainability and the Environmental Education Center's role in fostering that commitment. As each workshop filled up and the talks drew engaged crowds, it was clear that the event was not just a celebration but a pivotal moment in Greenhaven's journey towards environmental stewardship.

The Earth Day festival at the Environmental Education Center was nearing its end, and the success of the event was palpable in the air. As the afternoon waned into early evening, Alex, Elaine, and Michael gathered near the main stage, where the final presentation of the day—a panel discussion on community-led environmental initiatives—was about to begin.

"I think we've outdone ourselves this year," Alex remarked, watching as attendees began to take their seats for the panel. "The turnout, the engagement—it's been remarkable."

Elaine nodded in agreement, her eyes scanning the crowd. "Absolutely, and the feedback has been incredibly positive. People are not just interested; they're motivated to make changes. That's exactly what we hoped for."

Michael, checking the sound system one last time, added, "And the range of topics we covered today has sparked interest across the board. From solar energy to sustainable gardening, there's been something for everyone."

As the panelists took their seats on stage, a mix of local activists, business owners, and educators, the moderator, a well-known environmental journalist from Greenhaven, introduced the topic. "Today, we're here to discuss how communities like ours can lead the way in sustainability. Each of our panelists has been involved in creating or supporting initiatives that foster environmental responsibility."

The first panelist, a local business owner, shared her experience. "We started by assessing our operations to see where we could make immediate improvements—things like reducing waste and improving energy efficiency. It wasn't just good for the environment; it was good for our bottom line too."

A teacher from a nearby school spoke next. "In our school, we've integrated environmental education into our curriculum. But beyond that, we involve the students in real-world projects—like our school garden and recycling program—that teach them the importance of taking care of our planet."

"That's fantastic," the moderator replied. "It shows how education and action can go hand in hand. Alex, from the center here, can you share how initiatives like today's event play a role in community sustainability efforts?"

Alex leaned into his microphone, his voice clear and passionate. "Events like our Earth Day festival are crucial because they bring the community together for a common cause. We share knowledge, we inspire each other, and most importantly, we build networks of people committed to making a difference. It's about creating a culture of sustainability that lasts beyond just one day."

Elaine then added, "And it's important to remember that every small action counts. Whether it's choosing to bike instead of drive, conserving water, or supporting local green businesses, it all adds up to a significant impact over time."

The discussion continued with questions from the audience, who were eager to learn more about how they could contribute to the sustainability of their community. The panelists provided insights and practical advice, sparking ideas among the attendees.

As the panel wrapped up, Michael offered his thoughts. "Today has shown that there's a real desire in our community to take on the challenge of sustainability. It's up to all of us to keep this momentum going."

The audience applauded as the panelists stood, and the moderator thanked everyone for their participation. As people began to leave, many lingered to talk with the panelists or with each other, energized by the discussions.

Elaine, Alex, and Michael gathered their things, their conversation turning to the next steps. "We need to capitalize on the energy from today," Elaine said. "Let's think about a series of follow-up workshops and maybe a regular community update on our progress."

"That sounds like a plan," Alex agreed. "Let's keep pushing, keep engaging, and keep inspiring. This is just the beginning."

As the center emptied, the trio felt a profound sense of accomplishment and anticipation for the future. They locked up the building and walked together to the parking lot, discussing plans for the coming weeks. The setting sun cast long shadows across the ground, but the path forward was clear, illuminated by the collective commitment of the Greenhaven community to a sustainable future. The evening closed quietly around them, the day's success a promise of the continued efforts and achievements yet to come.

Chapter 17
Hidden Agendas

The fervor of spring had ushered in not only a blossoming of flowers across Greenhaven but also a burgeoning interest in the community garden initiative led by the Environmental Education Center. Under the guidance of Alex, Elaine, and Michael, the initiative was designed to expand urban green spaces and promote local food production through community gardens scattered throughout the city.

On a particularly vibrant morning, with the sun casting a warm glow over the newly tilled soil, the team met at the largest of these new garden sites, located on a once-vacant lot near the center of town. The area had been transformed into rows of potential—a blank canvas for the community's green thumbs.

"As you can see," Alex said, gesturing towards the neatly arranged plots, "we've set up the irrigation system, and compost bins are in place. Each plot is ready for planting."

Elaine, who was reviewing a list on her clipboard, nodded in agreement. "We have over fifty families signed up already. It's a great response, and I think as more people see the garden taking shape, even more will want to join."

Michael, checking the alignment of a new signpost, added, "We need to ensure there's a system in place for gardeners to share tips and resources. Maybe a monthly meetup here at the garden? It could serve as both a social and educational gathering."

"That's a good idea," Alex replied. "Engagement is key to keeping this project thriving. Plus, it fits perfectly with our mission of community involvement and sustainability."

As they discussed logistics, a local elementary school teacher approached with a small group of students, their faces bright with curiosity and excitement. "Good morning, Alex, Elaine, Michael," she greeted. "I brought the kids over to see the garden. We've been talking about plant life cycles in class, and I thought this would be a great real-life learning experience for them."

"Absolutely," Elaine responded warmly. "We're just discussing the community aspects of the garden. Kids, you're looking at what will soon be a lush space filled with vegetables and flowers, all grown by people right here in Greenhaven."

One of the children, a little girl with a sun hat too large for her head, looked up at Elaine. "Can we plant something today?" she asked with a hopeful glance at the rows of bare soil.

Alex chuckled, bending down to her level. "Not today, but very soon. We're going to have a big planting day, and you're all invited to help us get the first plants in the ground. How does that sound?"

"Awesome!" several of the children exclaimed, their enthusiasm infectious.

As the group of students toured the rest of the garden, discussing what types of plants they might see there soon, Alex, Elaine, and Michael continued their preparations. They set up information stands with leaflets on various gardening techniques and a calendar of upcoming garden events.

By the time the sun reached its zenith, the early framework of what would become a vibrant community hub was laid out. The site buzzed with potential, much like the bees that hovered over the nearby wildflowers, and as the team wrapped up their morning's work, they were satisfied with the progress.

"This is going to be something special," Michael remarked as they gathered their tools. "Not just for the adults but for the kids too. It's creating a living classroom."

"Yes," Elaine agreed, locking up the tool shed. "It's about growing food and beautifying the space, but it's also about growing a community."

They left the site, the promise of what was to come as palpable as the soft soil that would soon sprout Greenhaven's newest greenery. The day closed quietly, the setting sun casting long shadows over the garden, hinting at the growth and gatherings that were to take root in this communal space.

On a mild spring morning, the Greenhaven community gathered at the local community garden for the much-anticipated planting day organized by the Environmental Education Center. Families, individuals, and groups from nearby schools were all present, equipped with gardening gloves and enthusiastic smiles. Alex, Elaine, and Michael were on hand to guide the activities and provide support.

As volunteers started arriving, Alex addressed the group with a clipboard in hand. "Welcome everyone, and thank you for joining us on this beautiful morning to help get our community garden off to a great start!"

Elaine, standing beside a table laden with seed packets and garden tools, joined in. "Today, we have a variety of plants to put in the ground—everything from tomatoes to sunflowers. We'll start by assigning plots and then get right to planting."

Michael, checking the layout of the garden, called out, "If everyone could gather around for a moment, I'll show you where each section of the garden is and what we'll be planting where."

As people clustered around him, Michael pointed to a large map of the garden. "Here we have the vegetable plots, over there are the herb gardens, and along the back, we'll have some flowering plants that are great for pollinators like bees and butterflies."

A young boy, tugging at his mother's sleeve, piped up, "Can I plant carrots? I really like carrots."

Michael chuckled, nodding. "Absolutely, we've got some carrot seeds over on the table with Elaine. You can grab a packet and I'll show you to the vegetable plot."

As the planting began, Alex and Elaine walked among the rows, offering tips on planting depths and spacing. "Make sure you give each plant enough room to grow," Elaine advised a group of eager teenagers handling tomato plants. "Tomatoes like a bit of space, and they'll need to be staked as they grow taller."

One of the teenagers, holding a tomato plant, asked, "How often should we water them?"

Elaine answered, "Tomatoes like consistent moisture, so you'll want to water them whenever the top inch of soil feels dry. But don't overwater—tomato plants don't like soggy soil."

As families worked together to plant their plots, the garden quickly transformed from bare earth to a patchwork of green sprouts and colorful flowers. The sound of children's laughter mixed with the soft thuds of trowels digging into the soil created a lively atmosphere.

Towards the end of the event, as people began cleaning up, Alex gathered the group for a few closing remarks. "Thank you all for your hard work today. This garden isn't just a place to grow food; it's a place to grow community. We hope you'll come back often, not just to tend to your plants but to enjoy this space together."

A woman in the crowd, wiping dirt from her hands onto her jeans, smiled and said, "This has been a wonderful day, Alex. It's great to see the community coming together like this. How can we keep involved?"

Michael responded, "We're planning a series of workshops right here in the garden. Everything from composting to pest management. And of course, you're always welcome to come here and enjoy the space, or even just to check on your plants."

Elaine added, "And if you have any questions or need advice, don't hesitate to reach out. We're here to help, and we want to see both the plants and our community thrive."

As people started to leave, many lingered, chatting with new acquaintances and exchanging contact information. The community garden was already fostering connections and promising to be a lively hub in Greenhaven.

Walking back to the center, Alex, Elaine, and Michael reflected on the success of the day. "It's really coming together, isn't it?" Elaine remarked, a note of satisfaction in her voice.

"It is," Alex agreed. "Today was just the beginning. I can't wait to see how it all grows."

Their conversation drifted to future plans as they locked up the center, the garden behind them a tangible symbol of community and growth, its new shoots reaching up towards the spring sun, just like the aspirations of Greenhaven's residents.

As the community garden began to flourish, so did the bonds among the Greenhaven residents who frequented the space. The garden had become not just a place to cultivate plants, but also relationships and a shared commitment to the environment. Under the warm glow of the early summer sun, the garden was alive with activity, with residents tending to their plots, exchanging gardening tips, and enjoying the outdoors.

Elaine watched from the edge of the garden, her eyes reflecting pride and contentment. Beside her, Michael was busy setting up for the first of many planned workshops in the garden. Today's topic was natural pest control, a subject that had generated considerable interest among the gardeners.

"This workshop is going to be a great resource," Elaine commented as she helped Michael arrange the seating. "I've noticed a few people struggling with pests. It's all part of the learning process."

"Absolutely," Michael agreed, placing informational pamphlets on each chair. "The more they understand about managing pests naturally, the healthier their plants will be. And it's all information they can take home to their own gardens, too."

As the participants began to arrive, Alex joined Elaine and Michael, his gaze sweeping across the vibrant greenery. "It's amazing to see how much this place has grown—not just the plants, but the community's involvement. It's become a real hub of activity."

"It really has," Elaine said, smiling as she greeted a family approaching them. "And it's fostering a lot of interest in sustainable living beyond just gardening."

The workshop began, with a local expert explaining the benefits of using natural predators and organic methods to manage garden pests. Participants listened intently, asking questions and noting down tips. The discussion was lively, reflecting the community's eagerness to learn and implement eco-friendly practices.

After the workshop, Alex, Elaine, and Michael convened briefly to discuss the upcoming events scheduled for the summer. "We should keep the momentum going with more of these practical workshops," Alex suggested. "Maybe something on water conservation next? I've noticed quite a few questions about that during the last few days."

"That's a good idea," Michael responded. "Especially now that we're getting into the hotter months. Efficient water use is going to be crucial."

"And perhaps a session on harvesting and storing produce," Elaine added. "Many people are new to gardening and might not know the best ways to handle their crops once they start producing."

As they planned, children played along the garden paths, and other gardeners tended to their plots, the air filled with the sounds of a community garden at its best: laughter, conversation, and the rustling of leaves in the gentle breeze.

As the day drew to a close, the three friends paused to appreciate the scene before them. Families were packing up, children were helping to water the plants, and there was a general sense of accomplishment and belonging.

"This is exactly what we hoped for when we started this project," Michael remarked, watching a young couple proudly examine their thriving tomato plants.

"It's more than just growing food; it's about growing a community," Elaine reflected, her voice full of emotion.

Alex nodded, his eyes scanning the happy faces around him. "And it's just the beginning. Think of all the seasons to come, all the harvests, all the lessons we'll learn together here."

As they left the garden that evening, the sun dipped below the horizon, casting a golden light that lingered over the lush beds of vegetables and flowers. The day ended quietly, the soft buzz of the evening insects blending with the fading laughter of children. The garden, now a centerpiece of the community, stood as a testament to what could be achieved when people come together to care for the earth and each other.

The summer season was in full swing, and the Greenhaven community garden had become a verdant oasis teeming with life and activity. Alex, Elaine, and Michael organized a special event to celebrate the garden's first significant harvest. The day was set aside for a community potluck, where everyone was encouraged to bring dishes made from the produce grown in their plots. The atmosphere was festive, with tables adorned with colorful tablecloths and string lights twinkling in the background.

As they set up for the event, Elaine remarked to Alex, "It's incredible to see how much everyone's harvest has come along. This potluck is going to be a real testament to the community's hard work and dedication."

Alex smiled as he arranged the seating, "Absolutely. It's not just about sharing food; it's about celebrating the strong community ties we've forged here. Everyone's really taken ownership of their part in this garden."

Michael, checking the sound system for the music playlist, added, "And it's a perfect way to showcase the success of our natural gardening methods. Look at all the vibrant produce!"

As people began to arrive, carrying dishes brimming with colorful salads, homemade sauces, and fresh baked goods, the garden buzzed with excitement and chatter. "Look at this spread!" Michael exclaimed as he greeted the attendees. "Everything looks so delicious!"

One of the gardeners, a middle-aged man named Greg, approached Alex with a tray of stuffed peppers. "Alex, these are from the bell peppers I grew in my plot. I can't believe I actually managed to grow them so well!"

"That's fantastic, Greg!" Alex responded, admiring the dish. "They look amazing. It's all down to your hard work and what you've learned here."

Elaine, talking with a group of families, shared, "I brought a pesto pasta. The basil came straight from my section of the herb garden. I've never tasted anything so fresh!"

A young mother in the group, holding her daughter's hand, smiled and said, "We made a salad with the lettuce and tomatoes we harvested. My daughter, Mia, picked them herself. She's become quite the little gardener."

"That's wonderful to hear," Elaine replied. "It's amazing how gardens like these can instill a sense of responsibility and pride in kids."

The group laughed and shared more stories about their gardening adventures as children ran around, playing tag between the garden rows. The air was filled with the aroma of fresh food and the sound of laughter and music.

Later, as everyone gathered around the tables to enjoy the feast, Michael stood up to make a toast. "I want to thank everyone for coming out today and for bringing such incredible dishes. This garden is more than just a place to grow food; it's a place where we grow as a community. Cheers to many more seasons of harvest and happiness!"

"Cheers!" the crowd echoed, raising their glasses.

After the meal, Alex convened a small meeting with Elaine and Michael near the compost area. "Today was a huge success. We should think about making this an annual event. It could be a wonderful tradition."

Elaine agreed, "I think that's a brilliant idea. It's a great way to celebrate the fruits of our labor, literally and figuratively."

Michael nodded, "And it's an opportunity to reflect on what we've accomplished and what we can improve for next year."

As the sun began to set, casting a golden light over the garden, the community lingered, reluctant to leave the warmth and camaraderie of the gathering. Children helped collect plates and leftover food, learning early the values of community and stewardship.

The event wound down with people exchanging farewells and promising to return soon. Alex, Elaine, and Michael stayed behind to clean up, their conversation turning to plans for the future and improvements for the next growing season.

As they locked up the garden gates, the last rays of sunlight dipped below the horizon, leaving a sense of fulfillment and anticipation for what the next year would bring. The garden, now quiet, was a symbol of community strength and environmental awareness, its impact evident in every plant and every person who had come to call this place their own.

Chapter 18
Rallying the Troops

As autumn approached, the leaves began to display their fiery hues, and the Environmental Education Center was abuzz with preparations for the annual Greenhaven Environmental Festival. Alex, Elaine, and Michael gathered in the newly renovated community hall, surrounded by banners and displays awaiting installation. This year, the festival aimed to highlight innovative sustainability projects from around the community, including a special feature on recent advancements in renewable energy.

"I think it's essential we give these projects the spotlight they deserve," Alex said, unfolding a blueprint of the festival layout on the table. "These innovators are not just professionals; they're everyday citizens who are making a real difference."

Elaine, arranging the speaker schedule on her laptop, nodded in agreement. "Absolutely. And I've arranged for some of them to speak at the festival. There's Sarah, for instance, who installed a greywater system in her home that she's going to discuss during the Water-Saving Innovations session."

"That's fantastic," Michael chimed in, checking his notes. "And don't forget about the local high school's solar project. The students managed to reduce their school's energy bill by 30% this year alone. They'll have a booth and give a presentation at noon."

Alex smiled, pleased with the lineup. "It's impressive what they've achieved. We should make sure their booth is front and center. It's a perfect example for other schools and institutions."

Elaine glanced up from her laptop. "Speaking of schools, I've also reached out to the university's environmental science club. They're going to set up an interactive exhibit on urban biodiversity."

Michael looked up, interested. "What does that entail exactly?"

"They've created a model that simulates different urban environments and shows how various species can thrive in them," Elaine explained. "They'll have QR codes that visitors can scan to watch videos about each species and learn about small-scale interventions that can help support urban wildlife."

"That sounds engaging," Alex remarked. "I'm sure it will be a hit, especially with the younger attendees. Have we got everything sorted for the kids' corner this year?"

"Yes, that's all set," Michael replied. "We'll have eco-craft stations where kids can make bird feeders from recycled materials and a mini bug hotel workshop. Plus, the face painting booth will use natural, non-toxic paints this year."

Elaine smiled, visibly pleased. "I love how inclusive that is. It's important that the kids have fun while learning about sustainability."

As they continued to plan, the sound of volunteers arriving began to fill the hall. They came in with boxes of materials, ready to help set up.

"Let's make sure everyone knows what they're doing," Alex said, standing to greet the first group of volunteers. "Good morning, everyone! Thank you for coming to help out. Let's make this festival a great success."

Elaine joined him, clipboard in hand. "We'll start by setting up the main information booth here in the hall. We need signs pointing to each section of the festival, especially the workshops and main presentation areas."

Michael directed a pair of volunteers toward the back. "Let's get the speaker stage set up first. We need the audio equipment checked and ready before we do anything else."

As the volunteers dispersed to their tasks, the trio oversaw the setup, ensuring each element of the festival was meticulously prepared. The energy in the room was one of collective purpose, each person contributing to a cause greater than themselves.

The preparations continued smoothly, with Alex, Elaine, and Michael coordinating efforts, solving last-minute challenges, and ensuring everything was on track for the festival opening the next day.

As the hall transformed under their guidance, the anticipation for the event grew. This year's festival was not just a showcase of environmental initiatives but a celebration of community spirit and innovation. As they wrapped up for the day, the setting sun cast a warm glow through the hall's large windows, illuminating the fruits of their labor—a testament to what can be achieved when a community comes together for the planet.

The day of the Greenhaven Environmental Festival dawned clear and bright, a perfect autumn day that promised to draw a large crowd. As the early morning sun began to peek through the colorful foliage, Alex, Elaine, and Michael performed a final walk-through of the festival grounds, ensuring that every detail was in place for the day's events.

Michael, double-checking the setup at the renewable energy display, looked up as Alex approached. "All set here," he reported. "The solar panel models are hooked up, and the display monitors are running smoothly. We're ready to show off some cutting-edge technology."

"That's great," Alex responded, his voice carrying a note of satisfaction. "How's the setup going for the high school solar project presentation?"

"Right on track," Michael confirmed. "The students are really excited to share their work. It's impressive what they've managed to accomplish."

Elaine, joining them with a clipboard in hand, added, "And the university's urban biodiversity exhibit is attracting a lot of attention already. They've done a fantastic job making it interactive."

The trio continued their rounds, greeting vendors and speakers as they prepared for the influx of visitors. At the main entrance, Elaine paused to speak with a volunteer who was directing early arrivals. "Let's make sure everyone gets a program and knows where the key activities are located. It's important that our guests can easily find the sessions they're most interested in."

As people began to fill the festival grounds, the air buzzed with excitement and curiosity. Families, students, and environmental enthusiasts wandered between booths, engaged in lively discussions about sustainability and conservation.

At the community garden booth, Alex led a discussion on sustainable gardening practices. "Companion planting is not just about saving space," he explained to an attentive crowd. "It's about creating a mini-ecosystem where plants can support each other's growth and deter pests naturally."

A woman in the crowd, holding a notepad, asked, "Could you give an example of companion plants that work well together?"

"Certainly," Alex replied. "Take tomatoes and basil, for example. Basil helps to repel insects that might otherwise harm the tomato plants, and it's said that it can even improve their flavor."

As the morning progressed, Elaine took the stage at the central pavilion to introduce a panel on green building techniques. "Today, we have architects and builders who specialize in eco-friendly construction," she announced. "They'll share insights on how sustainable design not only reduces environmental impact but also saves homeowners money in the long run."

The panel was well-received, with many attendees staying afterwards to ask questions. One attendee, a local builder, inquired, "In terms of materials, what are some of the most cost-effective yet sustainable options available today?"

One of the panelists, an architect specializing in green buildings, responded, "Bamboo is a fantastic option. It's not only sustainable but also extremely durable and aesthetically pleasing. Recycled steel and glass are other materials that offer both environmental and economic benefits."

Throughout the day, Michael managed the children's area, where young attendees participated in eco-crafts and educational games. "Today, we're making bird feeders from recycled materials," he explained to a group of eager children. "It's a simple way to help wildlife and learn about the importance of reusing materials."

As the festival neared its conclusion, the community's enthusiasm was evident in the lively exchanges and the many plans for future initiatives being discussed. Alex, Elaine, and Michael reconvened to reflect on the day's events.

"We've sparked a lot of interest and, hopefully, inspired action," Elaine said, watching as the last of the visitors made their way out.

"It's been a fantastic day," Alex agreed. "Seeing the community come together like this, it reaffirms everything we're working towards."

As they began to help vendors and speakers pack up, the satisfaction of a successful event was mingled with their ongoing commitment to environmental education and community engagement. The festival may have been drawing to a close, but the conversations it started and the initiatives it inspired were just beginning, promising continued growth and engagement in the seasons to come.

As autumn deepened, the leaves in Greenhaven turned brilliant shades of red and gold, and the community's enthusiasm nurtured at the Environmental Festival continued to flourish. Inspired by the festival's success, Alex, Elaine, and Michael planned an initiative that would keep the momentum going—a series of seasonal workshops aimed at integrating more sustainable practices into everyday life.

The first of these workshops focused on energy conservation as the colder months approached. Held in the warm, inviting space of the Environmental Education Center, the room was set up with stations that demonstrated various energy-saving techniques and technologies.

Before the workshop began, Elaine reviewed the schedule with Alex. "We have the smart thermostat demo first, followed by the insulation techniques presentation. I think it'll give attendees a good grasp of how to effectively reduce their heating costs and environmental impact this winter."

"That sounds perfect," Alex replied, arranging pamphlets and information sheets on a table near the entrance. "Energy conservation is crucial, especially this time of year. It's important that we give people practical, actionable advice."

As the participants began to arrive, Michael greeted them at the door, offering warm smiles and workshop schedules. "Welcome! We've got a lot of great information to share today. Be sure to check out each station and ask plenty of questions."

The workshop was interactive, with attendees moving between stations, engaging with the displays, and discussing what they learned. At the smart thermostat station, a local HVAC expert demonstrated how to program and monitor the devices. "Smart thermostats are not just convenient; they're also a powerful tool for managing your home's energy use," he explained. "You can adjust the settings based on your schedule and even monitor your energy consumption in real-time from your smartphone."

At another station, Elaine led a discussion on the benefits of proper insulation. "Proper insulation doesn't just keep your home warm; it keeps your energy bills down," she explained. "Today, we're going to look at some eco-friendly insulation options that are both effective and sustainable."

The participants were particularly interested in the hands-on demonstration of window insulation techniques using eco-friendly materials. "Windows are a major source of heat loss in the winter," a volunteer at the station noted. "Using these materials can significantly improve your home's energy efficiency."

As the afternoon progressed, the workshop attendees became increasingly engaged, sharing their own experiences and tips with one another. The atmosphere was collaborative, with everyone from young homeowners to seasoned gardeners contributing to the conversation.

Toward the end of the session, Alex facilitated a roundtable discussion. "We've talked a lot about individual actions today, but I'd like to hear your thoughts on how we as a community can support each other in these efforts."

One attendee, a local schoolteacher, suggested, "Maybe we could start a community tool lending library. Not everyone can afford to buy smart thermostats or insulation materials, but if we pool resources, we could make these options more accessible."

"That's a wonderful idea," Michael responded, noting it down. "A tool lending library could really democratize access to energy-saving technologies."

As the workshop wrapped up, the participants lingered, exchanging contact information and discussing plans to implement what they had learned. The seeds of change planted during the festival were beginning to bear fruit, evidenced by the community's eagerness to continue making sustainable choices.

Elaine, Alex, and Michael stayed behind to tidy up, their conversation turning to the next workshop in the series. "Today was a great start," Elaine remarked. "I'm already looking forward to our next session on water conservation."

"Me too," Alex agreed as they turned off the lights and locked up the center. "It's clear that there's a real appetite for these kinds of practical, hands-on learning experiences."

As they walked to their cars under a sky streaked with sunset, they discussed plans for the upcoming workshops, each inspired by the community's enthusiasm and commitment to sustainability. The crisp evening air was a reminder of the approaching winter, but also of the warmth and vitality of a community united in purpose.

As the season transitioned from the vibrant hues of fall to the crisp chill of early winter, the Greenhaven Environmental Education Center prepared for its final workshop of the year, focused on sustainable holiday practices. The aim was to teach the community how to celebrate in an environmentally friendly manner, covering everything from gift-giving and decorating to food preparation.

Inside the center, decorations made from recycled materials adorned the walls and tables, demonstrating practical examples of the workshop's themes. Alex, Elaine, and Michael reviewed the agenda one last time before the participants arrived.

"We've set up stations for each aspect of sustainable holiday celebrations," Alex explained, pointing towards the different areas of the room. "Over there, we have eco-friendly gift wrapping techniques, and next to it, DIY decorations using natural or recycled materials."

Elaine nodded, adjusting the display on a table that showcased homemade candles and soaps. "These could make great gifts. We're also demonstrating how to make them, which adds a personal touch that's often more appreciated than store-bought items."

Michael, who was arranging pamphlets and resource guides on a side table, added, "And I think the food sustainability station will be a hit. We're discussing how to source ingredients locally and reduce waste during holiday meals."

As the workshop began, community members of all ages filtered in, greeted by the warm, inviting atmosphere. The room buzzed with conversations as participants explored the stations, engaging with the displays and asking questions.

At the gift wrapping station, a volunteer demonstrated how to use fabric and other reusable materials for beautifully wrapped presents. "Not only does this reduce waste, but it also turns the wrapping into a part of the gift itself," she explained to a group of intrigued attendees.

Meanwhile, at the decoration station, Elaine guided a family through making a wreath out of recycled materials. "You can use old book pages, fabric scraps, even natural elements like pinecones and branches," she instructed as they arranged their materials.

The food sustainability station was particularly popular, with Michael discussing how to plan holiday meals that were both delicious and environmentally conscious. "Consider a vegetarian dish or two," he suggested. "It reduces the carbon footprint of your meal and introduces guests to new, tasty options."

As the workshop progressed, Alex took a moment to speak with the attendees about the importance of carrying these practices beyond the holiday season. "What we're learning today can be applied throughout the year. Sustainability isn't just for the holidays; it's a lifestyle."

Participants nodded, many taking notes or discussing how they could incorporate these ideas into their holiday traditions. The workshop not only provided practical tips but also inspired a deeper consideration of everyday choices and their impact on the environment.

As the day wound down, the participants began to leave, thanking Alex, Elaine, and Michael for the insightful experiences. The team stayed back to clean up, their conversation turning to the impact of their year's efforts.

"This series has really brought the community together," Elaine reflected as she folded a tablecloth. "I think we've started something special here."

Michael, stacking chairs, agreed. "Absolutely. The engagement we've seen is promising. It's about more than just attendance; it's about real change in attitudes and behaviors."

Alex locked up the center, looking out over the snow-dusted landscape. "Let's keep this momentum going. Next year, we can expand our workshops and reach even more people."

As they left the center, the cold air felt invigorating, a crisp reminder of the winter ahead but also of the warm community spirit they had cultivated. Their steps crunched softly in the fresh snow, echoing the steady progress of their environmental mission, ever forward, into the new year and beyond.

Chapter 19
The Real Villain

As the new year began, Greenhaven welcomed it with a blanket of snow that added a silent charm to the town. The Environmental Education Center, spearheaded by Alex, Elaine, and Michael, was buzzing with new projects and renewed energy. The focus for the year was to initiate a "Green New Year's Resolution" program, encouraging community members to commit to sustainable practices throughout the year.

The trio met in Elaine's office, surrounded by posters and digital displays outlining their planned initiatives. Outside, the occasional sound of children sledding near the center broke the quiet of the winter morning.

"We need to kick off the 'Green New Year's Resolution' program with something that catches everyone's attention," Alex began, tapping his pen against his notebook. "Perhaps an event that showcases the simplicity and impact of incorporating sustainable habits into daily life."

Elaine nodded, pulling up a presentation on her laptop. "I like that idea. We could have a demonstration day—call it 'Green Living Made Easy.' We can show everything from installing energy-efficient appliances to composting and more."

Michael, looking over the schedule, added, "And we should tie it into a community challenge. Maybe encourage people to commit to one new sustainable practice each month. We could provide resources and support through workshops and online tips."

"That could really work," Elaine agreed, her eyes brightening. "Each month could have a theme. January could be about energy conservation, February about reducing waste, and so on."

Alex leaned forward, enthusiastic. "Let's make sure we keep the momentum going with regular check-ins and updates. Maybe a monthly newsletter that highlights community members who are excelling in their commitments."

"That's a great idea," Michael said, typing out some notes. "It could really help build a sense of community around the program. Plus, seeing real stories of people making changes could inspire others to do the same."

Elaine smiled, pleased with the plan. "I can start putting together the first newsletter. I already have a couple of community members in mind who have made significant changes after our holiday workshop."

As they continued to plan, a soft knock on the door announced the arrival of a volunteer, who poked her head in. "Sorry to interrupt, but there's a delivery of recycled paper and other materials for the event."

"Thanks, we'll be right out," Alex responded, standing up. "Let's finalize the details of this launch event. We need to decide on the location, volunteers, and exactly what demonstrations we'll have."

Elaine quickly outlined a proposal. "Let's use the main hall for the demonstrations and set up booths outside, weather permitting. We can cover topics like meatless Mondays, recycling correctly, and home gardening."

"Perfect," Michael said, checking his watch. "I'll coordinate with the volunteers to start setting up the spaces this week. We'll need signs and possibly some digital displays to make each booth engaging and informative."

As they wrapped up the meeting, the trio felt a renewed sense of purpose. The "Green New Year's Resolution" program wasn't just a series of events; it was a new chapter in Greenhaven's journey toward sustainability.

Leaving Elaine's office, they walked through the quiet halls of the center, now filled with the promise of active days ahead. The energy was palpable, a mix of anticipation and determination, as they stepped outside to greet the volunteers, ready to bring their plans to life in the chilly but invigorating winter air. The community was responding, the center was thriving, and the new year was off to a promising start.

The "Green Living Made Easy" event was set to be a pivotal day at the Environmental Education Center, designed to spark a year of sustainable actions among the Greenhaven community. As the morning of the event dawned crisp and clear, Alex, Elaine, and Michael were busy with the final setup in the center's main hall, which was bustling with volunteers arranging booths and setting up demonstration areas.

"Everything needs to be perfect," Alex said as he arranged the signage for the energy-efficient appliance demo. "These demonstrations are the practical touchpoints that can really drive the message home."

Elaine, organizing the literature on a table decked with pamphlets and reusable tote bags, nodded in agreement. "I've coordinated with the local utility company, and they've sent over someone to talk about incentives for home energy audits and upgrades. It should give people a real incentive to start making changes."

Michael was checking the audio equipment at the central stage. "How's the sound coming along?" Elaine asked, looking over to him.

"Almost there," Michael replied, adjusting the microphone. "We want everyone at the back to hear just as well as those up front."

As the first attendees began to trickle in, a mix of families and individuals curious about adopting greener lifestyles, Alex greeted them with a warm smile. "Welcome! We're thrilled to have you join us today. Make sure to visit each booth, there are lots of great tips and practical advice to take home."

One of the first demonstrations was on composting, a popular topic among both seasoned gardeners and novices. The volunteer leading the session was enthusiastic, explaining the basics and benefits of composting kitchen scraps. "Composting is easier than you might think, and it can reduce household waste significantly," she explained to an attentive crowd.

Nearby, Elaine led a discussion on reducing plastic use, showcasing alternatives like beeswax wraps, reusable shopping bags, and glass containers. "Every plastic item we avoid using is one less piece of waste that could end up in landfills or oceans," she told her audience, who listened intently, many nodding in agreement.

Throughout the morning, Alex, Elaine, and Michael circulated among the booths, answering questions and engaging with the community. The feedback was overwhelmingly positive, with many expressing surprise at how manageable many of the sustainable practices seemed.

At noon, Alex gathered the crowd for a special presentation. "Thank you all for being here today," he began, his voice resonant in the quieting hall. "These actions, whether big or small, contribute to a healthier planet. We hope that today's event inspires you to take the pledge for our 'Green New Year's Resolution' program."

Elaine then took the stage to explain further. "Our program is designed to support you throughout the year. Each month, we'll focus on a different theme related to sustainability, and we'll provide resources and workshops to help you meet your goals."

As the event drew to a close, Michael offered some parting words. "We're here to help and support each other. Sustainability isn't just about individual actions; it's about coming together as a community to make a difference."

The attendees dispersed with new knowledge and a sense of purpose, many stopping to thank Alex, Elaine, and Michael for an enlightening day. The trio stayed behind to tidy up, their conversation turning to the success of the event and their hopes for the future.

"This was just the start," Elaine said, packing up the last of the pamphlets. "I think we've really started something special here."

"Yeah," Alex agreed, turning off the lights in the main hall. "Let's keep this momentum going. Greenhaven is on its way to becoming a model for sustainable living."

As they locked up the center, the winter sun was setting, casting long shadows across the snow-covered ground. The day's success was a promise of the growth and engagement yet to come, an affirmation of the community's readiness to embrace a sustainable future.

As winter clung to the final weeks of its reign over Greenhaven, the buzz from the "Green Living Made Easy" event still echoed through the community. Inspired by the positive reception, Alex, Elaine, and Michael convened at the Environmental Education Center to plan the next installment in their series of sustainability workshops, focusing on indoor gardening and low-energy home solutions.

In the cozy warmth of the center's main workshop room, with diagrams and notes from the previous event spread out before them, the trio was deep in discussion about the upcoming session's structure.

"I think starting with indoor gardening is perfect for this time of year," Elaine began, pointing to a layout of the room on her laptop. "It's still too cold for outdoor planting, but people can start preparing seedlings indoors."

Alex nodded, examining the seed starter kits they planned to distribute. "Absolutely, and it's a great segue into discussing the broader implications of growing your own food, even in small, urban spaces. We should highlight how this reduces carbon footprints and promotes healthier eating habits."

Michael, arranging the chairs into a semi-circle for a more interactive session, added, "I've arranged for a local expert in hydroponics to come and demonstrate. It's a fantastic way to grow food indoors without using a lot of space or even soil."

"That will definitely catch people's interest," Elaine responded. "Especially for those living in apartments or with limited space. What about the low-energy home solutions? I think coupling that with indoor gardening could offer a holistic approach to sustainable living indoors."

Alex perked up at the suggestion. "We could set up a demo on LED lighting and other energy-efficient appliances that complement the indoor gardening setup. Showing how low-energy lighting can be used to help plants grow could tie the two themes together nicely."

Michael looked up from the seating arrangement, "I like that. And maybe include a segment on using programmable thermostats to maintain optimal temperatures for both plant growth and home energy savings."

Elaine began typing up a draft for the workshop flyer. "I'll make sure to outline the benefits clearly—how these practices not only save money but also create a sustainable living environment."

As they finalized the details, volunteers began arriving to help set up the space. Alex greeted them warmly, "Thanks for coming, everyone. Your help is invaluable to making these workshops a success."

One volunteer, a young woman who had attended the last event, shared her enthusiasm. "The last workshop really opened my eyes to how easy some of these changes can be. I'm excited to learn more today and help out."

Elaine handed her a box of flyers. "That's wonderful to hear! Could you help by placing some of these flyers at the entrance? We want to make sure everyone knows what's being covered today."

As the room began to fill with eager participants, Michael checked the audio equipment. "Alright, looks like we're almost set to start. Alex, do you want to do the opening again? You were a hit last time."

Alex laughed, straightening his notes. "Sure, I'd be happy to. Let's hope I can keep the streak going."

As the workshop began, Alex welcomed the attendees, "Thank you all for joining us today. We have a great session planned, focusing on sustainable practices you can adopt right inside your home. We're starting with indoor gardening, and then we'll explore some easy-to-implement, low-energy solutions for everyday living."

The attendees listened intently, their faces reflecting a mix of curiosity and motivation. The room buzzed with the energy of shared learning and community spirit.

Throughout the afternoon, as discussions unfolded and hands-on demonstrations took place, the sense of community and commitment to sustainability grew stronger. Participants exchanged ideas, shared personal experiences, and discussed plans to implement the new practices in their own homes.

As the workshop wrapped up, Elaine, Alex, and Michael stayed behind to chat with attendees and answer lingering questions. The positive feedback was overwhelming, reinforcing the trio's belief in their mission.

Leaving the center that evening, the three friends felt a profound satisfaction. The impact of their efforts was palpable, not just in the success of the workshop but in the strengthening bonds within the community. As they locked up and walked to their cars, their conversation turned to future plans, each idea building on the last, driven by the community's enthusiasm and the endless possibilities of sustainability.

The enthusiasm from the indoor gardening and energy-saving workshops had left the community eager for more, prompting Alex, Elaine, and Michael to organize a roundtable discussion to gather feedback and brainstorm future projects. The meeting was held in the main hall of the Environmental Education Center, now a familiar venue for such gatherings, where tables were arranged in an open circle to foster an inclusive and collaborative atmosphere.

As community members filed in, each was greeted warmly by the trio, who handed out agendas and pens for note-taking. "Thank you all for coming," Alex began, once everyone had settled. "Today is about reflecting on what we've accomplished and where we want to go from here."

Elaine took over, her tone enthusiastic. "We've seen fantastic engagement with our recent workshops, and we want to build on that momentum. Let's start by hearing what you think worked well and what could be improved."

A local schoolteacher raised her hand, smiling. "I loved the practical aspect of the workshops. It's one thing to hear about sustainability, but actually doing those activities makes a huge difference. My students and I started a small indoor garden in our classroom because of what we learned."

"That's wonderful to hear," Michael responded, jotting down notes. "Do you think there's a way we could further support educational initiatives like yours?"

The teacher nodded. "Perhaps more materials or even a kit that schools could use to start their own projects. Having a resource list or a small grant could help get more schools involved."

Elaine wrote this down, nodding thoughtfully. "Great suggestion. Let's think about how we can integrate that into our programming. What about others? Any thoughts on the topics or types of workshops you'd like to see in the future?"

A young mother, who had attended several workshops, chimed in. "I think a series on sustainable cooking would be fantastic. Showing how to use local, seasonal produce could tie nicely into the gardening projects."

"That's a brilliant idea," Alex said, excited by the proposal. "It could also include elements of reducing food waste, like using parts of vegetables that are often thrown away."

The conversation flowed freely, with community members proposing ideas ranging from water conservation workshops to community clean-up days. Michael facilitated much of the discussion, ensuring everyone's voice was heard. "These are all excellent ideas. How about partnerships? Are there local businesses or organizations we should consider collaborating with?"

An elderly man, a retired engineer, raised his hand. "There's the Greenhaven Tech Hub. They have resources and might be interested in partnering on projects that involve energy conservation or green technology."

Elaine was quick to respond. "That's a fantastic connection. I'll reach out to them. Partnering could expand our reach and provide more technical expertise for our workshops."

As the roundtable continued, Alex, Elaine, and Michael each took turns addressing questions and facilitating the discussion. The energy in the room was indicative of a community not just involved, but invested in the sustainability mission.

Wrapping up, Alex stood and addressed the group. "Thank you, everyone, for your invaluable input today. We've got a lot of exciting ideas to work with, and we're looking forward to making these a reality. Please, stay involved, reach out with any more ideas or feedback, and let's keep pushing forward together."

The meeting ended on a high note, with participants lingering to chat with one another and with Alex, Elaine, and Michael. Contacts were exchanged, and plans were made, the seeds of future projects already taking root.

As the center cleared out, the trio lingered, discussing the outcomes of the meeting. "There's so much potential," Michael said, gathering up the leftover papers and agendas.

Elaine, locking up the resource cabinets, agreed. "Today was incredibly productive. I'm excited about the direction we're heading."

As they turned off the lights and exited the building, the setting sun bathed the center in a soft, golden light. The evening air was crisp, and as they walked to their cars, their conversation never wavered from the future, from the community they were building together, one sustainable step at a time.

Chapter 20
Protecting the Sanctuary

As spring unfurled its fresh leaves and blossoms across Greenhaven, the Environmental Education Center was abuzz with preparations for a significant new project: the launch of a community-wide recycling initiative aimed at drastically reducing landfill waste. Alex, Elaine, and Michael were at the forefront, organizing an event to educate residents on the importance of recycling correctly and effectively.

The idea had sprouted during one of the previous workshops, where community feedback highlighted a general confusion about recycling protocols and what could actually be recycled. This had prompted the trio to think about a targeted campaign that would not only clarify these doubts but also encourage more robust recycling practices.

On a bright and brisk morning, the community center was transformed into an educational hub. Informative posters lined the walls, and stations demonstrating proper sorting techniques were set up around the room. Each station was equipped with bins labeled for different materials—plastics, metals, paper, and glass—each accompanied by detailed information on what items belonged in each bin and why.

Elaine supervised the setup of an interactive display that featured everyday items and asked participants to decide which bin they belonged in. This hands-on approach was designed to engage people more actively than a simple lecture. Nearby, Michael tested a small kiosk that would provide instant feedback on the recyclability of an item when its barcode was scanned, a technology they hoped to implement in local stores.

As the event started, Alex welcomed the attendees with a brief overview of the day's activities. "Today, we're going to take a closer look at what we throw away and how we can make smarter decisions to help our environment," he said, his voice filled with enthusiasm that mirrored the bright morning.

Throughout the day, residents of all ages filtered in and out of the center, participating in the activities and absorbing the wealth of information available. Children seemed particularly intrigued by the barcode scanning station, while adults appreciated the clarity the sorting stations provided.

The heart of the event was not just in teaching but in listening. Volunteers collected feedback on what residents found difficult about recycling, and what would make it easier for them to participate more effectively. This feedback would be crucial in shaping the ongoing campaign.

As afternoon gave way to evening, the crowd thinned out, and the trio gathered to discuss the day's outcomes. They walked through the center, reviewing each display and discussing the interactions they had observed. The general consensus was positive; the community was receptive and eager to improve their recycling habits.

Elaine, who had spent much of the day at the interactive display, shared her insights. "I noticed a lot of people were surprised to learn that certain plastics couldn't be recycled. There's definitely a need for more education around this."

Michael nodded in agreement as he packed up the last of the kiosk's equipment. "And the feedback on the barcode scanner was overwhelmingly positive. It simplifies the decision-making process, which is exactly what we need."

As they wrapped up, locking doors and turning off lights, their conversation lingered on the potential impact of the day. They had started a crucial conversation in the community, one that they planned to continue through newsletters, school programs, and more interactive events.

Walking out into the cooling evening, the setting sun cast long shadows across the now-empty parking lot. The day had been long and full of activity, but as they went their separate ways, each carried with them a sense of accomplishment and a renewed commitment to their cause. The seeds of change had been planted today, and they were eager to nurture them in the seasons to come.

In the weeks following the launch of the recycling initiative, the trio decided to hold a series of follow-up workshops aimed at addressing specific issues that had been identified during the initial event. The community's enthusiasm was palpable, and the center buzzed with anticipation as residents gathered for the first of these sessions, which focused on reducing contamination in recycling bins—a common problem that could undermine the effectiveness of recycling efforts.

As the residents settled into their seats, Alex opened the discussion with a welcoming smile. "Thank you all for joining us this evening. Today, we're going to tackle one of the trickiest aspects of recycling—contamination. Our goal is to ensure that what we place in our recycling bins is actually recyclable and not inadvertently causing more harm than good."

Elaine chimed in, holding up a variety of items. "Let's start by examining some common contaminants. For instance, pizza boxes. While they are cardboard, the food residue and grease can contaminate the whole bin. The same goes for plastic bags, which can't be processed at most facilities and often jam machinery."

Michael picked up the conversation, gesturing towards a display of properly and improperly sorted items. "Exactly, Elaine. Now, if everyone could come closer, we have set up some examples of common mistakes. Here we have a jar that still has food residue in it. It's glass, yes, which is recyclable, but the residue can contaminate an entire batch of recycling."

A woman in the front row raised her hand, holding a plastic takeout container. "So, what about this? It's plastic, but I've heard some types can't be recycled?"

"That's a great question," Alex responded. "Not all plastics are created equal. Look for the recycling symbols and numbers at the bottom of containers. In our community, numbers 1 and 2 are typically recyclable. This container, however, is a number 6, which our local facility cannot process."

Elaine added, "It's important to check with our local waste management services for specific guidelines. They can vary significantly from one place to another."

Another attendee, a young man with a notepad, inquired, "What's the best way to ensure we're not contaminating our recycling? Any tips?"

Michael nodded, ready with an answer. "First, always rinse out containers—food containers, bottles, cans. It doesn't need to be spotless, just free from major residue. Second, if you're in doubt about whether something is recyclable, it's better to throw it out. 'Wish-cycling'—hoping or assuming something is recyclable when it isn't—leads to more problems."

As the workshop progressed, more questions flowed, and the trio answered each with patience and detail, clarifying doubts and debunking common recycling myths.

Towards the end of the session, Elaine encouraged the group to spread the word. "You all are now more informed about proper recycling practices. Please, share this knowledge with your friends, family, and neighbors. The more people know, the more effective our efforts will be."

Alex closed the workshop with a note of gratitude and encouragement. "Thank you, everyone, for your active participation tonight. Remember, every little bit helps. Our next workshop will cover electronic waste recycling, which is another area where we can make a big impact."

As the residents began to leave, many stayed back to thank Alex, Elaine, and Michael personally, expressing their appreciation for the clarity the session had provided. Conversations continued in small clusters, with people animatedly discussing what they had learned.

As the center quieted down and the last of the attendees departed, the trio gathered their materials, their faces reflecting the fatigue of a long day but also the satisfaction of a job well done. They knew that each workshop added another layer to the community's understanding and commitment to sustainability, a vital step towards a cleaner, greener Greenhaven.

A few weeks after their successful workshop on recycling, Alex, Elaine, and Michael organized another session, this time focusing on electronic waste—a growing concern as technology continued to advance at a rapid pace. The session was set up in the community center's largest hall, where tables displayed various electronic devices, from old cell phones and batteries to larger items like monitors and CPUs, all intended to demonstrate proper disposal methods.

As the attendees filtered in, Michael greeted them with a friendly nod. "Welcome, everyone! Today we're diving into a very important issue—electronic waste, or e-waste, which has significant environmental impacts if not disposed of correctly."

Elaine, arranging the last of the display items, added, "That's right, Michael. E-waste contains hazardous substances like lead, mercury, and cadmium, which can leach into the environment when not handled properly."

Alex, checking the microphone setup, called the group to attention. "Let's start with a quick overview of what e-waste actually is and why it's so crucial to recycle it properly. Can anyone tell me what types of items are considered e-waste?"

A hand shot up from the back, a middle-aged woman speaking up. "Would that include things like old televisions, computers, and even our smartphones?"

"Exactly," Alex confirmed. "All those items and more. Basically, any product with an electrical cord or battery that you are no longer using becomes e-waste when you decide to discard it."

Elaine then steered the discussion towards the process of recycling these items. "Not all components of e-waste are hazardous. In fact, many contain valuable materials like gold, silver, and copper that can be recovered and reused. That's why proper recycling is not just good for the environment, it's also economically sensible."

Michael guided the attendees to a station with a dismantled computer. "Let's take a closer look here. This old desktop contains precious metals in its circuit boards, which can be extracted and recycled. However, it also contains toxic substances that must be handled with care."

A younger participant, a college student, looked intrigued. "So, how do we go about recycling this safely? I mean, it's not like we can just take it apart in our garage, right?"

"You're absolutely right," Michael answered. "It requires specialized facilities where they can safely extract these materials and ensure that no harmful substances end up in landfills."

Elaine chimed in, "And that's where certified e-waste recyclers come into play. It's important to use facilities that follow proper disposal protocols. You can usually find information about such facilities through your local waste management services."

Alex brought out a tablet and displayed a list of certified e-waste recyclers in the region. "We've compiled a list of all certified recyclers nearby. We'll share this with you at the end of the session, and it's also available on our website."

As the workshop progressed, the trio encouraged an open dialogue, answering questions and discussing the broader impact of e-waste on global pollution and health. The interaction was lively, with participants expressing a keen interest in learning more about how they could make a difference.

Towards the end of the session, Michael summarized the key points. "Remember, the goal is to keep these materials out of landfills and recover valuable components that can be reused. Every item you recycle helps reduce the environmental footprint of electronic waste."

Elaine concluded with a call to action. "Let's all make a commitment today to be more mindful of how we dispose of our electronic items. Share what you've learned with friends and family. Awareness is the first step towards change."

As the attendees started to leave, many stayed back to thank the trio and discuss how they could implement these practices in their homes and workplaces. The room buzzed with conversations about sustainability and responsibility, a testament to the community's growing commitment to environmental stewardship.

After the last of the participants had left, Alex, Elaine, and Michael gathered their materials, satisfied with the impact of their workshop. As they turned off the lights and closed the doors, they discussed plans for future events, motivated by the community's enthusiasm and eager to keep the momentum going. The evening closed on a hopeful note, with the promise of continued engagement and education in Greenhaven.

The Environmental Education Center was set to host its final workshop of the season, focusing on sustainable transportation options—a timely topic as Greenhaven was planning to enhance its public transit system and promote eco-friendly travel. Alex, Elaine, and Michael were eager to provide community members with insights into how small changes in their commuting habits could significantly impact the environment.

As attendees gathered in the brightly lit hall of the center, equipped with posters of cycling routes, electric vehicle charging stations, and transit schedules, Michael kicked off the event. "Welcome, everyone! Today, we're focusing on how we can transform our travel habits to benefit not only our environment but also our health and wallets."

Elaine followed up, "That's right. We'll look at everything from biking to work to using electric vehicles. Did you know that transportation contributes significantly to greenhouse gas emissions in our community?"

A young couple at the front seemed particularly interested. "We've been thinking about getting an electric car," the woman said, "but we're not sure if it's practical for us."

Alex, who had prepared materials on this topic, responded, "That's a great consideration. Electric vehicles have come a long way in terms of range and accessibility. Plus, there are incentives like tax rebates and reduced rates on electricity for charging during off-peak hours."

Another attendee, an elderly man, raised a point, "What about those of us who aren't driving much anymore? I'm retired and don't see the need for a car every day."

Elaine nodded, "That's a great point. For shorter, local trips, cycling or even walking could be fantastic options. We're lucky to have increasing bike-lane development here in Greenhaven."

Michael added, "And let's not forget about carpooling. It reduces the number of vehicles on the road, which decreases traffic congestion and pollution. Plus, it can be a more social and enjoyable way to travel."

The workshop continued with Alex showcasing a map of the city's planned improvements to public transit routes and discussing how these changes were designed to make public transport a more convenient option for everyone.

A younger participant, a local university student, chimed in, "I use the bus to get to classes, but the schedules aren't always aligned with my needs. Are there plans to increase frequency during peak times?"

"Actually, yes," Alex replied, flipping to a slide in his presentation that detailed the new transit schedules. "The city is adding more buses during peak hours and also looking into using smaller, more efficient vehicles during off-peak times to save energy."

Elaine took the opportunity to discuss the environmental benefits further. "By choosing public transit over driving alone, you can reduce your carbon footprint significantly. It's one of the simplest changes you can make with a big impact."

As the workshop drew to a close, Michael led a brainstorming session. "Let's think about personal action steps. What are some changes you could commit to this coming year to help make our transportation more sustainable?"

The group engaged enthusiastically, with attendees suggesting commitments ranging from trying out the new bus routes once they rolled out, to organizing local walking groups for short trips.

"We'll be here to support you," Elaine concluded, handing out information packets and free bus passes the city had provided. "And we'd love to hear about your experiences as you try out these sustainable transport options."

The attendees left the workshop energized, discussing amongst themselves the changes they planned to implement. Alex, Elaine, and Michael began cleaning up, pleased with the discussions and the proactive attitudes.

"This is how change happens," Michael said, stacking chairs. "One decision, one change at a time."

Elaine, turning off the projector, agreed, "And it's all about providing the right information and support. Today felt like a big step in the right direction."

As they locked up the center and stepped out into the cool evening air, their conversation lingered on future projects and the positive shifts they were witnessing in the community. The streets of Greenhaven were quiet as they went their separate ways, each filled with a sense of accomplishment and the quiet confidence of having sparked meaningful action within their community.

Chapter 21
Victory

As the crisp air of early spring rejuvenated Greenhaven, Alex, Elaine, and Michael embarked on their most ambitious project yet: the establishment of a community forest. The project was a natural extension of their ongoing efforts to promote sustainability and was set to transform an unused parcel of city land into a thriving green space. This forest was envisioned not only as a haven for local wildlife but as an educational resource where the community could learn about native species and ecosystem conservation.

The site chosen for the community forest was on the outskirts of Greenhaven, a plot of land that had lain fallow for years. It offered the perfect canvas for this initiative—a blend of open field and a small, existing copse that could be expanded into a more robust forest environment. As the trio surveyed the area, they discussed the layout of walking paths, informational signage, and benches that would make the forest both accessible and educational.

"We need to consider the variety of species that can thrive here," Elaine pointed out as she examined the soil quality in different parts of the site. "It's not just about planting trees; we need to ensure a biodiverse environment to support a healthy ecosystem."

Alex, who had been researching native species that could enhance biodiversity, nodded in agreement. "I've been looking at several native shrubs and wildflowers that attract pollinators. Planting these will help ensure our forest supports not only the trees but also the smaller yet crucial members of the ecosystem."

Michael, meanwhile, was busy sketching a preliminary map on his clipboard. "I'm thinking about how we can lay out the paths to maximize exposure to the different environments we're planning to create. We need to make sure the educational signs are placed strategically to teach visitors about the species and conservation efforts as they walk through."

The planning took on a life of its own as the project started to come together. The local schools expressed interest in participating, seeing the forest as an outdoor classroom for students to learn about biology and environmental science. Local businesses also offered support, donating materials and funds to help bring the project to life. The community forest was quickly becoming a symbol of Greenhaven's commitment to environmental stewardship.

As work commenced, volunteers from around the community came together, equipped with shovels, saplings, and a shared enthusiasm. Under Alex's direction, teams began the careful process of planting young trees, each selected for its suitability to the local climate and soil conditions. Elaine led another group in setting up the wildflower areas, explaining the importance of these plants in supporting the local bee and butterfly populations.

Michael coordinated the construction of the paths and benches, ensuring that access to the forest was easy for everyone, including families with small children and the elderly. "It's important that this space is welcoming to all. We want it to be a place where the entire community can come to relax, learn, and connect with nature," he explained to a group of volunteers.

As the day progressed, the empty field slowly began to transform. Paths took shape, weaving through areas that would soon be teeming with life. Saplings stood in neat rows, their branches slight but promising. Wildflowers dotted the landscape, their colors a stark contrast to the brown earth.

By the end of the day, the foundation of the community forest was laid. Tired but fulfilled, Alex, Elaine, and Michael took a moment to appreciate their work. The sun was setting, casting a golden glow over the newly planted area, the shadows long but the air filled with a sense of accomplishment.

As they packed up their tools and prepared to leave, the trio discussed the next steps: maintenance plans, educational programs, and the upcoming grand opening. The project was far from complete, but its roots were now firmly planted, much like the saplings they had just set into the ground.

Driving away from the site, they left behind the promise of what was to come—a new green space for Greenhaven, a project born of community effort and environmental hope, ready to grow and flourish in the seasons ahead.

As spring progressed, the community forest near Greenhaven began to take shape, each new leaf and blossom a testament to the community's dedication to the environment. Alex, Elaine, and Michael met early one morning at the site, coffee in hand, to review the progress and plan the next phase of development, which included installing educational signage and planning the grand opening.

Michael gestured toward the newly planted areas, now bristling with young plants. "The growth has been remarkable. It's incredible what can be achieved when the community pulls together like this."

Elaine, unfolding a set of blueprints for the signage, nodded. "Absolutely, and these signs will add so much value. We're not just creating a forest; we're creating an educational resource. Each sign will tell visitors about the flora and fauna they can see, as well as tips on how they can contribute to conservation efforts in their own backyards."

Alex, looking over Elaine's shoulder, pointed to a section of the map. "Let's make sure we place some signs along the main path here, where they're easily readable. And perhaps another set by the wildflower meadow. It's a key area for pollinators, and I think people will be interested in learning more about that."

"Good idea," Michael agreed. "We should also consider accessibility. Let's ensure the signs are at a height that's wheelchair-friendly and use clear, simple language that children can understand."

As they walked along the path, checking potential sign locations, they discussed the grand opening. Elaine shared her thoughts, "We need to make this event memorable. It's not just a celebration of this new green space but also of our community's commitment to the environment."

"What if we organize a series of mini-events throughout the day?" Alex suggested. "We could have guided tours, a few short talks from local environmentalists, and maybe some activities for kids."

Michael nodded enthusiastically. "I like that. Let's get local schools involved too. It could be a fantastic learning opportunity for the students. Maybe they could even contribute artwork or projects related to what they've learned about local ecosystems."

"That's brilliant," Elaine responded. "Involvement from schools could really underscore the educational aspect of the forest. I'll reach out to the principals and see if they're interested."

The discussion turned to the logistics of the grand opening. "We'll need to set up tents and arrange for some catering," Alex mused. "Something simple, maybe snacks and drinks that are eco-friendly—locally sourced, minimal packaging, that kind of thing."

"And let's not forget about publicity," Michael added. "We need a good turnout. I'll handle the press release and make sure we get the word out on social media and through the local newspaper."

As they finalized the details and locations for the signs, the trio felt a shared sense of anticipation and pride. They had seen the project through from conception to near-completion, and the upcoming grand opening felt like the culmination of not just months of hard work but of broader community engagement and environmental stewardship.

Elaine, securing a sign post into the ground, stepped back to admire their work. "This is going to be a beautiful place for education and relaxation. Seeing it come together like this is really rewarding."

Alex smiled, taking a moment to look around. "It really is. This forest is a testament to what we can accomplish when we work together for a common goal. It's a small step towards a greener future, but it's a significant one."

With the morning's work completed, they gathered their tools and prepared to head back. The forest, lush and inviting, was nearly ready to welcome the community into its leafy embrace. The path they walked back on was not just a trail through the woods but a journey towards a deeper connection with nature and each other. As they left the site, their conversation continued, already brimming with ideas for future projects and enhancements.

The grand opening of the community forest was set for a radiant Saturday morning, and as the early sun dappled through the young trees, Alex, Elaine, and Michael performed their final checks. The paths had been swept, the educational signs polished, and small flags marked the entrance, fluttering gently in the breeze. The forest, though young, was alive with the promise of growth, and the air hummed with the anticipation of the day's events.

Elaine was adjusting the last of the banners when Alex joined her, a clipboard in hand. "How's everything looking on your end?" he asked, scanning the area for any last-minute adjustments.

"Almost ready," Elaine replied, securing a banner. "The local bakery delivered the refreshments, and the face-painting booth is all set up. I think the kids are going to love it."

Michael was coordinating with a group of volunteers at the welcome table, making sure they were prepared for the influx of visitors. "Remember, everyone, the main thing today is to ensure our guests leave with a better understanding of our local ecosystem and the importance of this forest," he instructed, handing out brochures and event schedules.

As the clock neared the opening time, families began to arrive, their children's faces bright with curiosity. The volunteers greeted them warmly, handing out event maps and explaining the schedule of the day. The guided tour was the first major activity, designed to introduce the visitors to the various native species planted in the forest and the roles they played in local biodiversity.

Alex led the first group, pointing out the newly planted oak and maple trees, explaining their long-term benefits to the environment. "These trees not only provide habitat and food for wildlife but also help in carbon sequestration, which is crucial for combating climate change," he explained to an attentive audience.

Further down the path, Elaine took over, discussing the undergrowth species like ferns and wildflowers. "These plants are not just beautiful; they're vital for the health of our forest. They help prevent erosion and support a myriad of insects and birds," she noted, gesturing toward a butterfly fluttering nearby.

At the heart of the forest, Michael talked about the importance of such green spaces in urban areas. "Spaces like these act as natural air filters and significantly improve the quality of life in our city. They're not just for us; they're a legacy for future generations," he told his group, who listened, nodding in agreement.

Throughout the morning, other activities unfolded. Children participated in eco-crafts, creating small bird feeders from recycled materials, while parents engaged in discussions about sustainable living practices they could adopt at home. Local environmental scientists, invited as special guests, held mini-seminars by the seating areas, discussing topics from climate change to sustainable urban planning.

As the event drew to a close, Alex, Elaine, and Michael gathered near the refreshment tables, watching as families made their way out, chatting animatedly about their experiences. The feedback was overwhelmingly positive, with many expressing a new appreciation for the natural world and a desire to get more involved in conservation efforts.

"Today was a success on so many levels," Michael said, helping a volunteer collect signage. "Not only did we introduce the forest, but we also sparked a conversation about environmental responsibility."

Elaine smiled, packing up the leftover brochures. "And hopefully, it's just the beginning. The real success will be in seeing how this place grows, both the forest and its impact on the community."

As they finished their cleanup, the sun began to set, casting long shadows through the trees and bathing the forest in a golden light. The day had been one of celebration and education, a fitting inauguration for a project that symbolized hope and renewal.

Leaving the site, Alex locked the gate, looking back at the forest they had helped bring to life. "This is more than just a patch of green in the city," he reflected. "It's a statement of what we can achieve together."

Content with their efforts, they headed towards their cars, their conversation already turning to future projects and the next steps in their mission to foster a deeper connection between Greenhaven and its natural surroundings. The journey ahead was long, but like the forest they had planted, it held the promise of growth and endless possibilities.

The momentum from the community forest opening continued to build as Alex, Elaine, and Michael convened a few weeks later to discuss expanding their educational outreach. They gathered in the Environmental Education Center, where the morning light filtered softly through the windows, casting a serene glow over their meeting space.

Elaine opened the discussion with enthusiasm, her laptop open to a digital calendar. "The response to the community forest has been incredible. I think it's the perfect time to introduce more educational programs, especially for the local schools."

Michael, sipping his coffee, nodded in agreement. "Absolutely, Elaine. We should capitalize on this momentum. Maybe start with a series of field trips for students? We could tie it into their science curriculum."

Alex chimed in, "That's a great start. We could offer different themes for the trips, like biodiversity, the role of native plants, or even the science of composting. Each visit could focus on a different aspect of the ecosystem."

Elaine quickly typed a note. "I love that idea. Let's structure it so that teachers can choose which themes align best with their classroom activities. We can provide pre-visit materials and post-visit suggestions to extend the learning experience."

Michael leaned forward, his mind racing with possibilities. "And what about adding some interactive components? Like having the kids participate in planting or maintenance activities during their visit? It would give them a hands-on experience and a sense of ownership."

"That hands-on approach is key," Alex agreed, picking up a brochure from the table. "We could also develop a small workbook or app that students can use to track their observations. It might encourage them to notice more and feel more engaged."

Elaine nodded enthusiastically. "An app is a brilliant idea, Alex. We could include information points that they can unlock as they walk through different parts of the forest."

As they discussed, ideas flowed freely, each suggestion building on the last. "Let's not forget about the community at large," Elaine said. "We should plan some weekend workshops too, perhaps focusing on how individuals can apply what we're doing here to their own backyards."

Michael wrote down the idea. "Workshops on native gardening, creating wildlife habitats at home, or even sustainable home practices could draw in a lot of people."

Alex considered the logistics. "We'll need to coordinate closely with the schools and community groups to schedule these programs. And we should think about funding—perhaps some local businesses or environmental grants could support this expansion."

Elaine was already on it. "I'll draft some proposals for potential sponsors. There's a lot of interest in community-supported environmental initiatives right now."

The meeting continued with the trio outlining the steps needed to launch their expanded educational offerings. They divided the tasks: Alex would handle the development of the educational content, Elaine would pursue funding and partnerships, and Michael would organize the logistics and volunteer coordination.

As they wrapped up, Michael looked around at the plans scattered across the table. "This is going to take our project to the next level. It's exciting to think about the impact we could have."

Elaine closed her laptop, her eyes reflecting a deep commitment to their cause. "It really is. Educating the next generation about environmental stewardship is perhaps the most important work we can do."

Alex gathered the papers, a sense of accomplishment in his movements. "Let's get to work then. The sooner we start, the sooner we see the fruits of our labor grow."

As they left the center, the air outside was fresh with the promise of spring. The trees they had planted were just beginning to bud, a fitting metaphor for the educational seeds they were planting in the community. With plans in place and a clear vision for the future, they were ready to nurture both the forest and the minds that would help it thrive.

Chapter 22
New Beginnings Again

As summer approached, the vibrant growth of Greenhaven's community forest attracted not only local wildlife but also the attention of environmental educators and activists from neighboring regions. Inspired by the forest's success, Alex, Elaine, and Michael planned an inter-community environmental summit, inviting representatives from various environmental organizations to share ideas and strategies for sustainability.

On a sunny morning, with the forest as their backdrop, they prepared a welcoming area with rows of chairs and a podium. Elaine was checking the sound system when Alex approached with a stack of schedules and handouts.

"We've got a fantastic lineup today," Alex said, his voice full of anticipation. "After the opening remarks, we'll have a panel discussion on urban forestry initiatives, then break into workshops on various sustainability topics."

Elaine nodded, testing the microphone. "I'm really excited about the workshop on pollinator gardens. There's a lot of interest in expanding native plant areas to support bees and butterflies."

Michael, arranging the registration table, chimed in. "I think the composting workshop will be a hit, too. We've had a lot of success with our community composting program, and it's something easily replicated in other areas."

As the guests began to arrive, the trio greeted each person with warm smiles and handouts. The attendees were a mix of environmental professionals, community leaders, and passionate volunteers, all eager to connect and learn from each other.

The summit kicked off with Alex delivering the opening remarks. "Welcome, everyone, to our first inter-community environmental summit. Today is about sharing, learning, and growing together. Each of us brings unique experiences and insights that can benefit our collective efforts to foster a greener future."

Following Alex's introduction, Elaine moderated the first panel discussion. "Let's dive into our first topic: urban forestry initiatives and their impact on community health and biodiversity. I'd like to start with a question to our panelists: What are some of the main challenges you've faced in your projects, and how have you addressed them?"

One panelist, a director from a neighboring town's green initiative, responded, "Funding is always a challenge. We've had to be very creative, partnering with local businesses and applying for every grant imaginable. It's about showing the tangible benefits, not just to the environment but to the community's quality of life."

Another panelist added, "Engagement is another hurdle. It's crucial to get the community involved from the beginning, making sure they feel ownership of the project. We've found that educational workshops and school programs are great ways to stir up interest and participation."

As the discussion unfolded, the audience was invited to ask questions, leading to a lively exchange of ideas and solutions. Michael, leading one of the breakout sessions later, focused on practical applications. "Let's talk about how we can take what we've learned today and implement it in our communities. What are some small but impactful actions we can start with?"

One attendee suggested, "Community clean-up days are a great way to get people involved and aware. It's not just about picking up trash but about preventing it and educating the public along the way."

Another shared, "Water conservation efforts can also be impactful. Simple things like rainwater harvesting or fixing leaks can make a significant difference."

As the day progressed, the summit proved to be a fertile ground for collaboration. Ideas were exchanged, partnerships were formed, and plans for future joint projects began to take shape. The energy was palpable, with every conversation, every session adding to the momentum.

Elaine, reflecting on the day's events as they began to wind down, shared with Alex and Michael, "Today has been incredibly rewarding. Seeing so many dedicated people in one place, all committed to sustainability, gives me so much hope for what we can achieve together."

Michael agreed, "Absolutely. The connections we've made today are going to help us all be more effective in our work. It's about building a network, a community of practice."

As the guests departed, exchanging contact information and final thoughts, Alex, Elaine, and Michael stayed back to clean up, their discussion already turning to how they could support the newly formed partnerships and the next steps for their own community projects. The setting sun cast a warm glow over the forest, now teeming with more life than ever, both in its canopy and in the community it had helped to cultivate.

Following the success of the inter-community environmental summit, Alex, Elaine, and Michael focused their efforts on a new initiative inspired by the feedback and ideas exchanged during the event. They planned a "Green Technology Day" at the Environmental Education Center to showcase sustainable technologies and practices that could be implemented at a community level.

On the morning of the event, the center was buzzing with activity as exhibitors set up their displays. Solar panel setups, smart home systems, and water-saving devices were just a few of the technologies on show. Michael was overseeing the setup of the main exhibit, a small-scale solar farm model, when Elaine approached, clipboard in hand.

"Michael, how's the setup going? Are we on track?" she asked, surveying the bustling room.

"Looking good," Michael replied, wiping his brow. "The solar farm model is almost ready, and the smart home system guys just need another half hour or so."

"That's great," Elaine said. "I think the water-saving showerhead demo will be a big hit. It's ready, and it really shows how easy it is to save water with the right fixtures."

Alex joined them, carrying a box of brochures. "I've got the materials for the attendees. We've included information on tax incentives for green technology in homes. It should give everyone a good nudge towards making sustainable upgrades."

As the event officially began, community members of all ages streamed in, eager to learn about the technologies that could help them live more sustainably. Alex welcomed them with a brief introduction. "Thank you for joining us today! We're excited to show you how accessible and beneficial green technology can be. Each booth has experts ready to answer your questions and demonstrate how these systems work."

Elaine led a group to the smart home system display. "This setup not only reduces energy consumption but also provides data to help you manage your home more efficiently," she explained to an interested crowd. "You can control it all from your phone, which means you can adjust settings on the go to ensure you're always using energy in the most efficient way possible."

At another booth, Michael discussed the benefits of the solar panels. "These are not only great for reducing your electric bills but also for decreasing your carbon footprint. And with recent advancements, they're becoming much more affordable."

An attendee, a local homeowner, was curious. "How reliable are these systems? What happens when it's cloudy or raining?"

Michael responded, "That's a common question. Modern solar panels are quite efficient and can still generate power on cloudy days, albeit less than on sunny days. Plus, any excess energy generated on bright days can be stored in batteries, or you might even be able to sell it back to the grid, depending on local regulations."

Throughout the day, Alex, Elaine, and Michael facilitated discussions and workshops, each aimed at demystifying aspects of green technology. The community's response was overwhelmingly positive, with many expressing their interest in implementing what they learned.

As the event wrapped up, Elaine gathered feedback from the attendees. "What did you find most useful about today?" she asked a group that was lingering near the exit.

One of the attendees, a middle-aged woman, shared her thoughts. "I really appreciated the practical demonstrations. Seeing how these systems work in real-time makes the idea of integrating them into my home less daunting."

Alex smiled, pleased with the outcome. "That's exactly what we hoped for. We want these technologies to feel accessible because they truly are."

After the last of the guests had departed, the trio sat down to debrief. "I think we've sparked some real interest today," Michael noted, stacking chairs.

Elaine nodded, turning off the projector. "And hopefully, we've dispelled some myths about the cost and complexity of going green."

As they locked up the center, the success of the day was evident not just in the turnout but in the enthusiastic discussions and the promise of action it had inspired. The seeds of change had been sown, and as they walked away from the building, the fading light of the day reminded them of the ongoing journey towards a more sustainable Greenhaven.

The enthusiasm from the "Green Technology Day" spurred a surge of community interest in sustainable living, prompting Alex, Elaine, and Michael to launch a follow-up project: the Greenhaven Home Efficiency Challenge. Aimed at encouraging residents to adopt energy-saving upgrades, the challenge was a friendly competition with incentives for participants who made significant strides in reducing their household energy consumption.

Gathering in the community center, which was now adorned with posters highlighting energy statistics and success stories from local homes, the trio prepared for the challenge's kickoff meeting. Elaine was arranging the registration forms as Alex checked the setup for the presentation.

"Looks like everything's ready," Alex noted, glancing around the room. "We've got a good turnout expected based on the RSVPs. This challenge could really make a difference in how our community approaches energy use."

Elaine nodded, arranging the last of the handouts. "I think the practical tips and the competitive element will really motivate people. It's about making energy efficiency fun and rewarding."

Michael, setting up the projector, chimed in, "Plus, the prizes we've got lined up from local businesses will add an extra layer of incentive. Everything from energy-efficient appliances to home improvement store gift cards."

As residents began to arrive, filling the room with murmurs of curiosity and conversation, Alex stood to welcome them. "Good evening, everyone! Thank you for joining us for the kickoff of the Greenhaven Home Efficiency Challenge. Tonight, we're going to talk about how you can participate and make your homes more energy-efficient."

Elaine took over, clicking to the first slide of the presentation. "The challenge is simple. Over the next three months, we'll track your home energy usage. The household with the greatest percentage reduction will win our grand prize, but there will be lots of smaller prizes along the way."

Michael added, "We've partnered with local energy auditors to provide discounted audits to all participants. They'll help identify the best ways you can save energy in your home."

An attendee raised her hand, asking, "What kind of changes are typically the most effective?"

"That's a great question," Elaine responded. "Often, it's the small changes that add up. Sealing leaks around doors and windows, upgrading to LED lighting, and using programmable thermostats can all significantly reduce your energy use."

Another resident inquired, "Are there ways to monitor our progress throughout the challenge?"

Alex was quick to answer, "Yes, we're providing all participants with a simple app that can help you track your monthly energy consumption. It even gives tips and reminds you of ways to save energy daily."

As the Q&A continued, the trio provided detailed responses, ensuring each participant felt informed and ready to take on the challenge. Michael discussed the importance of water heating efficiency, pointing out, "Water heating can account for a significant portion of your energy bill. Simple adjustments like lowering the thermostat on your water heater can make a big impact."

Elaine concluded the session with a call to action. "We're all in this together, and every little bit helps. Not only will you see savings on your energy bills, but you'll also be contributing to a larger goal of reducing our community's environmental footprint."

As the meeting wrapped up, participants gathered around the registration table, signing up and picking up their informational packets. The room buzzed with excitement and a collective sense of purpose.

Alex, Elaine, and Michael stayed behind to answer any lingering questions and help with registrations. As they finally closed down the room, the streetlights outside casting a soft glow through the windows, the trio reflected on the night's success.

"We've got a good feeling about this," Michael said, locking the front door of the center.

Elaine smiled, looking out into the night. "It's more than just a challenge; it's a community movement. It's going to be exciting to see how much we can achieve together."

Walking to their cars, their conversation didn't dwindle; instead, it turned to ideas for maintaining momentum and ensuring the challenge led to lasting changes in Greenhaven. Each step they took was fueled by the knowledge that they were moving towards a more sustainable and connected community.

As the Greenhaven Home Efficiency Challenge neared its conclusion, the impact of the community's efforts began to materialize in tangible ways. Over the months, residents not only learned about energy efficiency but also implemented a variety of changes that transformed their daily lives and reduced their overall environmental footprint.

The closing ceremony of the challenge was scheduled at the Environmental Education Center, where Alex, Elaine, and Michael prepared to celebrate the achievements of the participants. The center was decorated with displays depicting before-and-after statistics of energy usage, photos of households making changes, and testimonials about the benefits experienced by the families involved.

On the day of the event, the air was filled with a sense of accomplishment and festivity. Community members arrived, sharing stories of their experiences and the changes they had made, from installing smart thermostats to replacing old appliances with energy-efficient models. The room buzzed with lively discussions about energy bills that had noticeably decreased and new habits that had formed, like turning off lights when leaving a room and managing heating and cooling more judiciously.

Alex stood at the front of the room, ready to address the gathering. "Welcome, everyone! Today, we not only celebrate your achievements over these past months but also the community spirit that made this challenge a success."

Elaine took a moment to highlight some significant statistics. "Together, we've managed to reduce our community's energy consumption by an impressive 15% compared to the same period last year. This is a fantastic result, showing what we can achieve when we work together."

Michael added to the celebratory mood by announcing the winners. "While everyone who participated made incredible strides, we have a few households who went above and beyond, achieving the highest reductions in energy usage. Let's give them a round of applause as they come up to receive their prizes."

As the winners were called up, the room erupted in applause, each recipient sharing a brief account of what they had done to achieve their results. The grand prize winner, a family that had cut their energy usage by nearly 30%, shared their simple yet effective strategies, like insulating their home and using natural light instead of electricity during the day.

The ceremony continued with Michael discussing the future steps to maintain the momentum created by the challenge. "We hope this challenge has sparked a lasting commitment to energy efficiency. Let's continue to support each other in making sustainable choices and exploring new ways to live more environmentally friendly lives."

Elaine encouraged ongoing community engagement. "We will be hosting workshops throughout the year to introduce more sustainable practices and technologies. This is just the beginning, and we look forward to seeing what else we can accomplish together."

As the event drew to a close, participants lingered, reluctant to leave the supportive community atmosphere. They exchanged contact information, promising to share tips and continue the conversation about sustainability.

The trio of Alex, Elaine, and Michael cleaned up the space, discussing the success of the challenge and ideas for future initiatives. They were committed to building on the foundation they had laid, confident in the community's desire to continue making positive changes.

As they locked up the center and walked to their cars, the sun set behind the newly planted trees of the community forest, casting long shadows across the parking lot. The challenge may have ended, but the journey towards sustainability in Greenhaven was far from over. With each new project and challenge, the community took steps closer to a greener, more sustainable future, inspired by the collective efforts and individual achievements of its residents.

Chapter 23
Proposal

In the heart of autumn, as the leaves turned a fiery palette of oranges and reds, Greenhaven embarked on its latest environmental venture—an ambitious city-wide initiative to enhance and connect the existing green spaces through green corridors. These corridors were designed to provide safe pathways for wildlife and to increase access to green spaces for all city residents. Alex, Elaine, and Michael gathered in the main conference room of the Environmental Education Center to map out the initiative with key community leaders and urban planners.

Elaine, spreading a large map of Greenhaven across the table, outlined the proposal. "Our goal is to create a network of green corridors that link our existing parks and green spaces. This not only benefits our wildlife by providing them with safe routes for migration and foraging but also enhances the quality of life for our residents."

Alex added, focusing on the map, "See here and here? These are potential corridors that could connect the northern parkland with the central city garden. We need to consider existing infrastructure and natural land contours to maximize effectiveness without disruptive overhauls."

Michael turned to the city's lead urban planner, who was nodding thoughtfully. "How feasible do you think this is, given our current city layout and budget constraints?"

The planner adjusted his glasses, pointing at the map. "It's certainly ambitious, but not impossible. We might need to look into phased development, starting with easier, less costly sections to gain momentum and public support. Grants and environmental incentives can also be explored to supplement the city's budget."

Elaine chimed in, "Public support is crucial. We should launch a series of public engagement sessions to explain the benefits of the corridors and gather feedback."

Alex looked around the room, his gaze settling on each participant. "It's also about connectivity—not just for wildlife, but for our community. These green corridors can be pathways that encourage walking and biking, reducing reliance on cars, and thereby reducing our overall carbon footprint."

A local environmental NGO representative leaned forward, enthusiastic. "I can see potential for educational programs as well. School children could learn about local flora and fauna directly through guided walks. We could integrate these corridors into our science curricula."

Michael nodded, jotting down notes. "Absolutely, and speaking of integration, we need to ensure these corridors are accessible to everyone. That means considering pathways that are navigable for wheelchairs and strollers."

The conversation shifted towards the technical aspects, with the city's engineer joining in. "We'll need to conduct thorough environmental impact assessments for each proposed corridor. It's not just about the green space, but also about managing stormwater runoff and maintaining the ecological balance."

Elaine summarized the points made. "So, we're looking at a phased approach, with ample community engagement and educational integration, keeping accessibility in mind, and ensuring environmental impacts are thoroughly managed."

Alex concluded, "Let's set up task forces for each phase—planning, community engagement, execution, and maintenance. We need champions for each sector to drive this forward effectively."

As the meeting wrapped up, the group agreed to reconvene in a month with updates on their assigned tasks. They left the room energized by the collaborative spirit, each participant committed to turning the vision of green corridors into a reality.

Outside, the crisp autumn air was invigorating, reminding everyone of the change of seasons and the changes they were bringing about in Greenhaven. Walking through the park on their way back, Alex, Elaine, and Michael discussed the potential challenges and their excitement about the project's positive impact on the community and environment. The path ahead was as clear as the day, lined with the promise of greener, more connected urban landscapes.

The implementation of the Greenhaven green corridors initiative had begun to take shape. As winter approached, the project's initial phases were underway, with Alex, Elaine, and Michael organizing the first of many public engagement sessions designed to inform and gather support from the local community. The session was set in the community hall, adorned with large maps and visuals of the proposed green corridors, and models showcasing how the corridors would weave through the urban landscape.

As residents filed into the hall, Elaine greeted them with a warm smile, handing out information packets. "Thank you for coming tonight. We're excited to share our vision for a more connected and environmentally friendly Greenhaven."

The room buzzed with curiosity as people took their seats. Alex began the session with an overview of the project. "Our aim with the green corridors is to create links between our parks and other green spaces that not only help our local wildlife but also provide you, our residents, with more accessible and enjoyable green spaces."

Michael projected images onto the screen, illustrating the expected benefits. "These corridors will facilitate safer migration routes for wildlife, helping to preserve our local biodiversity. They also mean cleaner air, as they help reduce urban 'heat islands' and improve stormwater management."

A hand rose from the audience, an elderly man looking intrigued. "How will this project affect our neighborhood directly? Are there going to be a lot of disruptions?"

Elaine responded, "Great question. We're planning construction in phases to minimize disruptions. We're also working closely with urban planners to ensure that the changes enhance the community spaces without taking away from the current uses of the land."

A young mother with a toddler in tow voiced another concern. "Will these changes make it harder for us to access the parks during construction?"

Alex reassured her, "We're very sensitive to maintaining access during construction. Temporary pathways and clear signage will be provided to ensure everyone can still enjoy the parks. Community safety and access are our top priorities."

As the session progressed, Michael detailed the timeline. "We're starting with the areas that require the least structural changes and will expand gradually. The entire project is expected to span several years, with constant updates and feedback opportunities like this one."

Elaine then shifted the discussion towards community involvement. "We're also launching a volunteer program for those interested in being more hands-on with the development of the green corridors. This could involve anything from planting days to educational outreach."

A teenager at the back, notebook in hand, asked, "Could this involvement count towards our school community service hours?"

"Absolutely," Elaine replied. "We're setting up partnerships with local schools exactly for that purpose. It's a great way to earn your service hours and contribute to a lasting legacy in your city."

The Q&A continued with residents expressing both enthusiasm and concerns, ranging from environmental impact to the specific types of plants being considered for the corridors. Alex, Elaine, and Michael addressed each query with detailed explanations and assurances of careful planning.

As the meeting concluded, many residents stayed behind to discuss their thoughts further with the trio, examine the maps more closely, or sign up for the volunteer program. Michael, packing up the last of the brochures, noted, "There's a lot of genuine interest and a few concerns, but it's clear people are excited about the corridors."

Elaine nodded as she folded up a banner. "It's about bringing the community together, not just through the corridors themselves but through the process of creating them."

The three of them left the hall, feeling satisfied with the evening's outcomes. The brisk night air was refreshing as they discussed the next steps, the paths illuminated by the soft glow of street lamps. Each step they took mirrored the progress they envisioned, binding the community closer through shared green spaces and collaborative environmental stewardship.

The enthusiasm for the green corridors initiative had grown significantly since the first public engagement session, with increasing numbers of Greenhaven residents expressing a desire to get involved. As spring approached, marking the start of planting season, Alex, Elaine, and Michael organized a special event to kick off the corridor planting. This event, crucial for the early success of the corridors, was designed to engage community volunteers in the actual planting of native trees and shrubs along the designated green corridor paths.

On a bright and crisp Saturday morning, volunteers gathered at the northern end of the first corridor, where Alex was giving out instructions, standing next to a pile of gardening tools and young saplings.

"Good morning, everyone! Thank you so much for joining us today. Each group will take a section of the corridor, and we'll plant a mix of these native species," Alex explained, gesturing toward the plants and a diagram on his clipboard. "These species are chosen for their adaptability and their benefits to local wildlife."

Elaine, handing out gloves and trowels, added, "We're also aiming to create a layered effect with trees, shrubs, and ground cover to maximize ecological diversity. It's all about creating a thriving habitat for insects, birds, and other local fauna."

Michael, organizing the groups, chimed in, "And don't worry if you're not an experienced gardener. We're all here to learn and help each other. Plus, we have some expert botanists here today to guide us."

As the volunteers began to work, digging and planting under the guidance of the experts, a local school teacher, Mrs. Thomson, who had brought along a group of high school students, remarked, "This is a fantastic learning opportunity for the kids. They're getting to see first-hand the impact they can have on their environment."

Alex, helping a group of students position a young oak, responded, "Absolutely, Mrs. Thomson. It's all about hands-on learning and seeing the real-world application of what they can do to help our planet."

As they worked, Elaine discussed the bigger picture with a group of volunteers. "Once completed, these corridors will connect our existing green spaces, making it easier for wildlife to move safely across urban areas. It's like we're stitching together a natural quilt that covers our whole city."

One of the volunteers, a retired engineer named Greg, shared his enthusiasm. "I've lived in Greenhaven most of my life, and it's initiatives like this that make me proud of our community. Seeing everyone come together to improve our city is really inspiring."

By midday, a significant portion of the corridor had been planted, and the volunteers took a well-deserved break. Michael took the opportunity to thank everyone involved. "Your hard work today is making a tangible difference. This corridor is a testament to what we can achieve when we come together as a community."

As the event drew to a close, the volunteers gathered to look over the day's work—a new green artery beginning to take shape, promising to become a vibrant part of Greenhaven's ecological network.

Elaine, packing up the leftover supplies, said, "This is just the beginning. Over the coming months, we'll continue to expand these corridors, enhancing connectivity and biodiversity throughout our city."

Alex, looking over the newly planted area, added, "And it's your continued support and involvement that will ensure the success of this initiative. We're grateful for every bit of effort you've all put in today."

As the volunteers departed, chatting excitedly about the next planting event, Alex, Elaine, and Michael stayed behind to survey the corridor. The late afternoon sun cast long shadows across the fresh plantings, the light playing off the young leaves in a promise of growth. Each new plant was a step toward a greener future, woven into the very fabric of Greenhaven by the hands of its own residents.

As the first phase of the green corridor project neared completion, Alex, Elaine, and Michael organized a celebratory event to acknowledge the community's efforts and to unveil the fully planted section to the public. Held in the heart of the new corridor, the celebration was an opportunity to showcase the thriving green space that had been cultivated through the dedication of countless volunteers and community members.

The event space was adorned with banners and informative posters that detailed the project's phases and highlighted the corridor's environmental benefits. As the community members gathered, the atmosphere was vibrant, filled with pride and anticipation.

Elaine, overseeing the final touches to the displays, turned to Alex, who was checking the sound system. "This turned out even better than I imagined. It's so rewarding to see the community come together like this."

Alex nodded, adjusting a microphone. "Absolutely. It's a testament to what we can achieve when we all work towards a common goal. Today isn't just a celebration; it's a thank you to everyone who contributed."

As the event officially began, Michael stepped up to the podium to welcome everyone. "Good afternoon, and thank you for joining us on this wonderful day. What you see around you is more than just new plantings—it's a new, living part of Greenhaven, a green corridor that connects and enriches our city."

Elaine took over, her voice enthusiastic. "This corridor is designed to be a safe haven for wildlife and a peaceful retreat for all of us. It's a place where nature and urban life meet, demonstrating our commitment to sustainability and biodiversity."

Alex then invited the mayor of Greenhaven to speak, who had been a strong supporter of the project. "This initiative is a fine example of what we can do when city management and the community collaborate. It enhances our city's green credentials and, importantly, the quality of life for all our residents."

Following the speeches, the trio led guided tours along the corridor, pointing out specific areas of interest. "Over here," Alex explained, "we used native shrubs that are particularly good at attracting pollinators. Not only do they help with the local ecology, but they're also quite beautiful when they bloom."

Elaine chimed in as they walked to a recently completed picnic area. "This space was designed with community input to be a gathering place. We envision families and friends coming together here, enjoying the outdoors right in the middle of our urban landscape."

As they moved along, Michael discussed future plans. "This is just the beginning. We plan to extend these corridors, linking more areas of the city, creating a network of green spaces that all can access and enjoy."

Throughout the event, attendees expressed their admiration and support. A local school principal approached Elaine, expressing interest in regular field trips to the corridor. "It's a perfect outdoor classroom. Our students could learn a lot from the biodiversity here."

Elaine, delighted, responded, "We'd love to coordinate with you on that. Educating young minds about the importance of these environments is key to our project's long-term success."

As the event drew to a close, the community lingered, reluctant to leave the new green space. Alex, Elaine, and Michael gathered for a final review of the day's activities, pleased with the turnout and the community's response.

Michael, looking over the filled space, remarked, "Seeing everyone come together today, seeing the interest and joy in their faces, it really drives home the impact of what we've done."

Elaine, packing up some of the informational pamphlets, added, "It's more than just planting trees and shrubs; it's about planting ideas and watching them grow."

As they walked back through the corridor, the setting sun cast a warm glow on the new growth, shadows stretching long and thin across the path. The day's success was a reminder of the progress they had made and

the continuous journey ahead to weave nature ever deeper into the fabric
of Greenhaven.

Chapter 24
Integration

With the green corridors flourishing, Alex, Elaine, and Michael now turned their focus to their next project: establishing a community rain garden initiative. This new endeavor aimed to tackle urban runoff and enhance water quality by using rain gardens throughout Greenhaven. To kickstart this initiative, they organized an informational meeting at the community center to engage residents and gather support.

As they arranged chairs and laid out informational brochures, Elaine checked the layout. "I think we should start with a quick overview of what rain gardens are and then delve into their benefits, particularly how they manage stormwater."

Alex nodded, arranging his notes at the podium. "Right, and we need to emphasize their role in preventing pollutants from reaching our rivers and lakes. It's also a chance to beautify property and support local habitats."

Michael, setting up a projector for a slideshow, added, "I've got some great before-and-after photos of rain gardens that can visually demonstrate their impact. Visuals always help in making the concept more tangible."

As residents began to fill the room, the trio greeted them warmly, their enthusiasm infectious. Once everyone was seated, Alex took the podium to begin the session. "Good evening, everyone! Thank you for joining us tonight. We're here to introduce an exciting new initiative that not only helps our environment but also enhances the beauty of our community— rain gardens."

Elaine took over, clicking to the first slide showing a beautifully designed rain garden. "Rain gardens are specially designed areas planted with native shrubs, perennials, and flowers. They are positioned to collect and absorb runoff from rooftops, driveways, and streets. This is crucial for reducing the burden on our storm sewers and preventing pollution in our waterways."

A resident raised his hand, asking, "How exactly do rain gardens filter pollutants?"

Michael responded, "Great question! The plants and soil in the rain garden work together to filter out pollutants. As runoff water soaks into the ground, the soil and root systems of the plants filter out contaminants before they can reach the sewer system or local water bodies."

Another hand went up, a woman at the back of the room. "What about maintenance? Are these gardens hard to take care of?"

Elaine smiled, "Another good question. Rain gardens are relatively low maintenance. They are designed with native plants, which are adapted to our local climate and soil conditions. This means they require less watering and care than traditional gardens."

Alex chimed in, "And to add to that, once established, rain gardens pretty much take care of themselves. They don't need fertilizer or pesticides and actually provide habitat for beneficial insects and birds."

A young couple in the front row looked at each other, intrigued. The man asked, "Where should one install a rain garden? Does it need a lot of space?"

Michael pointed to a diagram on the slide. "Not necessarily a lot of space. The key is to place them where they can effectively capture runoff—downspouts from your roof are ideal places. The size can be adjusted based on the area available and how much runoff you need to manage."

As the presentation concluded, Elaine invited the attendees to view the display tables where mock-ups of potential rain garden designs were shown alongside a list of suitable plants. "We encourage you to consider how a rain garden might fit into your property. We're offering free consultations for anyone interested in getting started."

The crowd mingled around the displays, discussing potential ideas for their own gardens. Alex, Elaine, and Michael moved among them, answering questions and discussing possibilities.

Michael, helping a resident with a layout question, summed up the spirit of the evening. "This project is about taking practical steps to protect our environment while adding beauty and value to our community. It's about all of us coming together to make a difference."

As the event wound down, many attendees expressed their enthusiasm for starting their own rain gardens, inspired by the benefits and the support offered. Alex, Elaine, and Michael gathered up their materials, satisfied with the turnout and the community's response. They stepped out into the cool evening, energized by the discussions and the potential impact of their new initiative on Greenhaven's environment.

Following the successful launch meeting for the community rain garden initiative, Alex, Elaine, and Michael organized the first hands-on workshop. This event was designed to provide residents with practical experience in designing and planting their own rain gardens. Held in a local park, the area was prepped with several demonstration plots, each representing different yard sizes and layouts.

As residents gathered, equipped with gardening gloves and enthusiastic smiles, Elaine welcomed them. "Good morning, everyone! Thank you for joining us. Today, we'll actually build a rain garden together. You'll learn everything from choosing the right location to selecting plants and proper installation techniques."

Alex gestured towards the first demonstration plot. "Let's start by discussing how to determine the best location for your rain garden. You want to place it at least ten feet away from your home to prevent any issues with water infiltration into your foundation."

A middle-aged man, notebook in hand, asked, "How deep does the garden need to be?"

"That's a great question," Michael responded, grabbing a shovel. "The depth can vary, but a typical rain garden is about four to eight inches deep. This allows it to capture runoff effectively without creating a standing water issue."

Elaine began demonstrating the layering of soil and compost. "You'll want a mix of topsoil, sand, and compost to ensure good drainage and support healthy plant growth. It's all about creating an environment where water can be absorbed efficiently."

As the group started to dig and shape the first plot, a woman in her thirties, looking puzzled, held up a plant. "How do we choose the right plants?"

Elaine, taking the plant from her, explained, "You want species that are both native and tolerant of wet conditions. Plants like swamp milkweed, blue flag iris, and cardinal flower are excellent for attracting pollinators and can thrive in the moist environment of a rain garden."

As they planted, Alex discussed maintenance tips with a small group. "Once established, your rain garden will be relatively low maintenance. You might need to mulch it annually and trim back dead foliage, but otherwise, it should sustain itself if you've chosen the right plants."

Michael, overseeing a group laying mulch, added, "And remember, the mulch helps to retain moisture and suppress weeds. It's important to maintain a layer about two to three inches thick."

The workshop continued with residents rotating through stations, each designed to teach a different aspect of rain garden construction, from initial soil preparation to final plantings.

As they worked, a young couple, clearly excited about the project, shared their plans with Elaine. "We have a spot next to our downspout that's always been a problem with runoff. This rain garden could be the perfect solution," the man said.

Elaine nodded, pleased. "Absolutely, it sounds like an ideal location. You'll not only solve your runoff problem but also create a beautiful feature in your garden."

By the end of the workshop, several rain gardens were taking shape, each reflecting the unique characteristics of the different plots and the personal touches of the participants.

As tools were cleaned and put away, Michael gathered the group for some final thoughts. "I hope today's workshop has shown you how feasible and beneficial rain gardens can be. We're here to help as you start your own projects, so don't hesitate to reach out with any questions."

The participants thanked Alex, Elaine, and Michael, many staying behind to discuss their plans or ask further questions about specific plants and techniques they had learned.

Walking back through the park as the event concluded, Elaine reflected on the day's success. "It's wonderful to see so much enthusiasm. Projects like these really bring the community together."

Alex, looking over the newly created gardens, agreed. "Yes, and it's just the beginning. Imagine how many gardens will spring up from today's effort."

Together, they left the site, satisfied with the knowledge that they had sparked a wave of enthusiasm for sustainable landscaping in Greenhaven, planting seeds that would grow into beautiful, functional rain gardens across the community.

As the community rain garden initiative gained momentum, Alex, Elaine, and Michael planned a follow-up event to monitor the progress of the newly planted gardens and to address any challenges the community members were facing. They decided to host a discussion forum at the Environmental Education Center, inviting all participants to share their experiences and learn from each other.

As community members filled the room, setting a lively atmosphere with their chatter about garden progress, Elaine welcomed them. "Thank you all for coming back to share your experiences. Today is all about learning from each other—what worked, what didn't, and how we can all improve our rain gardens."

Michael chimed in, projecting images of various community rain gardens on the screen behind him. "Let's start by looking at some of the gardens you've all created. Here's one from the Johnson family on Elm Street. You can see how they've incorporated native grasses and wildflowers."

A man in the front row, Mr. Johnson, beamed with pride. "Yes, that's ours. The biggest challenge was figuring out the right depth and slope, but we got a lot of help from the guides you provided. It's been amazing to see how it manages water during rains."

Alex nodded, taking notes. "Great to hear that, Mr. Johnson. Managing the water effectively is key. Does anyone want to share how they've handled overflow or heavy rain situations?"

A woman towards the back raised her hand. "I'm Linda, from Maple Drive. We installed a small overflow path lined with stones that directs excess water to a drier part of our garden. It was a tip I got from one of the workshops."

"That's a fantastic solution, Linda," Elaine responded. "Incorporating an overflow path can really help in managing unexpected or excessive rainfall. It also prevents water from pooling and potentially damaging plants."

Michael clicked to another slide showing a more challenging setup. "Here we have a garden that had some issues with pooling water. Can anyone guess what might have gone wrong here?"

A young man, Derek, offered an insight. "It looks like the soil might not have been amended enough to ensure proper drainage. Did they mix in enough sand and compost?"

"That's exactly right," Alex confirmed. "It's crucial to get the soil composition right to ensure that it can absorb and filter water effectively. For those who are experiencing similar issues, adding more organic matter and checking the garden's depth might help."

Elaine then steered the conversation towards plant selection. "Choosing the right plants is also vital. They need to not only survive but thrive in wet conditions. Has anyone experimented with different plants to see what works best in their garden?"

A middle-aged woman, Sarah, shared her experience. "We tried several types of perennials like bee balm and Joe-Pye weed. They've done really well, and the bees love them. The key was finding plants that could handle our local soil and weather conditions."

Michael nodded appreciatively. "That's great, Sarah. Attracting pollinators is another fantastic benefit of rain gardens. They become little ecosystems of their own."

As the forum continued, more participants shared their stories, each contributing pieces of wisdom and learning from the others. Alex, Elaine, and Michael facilitated the discussion, ensuring everyone who wanted to share had the chance.

To wrap up, Elaine gathered feedback on additional support the community might need. "We're here to help you all succeed with your rain gardens. What other resources or information would be helpful for you moving forward?"

Several hands went up, with requests ranging from more detailed planting guides to workshops on maintaining rain gardens through the changing seasons.

"Thank you for your feedback," Michael concluded. "We'll work on developing those resources. Remember, every small step you take contributes to a larger impact on our community's sustainability efforts."

As the event ended and participants slowly filed out, engaging in smaller conversations about their gardens, Alex, Elaine, and Michael stayed back to discuss the success of the forum. They were pleased with the engagement and the community's commitment to improving their local environment. Each shared a sense of accomplishment and a renewed sense of purpose, eager to continue supporting Greenhaven's transformation into a greener, more sustainable community.

The community rain garden initiative was now in full swing, with many residents actively involved and witnessing the benefits firsthand. Alex, Elaine, and Michael decided it was time to evaluate the progress and plan future expansions. They scheduled a town hall meeting to gather input on the initiative's next steps, inviting all stakeholders to participate.

As residents settled into their seats at the community center, Elaine opened the meeting with a warm smile. "Thank you all for joining us this evening. We're here to discuss the progress of our rain gardens and to explore how we can expand this project to have an even greater impact."

Michael then shared some success stories on the screen. "Here's a look at some of our thriving rain gardens around Greenhaven. As you can see, these gardens are not only functional, reducing runoff and improving water quality, but they've also become beautiful additions to our properties."

Alex followed up, encouraging feedback. "We'd love to hear from you all. What are your thoughts on how the initiative is going? Any challenges or successes you'd like to share?"

A woman in the third row raised her hand. "I've noticed a significant decrease in the amount of standing water on my property since installing the rain garden. It's been a great success for us, especially during heavy rains."

"That's fantastic to hear," Elaine responded. "Reducing standing water not only helps with managing runoff but also reduces mosquito breeding sites, making your outdoor spaces more enjoyable."

A man towards the back spoke up. "I've had some challenges with choosing the right plants. Some didn't survive the first few weeks. Maybe we could use more guidance on plant selection and care?"

Michael took note. "That's valuable feedback. We can certainly improve our resources on plant care and selection. Perhaps a workshop dedicated to that topic would be useful?"

The crowd murmured in agreement, and a young couple suggested an idea. "Could we possibly set up a mentorship program? Those of us who are new to this could really benefit from the advice of more experienced gardeners."

"That's an excellent idea," Alex said, jotting it down. "A mentorship program could really strengthen our community's knowledge and involvement. We'll definitely look into setting that up."

Elaine then steered the discussion towards future plans. "Looking forward, we're considering expanding the rain gardens into public spaces like schools and libraries. What do you all think about that?"

A teacher from a local elementary school was quick to respond. "I think that would be wonderful. It could serve as a practical learning tool for students, teaching them about water conservation and native plant species right in their schoolyards."

"Great point," Michael acknowledged. "Educational integration is key to fostering a long-term appreciation for these practices."

The discussion continued, with community members expressing enthusiastic support for the expansion and offering various suggestions for locations and designs. Alex facilitated the conversation, ensuring that everyone who wanted to speak had the opportunity.

As the meeting drew to a close, Elaine summarized the key points and action items. "Thank you, everyone, for your insightful contributions tonight. We have some great ideas to move forward with, including improving our plant selection guidance, starting a mentorship program, and expanding into public spaces."

Michael added, "We'll organize follow-up sessions on these topics and begin the planning process for expanding our rain gardens to public areas. Your continued involvement and feedback will be crucial."

As people started to leave, many stayed back to chat with Alex, Elaine, and Michael, discussing personal tips and experiences with their rain gardens. The trio felt a renewed sense of motivation from the community's enthusiasm and support.

Walking out of the community center together, the three discussed the evening's successes. The air was brisk, and the streets of Greenhaven were quiet, but the path forward for the rain garden initiative was clear and promising, lit by the community's collective commitment to a more sustainable future.

Chapter 25
A Rare Sight

In the vibrant heart of summer, the success of Greenhaven's rain garden initiative had inspired Alex, Elaine, and Michael to embark on their next project: developing a sustainable urban agriculture program. They planned to integrate community gardens and small-scale farming operations throughout the city, providing fresh produce to residents and further enhancing Greenhaven's green spaces.

The trio organized an exploratory meeting at the community center to gauge interest and gather input on potential locations and practices for these urban agriculture sites. As the local residents began to arrive, the room buzzed with curious chatter about the benefits of urban farming.

Elaine opened the meeting with a bright smile, addressing the crowd. "Welcome, everyone! We're thrilled to see so much interest in sustainable urban agriculture. This initiative is not just about beautifying Greenhaven but also about strengthening our food security and reducing our environmental footprint."

Alex added, "Our goal is to use underutilized spaces around our city for growing food. This could include rooftop gardens, vacant lots, and even park edges. We want to hear your thoughts on where these could be set up and how they could be managed."

Michael, standing next to a large map of the city marked with potential sites, invited participants to come forward and place stickers on areas they felt were suitable. "These stickers represent your input on where you think community gardens could thrive. Don't hesitate to suggest new locations as well!"

A middle-aged woman, Ms. Harper, raised her hand. "I love the idea of using vacant lots, but what about water access? How do we ensure these gardens are properly irrigated?"

Elaine nodded, acknowledging the concern. "That's a great point. We're considering installing rainwater harvesting systems to tackle that issue.

This would not only provide a sustainable water source but also teach the community about water conservation techniques."

A young man, Derek, who was involved in local school programs, suggested, "What about involving schools? Students could learn about agriculture and sustainability firsthand, and it could also provide fresh produce for school meals."

"That's an excellent idea, Derek," Alex responded enthusiastically. "Incorporating educational programs will be crucial. It can help foster a new generation of environmentally conscious citizens."

As the discussion continued, several attendees voiced their enthusiasm and offered various skills, from gardening expertise to community organizing. Michael took notes diligently, ensuring all suggestions and offers of help were recorded.

Elaine facilitated a discussion on potential challenges. "What are some obstacles we might face with this initiative, and how can we address them?"

An elderly gentleman, Mr. Thompson, commented, "One challenge might be maintenance. Who takes care of these gardens, especially if they're spread out across the city?"

Michael replied, "That's valid, Mr. Thompson. We're considering a volunteer-based model with support from local gardening clubs and perhaps partnerships with environmental organizations. Regular workshops and training sessions could help maintain community involvement and care."

As the meeting neared its end, Alex summarized the next steps. "Based on tonight's feedback, we'll start small with pilot gardens in the most agreed-upon locations. We'll assess their success and sustainability before expanding further."

Elaine concluded, "We'll also start reaching out to potential partners and sponsors. The more support we have, the more robust our program will be. Let's make Greenhaven a model city for urban agriculture."

The residents left the meeting energized, many staying behind to speak with Alex, Elaine, and Michael, discussing personal contributions and expressing excitement about the initiative's potential. The evening had laid the groundwork for a project that promised to enrich Greenhaven's community and environment significantly.

As they locked up the community center, the trio felt a shared sense of anticipation about the transformative potential of urban agriculture in Greenhaven. The streets were quiet as they walked to their cars, but the air was alive with the promise of growth—both for the crops they planned to cultivate and for the community at large.

The initial success of the community input session for Greenhaven's urban agriculture program had spurred Alex, Elaine, and Michael to organize a detailed planning workshop. Held at a local park earmarked for one of the pilot community gardens, this workshop aimed to delve into the specifics of garden design, crop selection, and the integration of sustainable practices such as composting and rainwater harvesting.

As community members gathered around several tables laden with maps, design tools, and agricultural brochures, Michael greeted them warmly. "Welcome back, everyone! Today, we're going to get our hands dirty with planning. By the end of this workshop, we hope to have a concrete plan for our first community garden right here in this park."

Elaine quickly chimed in, "Let's start with the layout. We want these gardens to be not only functional but also beautiful and inviting. Any thoughts on how we should design the layout?"

A young landscape architect in the group, Jenna, suggested, "I think raised beds would be great. They're easier to manage and maintain. Plus, we can design them in a way that makes the space look organized and aesthetically pleasing."

"That's a fantastic idea, Jenna," Alex replied, sketching some rough outlines on a pad. "What about pathways? We need to ensure that they are accessible to everyone, including those with disabilities."

"I recommend gravel pathways," Jenna continued. "They are permeable, which is great for drainage, and they're also wheelchair accessible if laid out properly."

Elaine noted this down and then transitioned to the next topic. "Now, let's talk about what we're going to grow. We need to consider crops that are suitable for our climate and soil conditions here in Greenhaven."

A seasoned gardener, Mr. Brooks, raised his hand. "We should focus on easy-to-grow vegetables and herbs to start. Things like tomatoes, peppers, zucchinis, and basil. They don't require too much special attention and are popular with most families."

Michael nodded in agreement. "Good point, Mr. Brooks. And we should also think about including pollinator-friendly plants to help attract bees and butterflies, which are vital for a healthy garden."

The group then discussed sustainable practices. Elaine brought up composting. "It's essential we include a composting area. Not only will it reduce waste, but it will also provide us with rich soil for the gardens. Any volunteers to help set up and manage the compost?"

Several hands went up, including a young environmental science student, Lisa. "I'd love to help with that. It's a great way to make our garden sustainable and educate the community about the benefits of composting."

"Excellent, Lisa," Alex said with a smile. "What about water management? We talked about rainwater harvesting during our last meeting. Any thoughts on how we can implement that here?"

Jenna responded again, "We could install rain barrels under the downspouts of nearby buildings. The water collected can be used for irrigating the garden, especially during dry spells."

The discussion was fruitful, with everyone contributing ideas and expressing their visions for the garden. As they wrapped up, Michael summarized the decisions made. "Thanks to all your great input, we now have a solid plan for our first community garden. We'll have raised beds, gravel paths, a variety of crops, and sustainable practices like composting and rainwater harvesting."

Elaine concluded, "Our next step is to put these plans into action. We'll start setting up the garden next weekend. Please feel free to join us and bring anyone else who might be interested. The more, the merrier!"

As the workshop ended, the participants lingered to discuss personal tips and ideas for the garden, their enthusiasm palpable. Alex, Elaine, and Michael were filled with a profound sense of community spirit, ready to bring the collective vision to life. They left the park with a clear plan in mind, the conversations continuing as they walked together, each step taking them closer to creating a greener, more connected Greenhaven.

With the plans for Greenhaven's first community garden solidified, Alex, Elaine, and Michael initiated the physical setup of the garden. They organized a community planting day, inviting all those interested to help bring the project to life. As residents gathered at the designated park site, equipped with gardening tools and enthusiastic spirits, the trio distributed tasks, ensuring everyone knew their role.

Elaine, overseeing the layout, directed the volunteers. "Let's start by marking out where each raised bed will go. We want to make sure there's enough space for the paths between them for easy access."

Alex, handling the supplies, handed out seedlings and gardening gloves. "Here are the plants we'll be starting with. We have a variety of vegetables and some herbs. Let's make sure each bed gets a good mix."

Michael coordinated the younger volunteers, assigning them to simpler tasks. "You guys can help with spreading the mulch around the beds once they're set. It'll help keep the weeds down and keep the soil moist."

As they worked, the community's excitement was palpable. A retired teacher, Mrs. Thompson, shared her thoughts with Elaine. "This is such a wonderful project for Greenhaven. It's great to see so many people, especially the young ones, getting involved."

Elaine smiled, wiping her brow. "It really is, Mrs. Thompson. We're not just planting a garden; we're planting seeds for the future—teaching responsibility and sustainability."

Alex, working alongside a father and his young daughter, discussed the importance of their efforts. "Each plant here not only contributes to our community's health by providing fresh produce but also helps educate our children about where food comes from."

The father nodded, helping his daughter place a tomato plant in the soil. "We've been so excited to get involved. It's a great learning experience for her and a way for us to do something meaningful as a family."

As the day progressed, the empty lot slowly transformed into a vibrant garden. Raised beds filled with rich soil and young plants began to form a lush green grid. Michael, taking a break with a group of volunteers, reflected on the impact. "Look at what we've managed to do in just one morning. Imagine what this place will look like by the end of the season."

A young couple, new to the area, expressed their appreciation to Michael. "We just moved here, and getting involved like this has made us feel really connected to the community."

"That's exactly what we hoped for," Michael responded. "Community gardens are as much about growing produce as they are about growing community ties."

Towards the end of the day, Elaine gathered everyone for a brief talk. "Thank you all for your hard work today. This garden isn't just a testament to what we can achieve together—it's a promise for sustainability and community spirit. And remember, this is just the beginning."

Alex added, "We'll need ongoing help to maintain the garden, so please feel free to come down anytime. We'll have scheduled days for group gardening, but the space is always open for anyone to enjoy and contribute."

As tools were cleaned and stored away, and the last plants were settled into their new beds, the volunteers shared refreshments, their conversations buzzing with plans for the next steps and the garden's future. Michael, Alex, and Elaine thanked each person individually, their expressions one of genuine gratitude and pride.

The sun began to set, casting a golden glow over the new garden, its beds neat and promising under the gentle evening light. The day ended not just with a new green space in Greenhaven but with strengthened community bonds and shared commitments to nurture and sustain this new urban oasis.

As the community garden began to thrive, yielding its first harvests of vegetables and herbs, Alex, Elaine, and Michael saw an opportunity to further educate Greenhaven's residents about sustainable cooking and food preparation. They decided to organize a "Garden to Table" cooking demonstration to be held right in the community garden, inviting local chefs who specialized in using fresh, locally-sourced ingredients.

On the day of the event, tables were set up amidst the rows of lush garden beds, each station equipped with cutting boards, cooking equipment, and an array of fresh produce picked straight from the garden. Residents gathered, eager to learn how to transform the fruits of their labor into delicious, healthy meals.

Elaine welcomed the crowd, her voice full of excitement. "Thank you for joining us today! We're going to show you how to use these wonderful vegetables we've all worked so hard to grow. We hope you'll take away not just some great recipes but also a deeper appreciation for what it means to eat locally and sustainably."

Chef Mara, one of the participating chefs, started her demonstration by picking some herbs. "Fresh herbs like these are a game-changer in cooking. They add incredible flavor without the need for much salt or fat, which makes your meals healthier and more aromatic."

As she chopped vegetables for a salad, she continued, "The key to using garden vegetables is to let their natural flavors shine. A simple vinaigrette with olive oil, lemon juice, salt, and pepper is all you need for a dressing that complements the fresh produce without overpowering it."

Michael, overseeing the setup of another station, called over to a group of young parents. "Over here we have Chef Luis preparing a quick vegetable stir-fry. It's a great, fast way to use a lot of different vegetables from the garden."

Chef Luis greeted the group, tossing bell peppers and zucchini in a large pan. "Stir-frying is perfect for weeknight dinners. It's quick, and you can use almost any vegetable you have on hand. The high heat keeps everything crisp and vibrant."

Meanwhile, Alex engaged with a family at a station where Chef Ana was assembling vegetable wraps. "Chef Ana is using collard greens as a wrap instead of bread, which is a fantastic gluten-free option and another clever way to use your garden's bounty."

Chef Ana smiled, handing a wrap to a young girl. "Collards are sturdy and have a mild flavor, making them perfect for wraps. Just blanch them briefly to make them pliable, then you can fill them with whatever veggies you like!"

Throughout the afternoon, residents moved from station to station, tasting dishes, and taking notes. Elaine, chatting with a group of elderly residents, shared, "We also have recipes available for all the dishes being demonstrated today. We encourage you to try these at home and experiment with the produce from your own gardens."

As the event drew to a close, Michael gathered feedback from the attendees. "What did you all think? Were the recipes easy to follow? Is there anything else you'd like to learn about in future cooking demos?"

The feedback was overwhelmingly positive, with many expressing interest in more such events. "Maybe next time, we could do something with fruit," suggested one resident, "like jams or baking?"

"That's a great idea," Alex responded enthusiastically. "We could definitely plan something around that. It's all about making the most of what we grow and reducing food waste."

The day concluded with the community lingering in the garden, enjoying the last of the food samples and the late afternoon sun. The success of the event was evident not just in the enthusiasm of the participants but also in the deeper connections they forged with the food they grew and the community they were part of.

Elaine, helping to clean up, reflected on the day with Alex and Michael. "This was about more than just cooking. It was a celebration of community, sustainability, and the joys of gardening. It's wonderful to see how much everyone has embraced this project."

As they left the garden, the trio discussed plans for future workshops and how they could continue to support the community's journey towards sustainability. The garden was quiet now, but the ideas and inspiration it had fostered continued to grow, much like the plants that filled its beds.

Conclusion

As the seasons changed, the community of Greenhaven continued to thrive, fueled by the initiatives led by Alex, Elaine, and Michael. The community gardens blossomed, turning into hubs of life and activity, not just for the cultivation of plants, but for the growth of community spirit and environmental awareness. The green corridors, once mere sketches on a planner's map, now wound through the city, connecting parks and neighborhoods with ribbons of green, alive with birds, butterflies, and the footsteps of residents enjoying their new paths.

The "Garden to Table" events became a beloved monthly fixture, celebrating each season's harvest with cooking demonstrations that transformed the yield of the gardens into fresh, delicious meals. These gatherings were about more than food; they were a testament to the power of community and the shared commitment to sustainability. Each event spun off new ideas and projects, from rainwater harvesting workshops to composting clinics, each initiative building on the last, weaving a tighter fabric of community involvement and ecological responsibility.

Meanwhile, the rain garden initiative had not only beautified the city but had significantly reduced urban runoff, improving water quality in local streams and rivers. The success of these projects became a model for neighboring cities, inspiring a regional movement towards more sustainable urban living practices.

Alex, Elaine, and Michael, once driven by a shared vision, now stood as leaders of a vibrant community movement. They continued to innovate and inspire, always looking for new ways to enhance the environmental health and communal strength of Greenhaven.

One brisk autumn evening, the trio met at the community center to reflect on the journey they had embarked upon. Around them, the walls were adorned with photos and stories of their community's achievements—each picture, each story, a testament to the change they had fostered.

Elaine looked around at the smiling faces in the photos and then at her friends. "When we started, I hoped we'd make a difference, but I never imagined we'd come this far."

Michael nodded, his eyes scanning the same images. "It's amazing, isn't it? It feels like we started with small steps, but now, look around. We've started a movement. This community is living proof that change is possible when people come together."

Alex leaned back, his thoughts turning to the future. "What's next for us?" he mused. "There's so much more we can do. This is just the beginning. We have a responsibility to keep this momentum going, not just for us, but for future generations."

They agreed to start planning a new series of initiatives, each designed to further integrate sustainable practices into daily life and to ensure that every resident of Greenhaven could participate in and benefit from the greener choices the community embraced.

As they left the community center that evening, the setting sun painted the sky with streaks of orange and pink, casting a warm glow over Greenhaven. The streets were quiet, but the air was filled with the promise of continued growth and renewal. In Greenhaven, change had taken root in the fertile soil of community and care, promising a future as lush and vibrant as the gardens that lined its green corridors.